REQUIEM FOR THURSDAY

A SUPERNATURAL MYSTERY

DOUGLAS COCKELL

For Mary

*With many thanks to Sharon Purtill
for her wise guidance.*

Copyright © 2020 Dunhill Clare Publishing

Requiem For Thursday

A Supernatural Mystery

By Douglas Cockell

First Edition

dunhillclare@gmail.com

All rights reserved

Edited by Jody Freeman

This book is a work of fiction. Any omission, or potential misrepresentation of, any landmarks or companies is entirely unintentional. As a result of changing information, conditions or contexts, author and publisher reserves the right to alter the content at their sole discretion impunity.

It is illegal to copy, distribute, or create derivative works from this book in whole or in part. No part of this book may be reproduced or transmitted in any form whatsoever, electronic, or mechanical, including photocopying, recording, or by any informational storage our retrieval system without expressed written, dated and signed permission from the publisher, except within a brief review or mention.

Published in Ontario, Canada

Hardcover ISBN: 978-1-989733-11-0

Paperback ISBN: 978-1-989733-12-7

Ebook mobi version ISBN: 978-1-989733-14-1

Ebook epub version ISBN: 978-1-989733-13-4

Library and Archives Canada Cataloguing in Publications

CHAPTER ONE

Once, Carly had been standing in the arrivals gate at Pearson Airport in Toronto when Hugh Jackman walked out, looked around and stood quietly as though waiting for someone. His driver probably. What made the situation weird was that there didn't seem to be anyone else around. It was just she, Carly Rouhl, in a black and white plaid skirt and wedge sandals, and Hugh, standing alone side by side. She'd been too introverted to gush and ask for an autograph, so absolutely nothing happened. It was kind of exciting, but a non-event at the same time, and one that dies in the telling.

Carly figured people would be impressed with *this* story though. This one was better: it too had a celebrity, and it was taking place in a cemetery. There she was, standing alone by her green Mazda, waiting for celebrated best-selling author, A.L. Rouhl, to come out of a tomb—some goddamned spired and buttressed mausoleum.

Okay, so A.L. was her father, but as she stood there watching autumn leaves and old silk flowers blow through the monuments and headstones, even she could appreciate the irony. Knowing the gloomy cynicism of his later work, people would figure Alistair Rouhl was doing research for his next book, right? Rouhl had always loved moody gothic settings and nuanced weather—even in the early books when he'd had a sense of humour.

But Carly Rouhl knew something the public didn't: that now the old man's writing days were over. They didn't know that in the last few months her father had wasted away to a walking spectre who could barely make it up those red granite steps, who could only pull open the heavy iron door of the mausoleum with her help—in this case, her grudging help.

She'd never been able to stand up to him, not when she was a kid and they had named her grade school after him, much less now, knowing that she would lose him before the year was out. At least today she'd drawn the line at going in there with him. Let him get his so-called research and then she could drive him back to his home, to the seamless rotation of nurses who were keeping him alive and out of intensive care.

She looked at the glow of her cell phone in the dishwater twilight that sulked over the bay. Her father had been in there about twenty minutes now, and she was beginning to feel guilty about leaving him to stumble about in a space lit only by narrow piercings of stained glass. The idea of the great A.L. Rouhl collapsing on the stone floor of somebody else's tomb sounded too much like his own ironic prose for her to dismiss.

So when she heard the sharp creak of an iron door and looked up at the steps of the tomb, her heart made a cold leap in her chest. In the dusky shadows, warmed to a lavender shade by the red granite stonework, a stooped figure in a grey coat was standing. There was a dog at his side. Carly had a bad moment, panting in time with the dog as a scatter of leaf-meal drifted in from the rows of headstones and gusted about her feet.

The stooped figure lurched forward into a puddle of light and Carly could see her frail old father. His right arm was trembling, jerking out as though he were about to step forward into a little dance routine.

"Easy, Car. Your nerves are shot." The old man's voice settled through the gloom, gruff and sardonic as usual. "It's just this damn iron door. Bugger creaks like the hinges of hell."

"Hinges of hell. Great." Carly took a breath, holding her ground, compelled to stare up at him. She wondered if her father understood how for her this little vignette of him standing in the doorway of a tomb pre-figured his own death.

Who was she kidding? Of course he did. This was A.L. Rouhl, master of the telling moment. She watched him glance down at a smear of rust on his scarecrow coat. Then he grinned. "I suppose this little outing must strike you as a bit...sinister?"

Of course it bloody did. "Jesus, Dad. I thought you just wanted to see Mum's gravesite again. That's why I brought you here."

"And I did, didn't I? I paid my respects. Thank you for that. The mausoleum? Well, this is just business. I figured while we were here..."

"You don't seem to realize, you don't have the stamina for this anymore. You're about one bad cold away from peeing through a tube."

"Yes, charming thought. But look, I'm done now."

She swept her dark hair behind her left ear. "How did you get permission to be in there anyway? It's not open to the public."

"Ah, yes, well, I had to do a little financial bullying, but the trustees agreed to let me take a few photographs around the tombs and in the mausoleum. After I signed their damned waiver, of course. They were worried about me expiring on the premises. Quite right, of course. I wouldn't care for that either. I'd hate to be *stuck* here."

"Stuck here?" She looked around at the rows of tall tombstones cross-hatched in their own shadows. My God. The ironies just kept on piling up. "A whole *lot* of people are stuck here."

"I see what you mean, dear. Very droll. But they didn't *die* here, you see, and that's what counts. They're busy haunting other…uh…venues."

"Do I really want to know what you're talking about?"

"Oh, come on now—scholar to scholar. You know—that little theory of mine about ghosts? God, Carly, haven't I told you this?"

"Dad, not now…"

"I'm sure I have. The way that in all the stories, the ghost is stuck at the actual place of his death? You know; haunting a particular castle or New England farmhouse or some such? And that territorial thing always made a kind of sense to me. But the way I see it: it's not the *place* the phantom is stuck in. No—it's the *time,* don't you see. The ghost is bound to the actual moment of his dying. That's what tethers him to the earth. The tyranny of time ends at the moment of death, so sure, the ghost stays where he died, but he's fixed not to the place where it happened, but to the moment—the moment at which, for him, the passage of time ended. In a sense, the ghost lives on…but only in the moment of his death. Perhaps for him, that moment is as spacious as… as Aunt Matilda's parlour. After all, we're getting used to the idea that time and space are relative ideas, aren't we? Well? What do you think?"

"What do I *think*? Well, let's see. Place? Time? What the hell difference does it make? I think I'm cold, and you need to be in the car."

"Where's your subtlety of mind, girl? You and I—we're writers discussing a plot device."

"Yeah, well, speaking of plots, I think the cemetery board would actually love it if you passed away on their grounds. Imagine the publicity. Another piece of local history to tell their prospective clients. You'd probably make it into their brochure, right beside Whatshisname, here."

"Ah yes, Lafayette. The *Great* Lafayette." A.L. turned in a stiff shuffle and looked back at the tomb. "The old boy was an immensely popular stage magician, you know. Imagine how wealthy he must have been to throw together this heap of masonry. Anyway, the trustees let me have the key to his greatness's last resting place. This is the tomb I had to see. Lafayette must have been quite devout; there's a little chapel inside."

To prove his claim he hefted a key of operatic size, and then with a little cautious balancing, he started down the steps, shuffling sideways the way someone who is disabled might do. Each step, though, was a plunge, his right elbow flapping, and he grimaced with each footfall.

Carly tried to shake off her righteous resentment and remembered that under his arm her father had a leather camera case which had a folded tripod between the carrying straps. The camera was digital, but with all those extra lenses and whatnot, it was heavy enough. She'd hefted it up the steps for him.

A.L.'s withered left hand held the big key and several loops of a ribbon dog leash. It took a second for her mood to soften into concern, but then she started to mount the steps. "Here, give me the case. Let me give you a hand."

The old man let Carly take the weight of the camera equipment and, buying time to steady his breathing, he glanced up at the iron doors. "You're right though; the trustees wouldn't let just anybody in there—not without supervision. Truth is, they expect to make a good deal of money from me someday."

Carly closed her eyes. "No shit," she said. *Someday soon,* she thought.

Ever the sensible one, she'd begun looking at her father's papers, but she couldn't recall any directions about his funeral arrangements. She'd known all along that it would fall to her to decide it all and wondered if he had brought her here with this in mind. The old man had always loved ambiguity, had loved saddling her with some quandary or other as though it might teach her something. So far she hadn't steeled her heart to ask him outright. And she wasn't about to do it here and now. She wasn't in the mood to play his morbid game.

While they talked, Indy, a tan, medium-sized lab with a handsome profile, started shifting and forth, as though wary or anxious. Indy's long time master had been stocky once, but now A.L.'s clothes hung on his shoulders as though on the hinged sticks of a marionette. But somehow, with elbows flying, his high forehead furrowed with effort—A.L. managed to jolt down to the last step.

Carly mimed patience; at least the old man hadn't faded to a transparent wisp leaving a quavering moan hanging in the air—he might not be long for the world, but the leaves still scattered sensibly aside as he shuffled, and his dog sniffed the leaves for real squirrels.

"You said these pictures you were taking were research for a book?" she said, not bothering to hide her skepticism.

"Research? Did I actually say that? Well, I suppose that's what you'd call it. I thought there might be a picture here you could use for the memoir. I gave you all my old photos—I thought I'd give you a few new ones to choose from...a nice gloomy tomb for the last page, perhaps. You always have to plan the ending, you know." A.L. chuckled, but Carly just shook her head. Plan the ending? How many times had she heard *that* piece of advice?

After a great shuffling of key and camera case, Carly got the Mazda loaded and Indy bounded into the back seat. The old man shuffled around and opened the passenger side door before Carly could help, and then stood there looking back at the mausoleum: an umbrella rack of gothic shadows in the failing light. "What's the matter with you, Car? I thought you *liked* ghost stories," he said, leaning on the door.

"Oh, for... Give it up, Dad. You're killing me here. You're a cynical atheist. Don't talk to me about spirits."

"How did you get to be such a hardass? Not all metaphysics are religious, you know. Just listen. You'll enjoy this. You see that old pile of granite? The Lafayette Tomb? That damn place just took a picture of *me*. Now, what do you think of that?"

"Excuse me?"

"My camera—it was sitting on the tripod all by itself, six feet away from me. I'm groping around in the light from the door and then, whoosh, the flash goes off in my face. I damn near wet myself. Well, not really. These days it takes me ten minutes to get a good pee going."

"You must have tripped the self-timer."

A.L. waved a hand impatiently. "Yes, yes, the timer. I thought of that. After all, a ghost can't actually *do* anything, can he? Not in the world of the living. Poor fellow can't even push the button on a camera. His existence is trapped inside a nanosecond of time. And if he strays from that instant, he does so as no more than an insubstantial wisp of ectoplasm. You know, when you think about it, that's the problem with *all* ghost stories, isn't it? Your ghost can moan and thrash about all he wants, but how does the writer get him to throw a rock or pull a trigger? How could he *do* that?" A.L. was thoughtful for a moment and then blinked his eyes wide. "Still, I can tell you, it was a nice piece of melodrama in there. Good old Lafayette. What a showman."

Without quite abandoning his frown, A.L. let his smile return and then looked back at Indy who was pawing the front seat, prepared to drive if no one else would. He crumpled one of the dog's ears affectionately. "Ready to go home, Indy?"

Carly watched with concern, but the old man seemed to manage a controlled collapse into the passenger seat, so she straightened and, wanting to check that the tomb had been properly secured, she glanced upward. It was hard to tell with the web of shadows obscuring the lock. "Give me a second, will you? I just want to make sure you…"

"Oh, for God's sake, Carly. Don't fuss."

She took the steps two at a time, her long legs making it look graceful. At the top, she tugged at the great portal, but the old man had somehow managed to shut and lock the doors. On a whim, she turned for a moment to take in the view of Burlington Bay from the top step. Protected from the wind by the pointed archway, she allowed herself to lean back until she could feel the cold rivets of the iron door through her coat. As she glanced around she noticed how the gardens were laid out on a slope towards the water, and in the distance, she could see the Skyway bridge to Hamilton and Niagara soaring over the harbour. Just below that were the squat towers of the smaller lift bridge and the high tension lines along the beach strip.

The overcast was low and sullen, and there was a sweet winter sting in the wind, which resembled the smell of lightning leaping from damp soil. Carly took a curious sniff. But she'd skipped the optional college course on Vaudeville.

So, she doesn't know that the sudden ozone all about her has the distinctive smell of a limelight arc. She doesn't know that the cloying, musky undercurrent of perfume that forces itself upon her rises from a time when theatre goers bathed seldom and covered themselves with masking scents.

Behind her, one of the doors booms as her weight pops the metal sheeting. The wind gusts suddenly, lifting a flurry of leaves—and it's as if a hundred hands are applauding the trick.

CHAPTER TWO

Most men look on death and are afraid, but Brian Maitland had completely *missed* that about Marcella Cole. He was just tired of the whole affair. The night she finally gave Brian Maitland what he wanted she had worn a semi-transparent white blouse that buttoned high on her slender neck and tight at her wrists as though she were covering up as much of her pale winter skin as possible. Her skirt was straight and simple but not too short, and when she finally let him drop it to her ankles, it slid down revealing a lace slip with a side split that showed her legs off. Maitland should have picked up on her meticulous planning of the striptease, her careful staging of everything within a hundred yards of them.

If Maitland had lived long enough to think about it, he would have realized that Marcella never let him see her naked, but with exquisite timing, she'd revealed herself in a tight satin bodice that was more interesting to him than her cool skin. He could feel the ribbed harness in the dry heat of her bedroom, and he spent a few seconds figuring out the challenge it represented: four long garters to loosen…and then a ribbon of nylon to tear away.

When they finally made love it was spectacular, leaving his common sense in tatters and his petty resentments blunted. His excitement had spiked a couple of times already following her drawn out script, but at the climax she moved well, raising her hips and drawing her nails down his back. When he started to think again he had to acknowledge the mutual selfishness of their passion. He had never had the sense that she cared for him, and he had been drawn to her by his own uncritical hunger.

Afterwards, he lay back with his mouth open and relief on his brow. No smile. Just his rational thoughts flooding back as he squinted in the darkness at the brass nipple of the light fixture. The cold clear night outside seemed to take a step closer, the feeble blue light from the window draped across the quilt.

Suddenly Marcella stirred and got up. It must have been two in the morning or so. There was a puff of warmth from the bed, then she grabbed her clothes from a chair and was out the door and padding down the hall in her stockings before he had a chance to say a word.

Maitland sighed and sat up; he already had a sense that it would soon be over between them and he found himself making an assessment: in a way, this was the most adult relationship he'd ever been in. Marcella Cole had never been clinging or curious about his personal life—at least so he believed. She'd barely even flirted, but he had to admit she'd read him like a book, drawing out his tastes and fantasies while giving nothing away about herself—except perhaps a hint of willingness. And in the end, that was all he cared about.

If he'd read her coolness and reserve correctly, he might have acted differently. Perhaps she wouldn't make a fuss about him moving on. That would be good. The only illusion she seemed to harbor was her own air of superiority and entitlement. Clever bitch; she'd probably make the break-up sound as though it was her own idea.

As to that, it was time for him to get dressed too. Time to tell her it was over.

Still tucking a tie under his shirt collar, he followed the hallway down to her living room with its towering fireplace, half expecting her to be standing before the hearth in the glow of the embers, striking a pose. Instead, he spotted her right across the room, fully dressed now and looking back at him from the entryway. To her right and just out of Maitland's sight was the front door to her home.

"Marcella, what's going on? Where are you going? Come here. We need to talk about things."

She stared back, beautiful but unreadable. "Let's not," she said in her slightly accented patrician voice, without emotion or nuance.

Maitland took a step towards her and glanced in the direction of the front door. "What is this, Marcella? Are you saying you want me to leave? Is that what this is about?"

"I'm saying that this isn't going to be settled by talk."

"Then what…" He frowned, trying to read the situation; another one of her damn tests, he supposed. She wasn't dressed to go out herself. In fact, it was the same skirt and blouse she had worn earlier, buttoned up to her throat, and as thin as gossamer. For all that, she turned and walked out of sight towards the entrance before he could say more, leaving Maitland standing in her living room, straightening his tie as if neatness could restore his composure.

"Marcella, for God's sake…"

He followed her, slowed by indecision, crossing the tufted carpet with his hands in his pockets. And there she was—by her own front door, one hand on the knob. She had pulled a heavy gold-coloured cardigan off a coat hook and was wearing it, open. At first, Maitland just narrowed his eyes at her, then he gave a humourless laugh. "Okay. Fine. I get it. You're showing me the door."

She opened it with a sweep of frosted glass and burnished oak, and Maitland could feel the outside air dump an icy treacle past his ankles, but instead of holding the door for him and waiting, Marcella Cole stepped outside herself—and went on stepping down to the front walk—out into the perishing moonless night. Glancing at him over her shoulder, she turned along the path and walked from the coach lamps at the foot of the steps into the starlight and out of sight.

"What the hell..." All he could think was that he had to follow her, take her a coat or something. Didn't she know how fucking *cold* it was tonight?

In a way, though, Maitland was grateful. He hadn't expected tears from her; she wasn't the type. But there was a cruel side to her cleverness, and in a shouting match, she would have known how to hurt him, how to make him feel foolish. Instead, she had gone out into the goddamn freezing night. Why? To stare hurtfully at the stars? To make him feel like shit?

Fine. He would take his time following her. He grabbed his suit jacket from the couch in the living room and pulled the drapery aside until he could press his nose against the triple-glazed window. At first, all he could see was his own reflection: his thick brown hair as neat as a furrowed field, the veteran's tie knotted neatly under his parade ground jaw. He shaded the glass with his hand, but even then, despite the yellow light of the coach lamps along the driveway, Maitland didn't see Marcella Cole.

"Where the hell..."

Then, out of the corner of his eye, he caught her moving, not out between their cars where he might have expected her to go, but way over by the snow fence to his right. She was at the end of a narrow pathway, a trail cut through the snow to a clearing piled with neatly stacked firewood. Maitland could see her stop and glance back, and he watched her with a bitter smile.

Marcella, in turn, saw him at the window and surprised him

by giving a half-hearted wave. Maitland stopped smiling and scowled.

She was calling out to him. He couldn't hear the words, but the muffled sound of her voice and the gesture seemed clear. "Here. Come on, out into the cold for me," she was saying, without a hint of anger or recrimination.

She called again. He could barely hear her, but it didn't seem right to just stand here watching her shiver.

Everything about Marcella and the situation was odd. In the script Maitland had expected, she would have turned her back on him, maybe put her hands on her hips to show her fury. But when had she ever been predictable? Instead, this—whatever the hell it was. And there she was, standing over by the woodpile, her bare hands plunged deep in her cardigan pockets, her shoulders hunched, waiting. Waiting for him. She was saying something, but this time Maitland couldn't even hear the sound of her voice. There was no wind. There didn't have to be. The cold was lying on the snow as heavy as chilled vodka. He could see the ice crystals beyond the window glass.

Maitland tried to imagine what was going on in Marcella's head as she stood out there in the darkness. "You're curious, aren't you?" she might be saying to herself in a quiet bedroom voice at odds with the night and the sweep of city lights below the escarpment. "After all, you still want me. You just hate the idea of me calling you, making demands. You want an on again off again relationship on your own terms."

"What did you say?" he shouted at the glass. Damn it. "See? There she goes again." Now he was muttering to himself in a frustrated undertone. "Can't tell if the damn woman's talking to me or herself."

Maitland cursed under his breath as he put his suit jacket on and stepped from the window towards the entranceway, sweeping his car coat off a hook in the hallway as he passed. He'd wear it—and then, when the time was right, put it around her shoulders to bring her back inside. Talking to herself was just one of her little manipulative tricks. Out there, she had to be freezing; the coat would give him the advantage.

Out on the front steps, the cold struck him, and he wanted to turn and go back in; his coat wasn't heavy enough—but the sight of her standing out there at the edge of the light in that flimsy blouse and cable knit cardigan shamed him. Fine, he'd let her play her little game until the cold won it for him.

He spoke, lifting his chin at her. "What, you getting wood for the fire or something?" Maitland didn't have to raise his voice now. Out here the air was standing and crystalline, the forest an intimate room pressing close on two sides. "You *do* know there's still some wood in the firebox."

As a strategy, saying nothing was surprisingly effective. Fuck, the woman had a strategy for everything. It had taken him a few weeks to catch on. Now, out there, she was playing for sympathy, letting the cold do the talking for her. The witch would freeze to death just to manipulate him.

At last, her voice came in little waves lapping up and down below his hearing. He half-heard, half-imagined: "All you have to do is come to me. Then we kiss, and then, what? You think you can go away, keep my number on your cell? Call me when you feel like it? *Keep coming.*"

Maitland glanced back at Marcella's house, the windowpane alive with the crumbling embers in the fireplace, and then at her lean, long-boned figure, arms pressed tightly to her sides. She waited there at the end of the path, at her feet an orange power cord running from a small electric chainsaw back to her garage. She had always struck him as odd, but women like her held a particular fascination for some men, (and for him) appearing seductively old-fashioned: a 1950s fetish object. Her red lips, her perfect, carefully curled hair, the rosy almond scent of her. And here he was, starting up the path towards the clearing with its carpet of fresh sawdust.

The path had been cut deeply into the clean snow, probably by a single pass with a snowblower because the edges were vertical and precise. There was no way to stray off the path. A few more steps and now he was close enough to wonder about the eagerness in her eyes. He paused.

In a sudden twist of elbows and shoulder, she dragged the cardigan off and flung it behind her. It settled on the snow, bleeding warmth, the gold of the wool the only heat on the cool palette of the night.

"What the hell do you think you're doing? This cold'll kill you. You're just a kid holding her breath to get attention." Under the gossamer of that high button blouse, its folds as blue-white as the mounded snow, he could see the stays of that fantasy bodice. His fingers twitched and his belly tightened as he remembered its rigid sheen. He could almost see her warmth bleeding away into the night. There was something unaccountably sexy about this slow suicidal exposure of hers, a tease more compelling than the fall of her skirt in the bedroom.

"Don't worry, Brian. I'll keep you warm," she whispered, once again giving the impression that his being able to *hear* what she was saying was of no real interest to her.

He looked around at the snow, uncertain, desperately trying to intuit the rules of her game. She followed his eyes.

"Why are you stopping?" she said. "The chainsaw? What? You think the crazy bitch'd come at you with a chainsaw? God, look at you, eyeing that log, thinking how you could pick it up if I went crazy and came at you."

"Marcella, for Christ's sake. Where do you get this stuff? I wasn't... What are you doing leaving a chainsaw lying out here in the fucking snow anyway? Planning to cut more wood in your damn bra? There's a *ton* of wood out here. Look at that goddamn pile. And it's fucking *cold.*"

She said nothing, her shoulders tight in a kind of clenched

shrug; it must have been controlled shivering that forced the micro-movements of her shoulders and neck.

"God, you know what? I shouldn't have come up here to your place at all tonight." Maitland had stopped just short of the clearing. She stood on the other side where the narrow plowed path resumed, not twenty feet away. "We could've cleared this up on the phone. I told you…I'm not saying we can't see each other anymore. I just have to cool it for a while. My wife is getting suspicious. Jesus, it's cold. You have to be in agony, out here."

"Your wife? Your *wife*?" Marcella Cole never laughed, but she was good at scornful amusement. "You think I'm *stupid*? First thing I *did* was find out everything about you. I watched your house, followed you, and spoke to people who knew you. I know all *about* your *wife*."

"You…you…What?"

Between them, there were only a few yards of pathway; the wall of cut logs was neat, the sections lined up and sized as though by a machine—or by a merciless compulsion. He and Marcella might as well have been orbiting through the dark, each on a separate planet of ice. There had never been any real communication between them. She was, of course, as kinky as Edwardian porn and more than smart enough to dominate him, and that had been exciting: this little affair had always been about his pecker and his taste for novelty. He'd promised her nothing else, and she'd allowed him to ravage her stiff, set curls and gartered thighs while they made mutually selfish love.

And of course, it had nowhere to go after that. The truth was, his estranged wife hadn't a clue about the affair, and he hadn't heard from her in weeks.

"No, don't stop. All you have to do is keep coming towards me," she said.

Bloody woman. Even now, she wouldn't show him an unambiguous emotion he could react to—anger, resentment, hurt pride. Just this mocking indifference. She just stood there at the far side of the clearing beside the woodpile, waiting, her swallow-wing brows slightly raised as though wondering what was keeping him. He realized with a slight start that this was the same kind of ironic childishness that had started their affair in the first place: that come hither—I dare you—that somehow held scorn and a carnal promise in one enigmatic look. Even now, after he'd as much as told her it was over, the woman was a slate asking to be scrawled on.

He shivered, folding his arms across his chest. If there had been any wind at all, this would have been unbearable. As it was, the cold was wicking heat from his back and chest, and his ears were losing sensation. "I don't believe this. It's fucking forty below out here." He glanced about, filling her silence, wondering what to do. "Why did you put the damn woodpile way out here anyway? Would have made more sense to put it by the back door. If you're going to live up here in the sticks, you need some common sense."

"The wood pile's out here for a reason. Just here. Right at this spot. You have no idea how meticulous I am, do you? How careful. *Keep coming.*"

"What? What are you talking about?"

But she became silent again. She just went on staring at him through her lashes and then, unaccountably, she backed up, taking two small steps away from him. It was as mad and incongruous as the cardigan abandoned on the snowbank. He blinked at the utter pointlessness of it. The bloody woman's body language was a mystery. She was either borderline autistic or a sociopath—he honestly wasn't sure which. Was she showing him her toughness? Or was it the other game? The one where she's weak and in peril. Did she want him to go to her, to supersede everything with some swooping, romantic gesture? Was this all about body heat? Did she want him to take her in his warm arms and protect her from the brutal night?

"You can feel my power, can't you?" she said.

When Maitland finally answered, his jaw tight with the cold, the recrimination had gone from his voice. And when he said, "Shit. What's the matter with you," it wasn't a question, more an expression of wonder. There was even tenderness in his voice. "How can you stand the cold?"

"Yes, that's it. See the frail woman. You have no idea how strong I can be."

He paused a moment more as the silence and the cold worked on him, and then, miraculously, she had won. Whatever her maddening, beguiling game, he had to go to her: one, two big strides…

And with that, the ground gave way beneath Brian Maitland's feet. The sawdust parted with a whisper of slush and he tumbled forward and down, gasping and windmilling his arms to stop his fall. But the sawdust carpet crashed like foam on surf and he was down deep in water so hellishly, violently cold, it seemed to skin him. Maitland tried to scream but was too busy gasping for breath. Arching back above the surface, flailing at the sawdust, trying to find something solid to grab onto, he hadn't noticed her bright eyes as she stepped forward and reached down for the chainsaw.

She unplugged the orange power cord from the saw.

Being careful not to pass a point on the path marked by a twig, she gathered five or six feet of the extension cord in perfect, even coils.

"For… God's…s…sake. Woman. Help. Me. *Help*…me." His words were racking gasps, his breathing convulsive.

"Yes. Yes. Better than last time. Smoother edges this time. Everything is ready for you. Just so."

"Are you trying to k-kill me for God's sake?"

"You're already dead. You just haven't caught up yet."

Taking her time as though the toss had to be well-aimed, she threw the coils of electrical cord to Maitland. And…the desperate figure lashing wildly in the frigid water actually reached up to take them in his hand!

Afterwards, when she was standing by the fire and the feeling was returning to her ears and fingers, she wondered about that. Is it possible that even then, in the panic of the moment, Brian Maitland was ambivalent? Did he have time to feel horror at the fall of the bright orange cord? Or to convince himself that the electrical cord was a lifeline and couldn't *possibly* be live? That no sane person would make such a mistake?

Of course, he stopped struggling the second the empty socket touched the water. The lights along the driveway blinked out as the outdoor circuit was cut off by the breakers.

It went pleasantly quiet then. She waited a minute longer in the dark before nodding in tight-lipped satisfaction. Maitland's clothes were drinking in the freezing water from the old septic tank, water salted and stirred with antifreeze, and his head was settling down into the daiquiri of slush and sawdust. Oddly, his eyes had only partly closed, and his expression conveyed bland indifference, making it seem as if, like some tough critic, he had simply lost interest in his own melodramatic death scene.

Of course, it was possible Maitland was still alive, his mind mercifully shut down against the ice and the horror, but hypothermia would finish him off in a few minutes... (she watched as his parted lips settled out of sight) ...if he didn't drown first.

CHAPTER THREE

Even if he hadn't taken the call, Eilert Weiss would have been able to tell at a glance that something was going on beneath the lift bridge. Knowing what he would find on the pier supporting the bridge, Weiss barely noticed the falling snow, or that it was unpleasantly stuffy in the car; the heater had been noisily blowing away at his feet since he left the precinct lot on Hampton Road.

This time of year, the lift bridge on Eastport Drive should have been down, with only the aircraft warning lights flashing red at the overcast. Soon, thickening ice would bind the rust and concrete gap from the lake into Hamilton harbour, and the channel wouldn't be navigable at all. But tonight there was an unfamiliar pool of white light on one of the piers under the bridge, and a curious stirring of headlights around the lift towers.

The light at the intersection of Lakeshore and Eastport changed and he turned left, following the shore strip that spanned the narrowing end of Lake Ontario. The road skirted beach properties and the occasional mansion that the conspicuously wealthy still called cottages. On these gated estates, nineteenth-century wreckers had once built bonfires to mislead ships in the fog. Time had changed everything but the fog and the venality.

In a few minutes, Weiss was rumbling across the steel frets of the lift bridge. He turned off the main road on the far side, following the path down and around to the foot of the old stone lighthouse. In the gloom of the parking lot, he saw an EMS truck, a plain white panel van, and four red and blue striped Halton District police cruisers.

As soon as Weiss climbed out of his unmarked Ford cruiser, the sounds of the night came to him from everywhere: frigid waves driven in from the open waters, the wind blustering through the green painted girders of the bridge towers. One rubber rumble after another shook the lattice roadway overhead.

Weiss came out from its lacy shadows, the only thing slowing his walk out under the bridge, a gritty puddle of black ice in the concrete of the pier. Beyond that, uniformed officers hung back in the shadows behind pole mounted work lights while two men, white plastic coveralls stretched tight over their winter coats, crouched near a heap of sodden rags.

Detective Prem Joshi got up off a stone breakwater. Eilert Weiss was a bit above average height, his long brush cut and narrow face elongating his frame; his partner was a comfortably stable cone, firmly rooted on the ground. The other thing that set them apart was Weiss's mustache; only county seniority gave you the nerve to sport that kind of bottle brush.

Joshi was unscrewing the top of a thermos. "It's tea with skim milk. It gets weird tasting in a flask. Want some?"

"Nice sales job, but no thanks. Did you find out who it is?"

"Yeah. His name is Brian Maitland. Had money, a wallet and credit cards. What you'd expect in an accidental drowning."

Weiss circled the halogen light until he could see the white of the dead man's face. It glistened. Everything else on the bridge was a tattered pile of matte grey fabric shredded by a succession of boat hooks and grapples, but the face was mother-of-pearl, except that the eyes were gone, taken by fish. Maitland's hands were lost in sloppy woollen folds, only the blue fingertips exposed.

It was almost as if Weiss was prepared for the fleeting moment of remembered grief that came over him at that moment; after all, it had happened before. It felt like a wave of nausea. All he had to do was screw his eyes shut against it and let the image fade. There: the sensation was passing... just enough time to remember a woman's body on the deck of a police rescue boat. A woman wearing Weiss's own clothes. Five years ago, his wife's face had reflected the police lights the same way.

Then the replay was gone and the body of Brian Maitland was back, patiently dripping oily water on the pier.

Weiss's shuffling examination brought him back to Joshi. Weiss pointed to a puddle of water at the corpse's feet that was already crusting over with ice. "Nice shoes," he said. "All set for the big dance at the Marriott."

"Shoulda had flippers," Joshi said.

"I'm the same way. Never have an umbrella when it rains."

"The floater was spotted by the bridgemaster in the control room up there." Joshi indicated by motioning towards looming angled windows on the nearest bridge tower that reflected the halogens back at them.

"Anything else on the body?"

"Nice shirt, pullover. Expensive slacks. Sawdust."

"Sawdust?"

"Big flakey sawdust in the folds and pockets. And there's a shallow puncture wound in the armpit."

"Ouch."

"Probably done by the EMS guys with one of their hooks. There are a couple of tears in the coat too."

Weiss nodded. "Right. When they were trying to finesse him out of the canal with hooks." He crossed his arms and looked down. "Any of those hooks around?"

Joshi tilted his chin at the control tower. Two long poles rested against the brick wall, and Weiss stepped over work light cables to take a closer look. A technician in baggy white overalls moved away as though distancing himself from the deed. "They're kind of harmless looking. Shepherds' crooks that could encircle an arm, but not pointed. With the skin softened by immersion, I guess they *could* penetrate. Funny, though. The hooks don't look up to tearing the coat material."

In the metal cap of Joshi's flask, the tea steamed. "They had to get the poor sod out of the water and hoist him up the wall, remember."

"Anyway," Weiss nodded at the poles with their rubberized tips, "I've got an idea. You freeze your toes off here, and I'll go up to the nice warm control room, and talk to the bridgemaster."

He turned towards the lattice bridge tower. Inside hung a counterweight the size and shape of a boxcar.

Joshi sipped the rapidly cooling tea and began to amble back to the breakwater wall. "Fine," he said. "You're doing the paperwork."

"Oh Prem, one other thing. Did you send me a bottle of scotch and a card?"

Joshi half-turned and looked around at the gravelled ice as though making sure Weiss meant him. "You've got to be kidding."

"'Cause if you did, you still can't touch my ass."

"You can keep your Prussian ass. It wasn't me. What did the card say?"

"It was a thank you card, handwritten but unsigned. Classy. Not really your style, come to think of it."

"Did it have big, googly eyes that roll around when you shake the card?"

"No eyes."

"It wasn't from any of *my* friends then."

"I've got no idea who'd send me something like that. I asked Jerry Sales and he said the bottle was a single malt scotch from Islay. Very expensive."

Joshi continued to stare. Weiss began to back off, shrugged with one shoulder, and then, frog marched by the wind from the bay, he started back along the pier. As he shuffled out from beneath the roadway span, he managed to look up. The lift bridge control room, against the cool, distant lights of the city, was a warm, tungsten yellow.

He was still walking when his phone rang in his jacket. He stopped, checked the caller ID and frowned. "It's Eilert, Toni. What's up?"

A woman's voice, tired and drawn out: "Don't sound so surprised. Don't I always look out for you?"

He smiled, acknowledging the truth in that and picturing her smirk. "Yeah yeah. You're my guardian angel. Except you carry a gun and look sexy in Kevlar. So, do I *need* help tonight?"

"I heard you'd drawn a floater down by the canal. That right?"

"Yeah. Under the bridge into the harbour. Just got here. You interested?"

"Maybe. Are you thinking accidental drowning?"

"Pretty much."

Weiss thought that the connection had broken, but just as he was about to check the screen of his phone Detective Toni Beal's voice seemed to unfold out of an elaborate sigh. "I may be stepping over some line here, but is there anything... Does anything bother you about the scene?"

Weiss took his time. "Well, you know... Couple of things. Why?"

"Probably nothing. All the same, I think we should compare notes on this. I handled the floater last winter, remember?"

Weiss's memory called up a gray newspaper photo. "Oh, right. Common denominator, a hell of a lot of water. Sure. I can see where you're going with this."

"Don't be sarcastic, Eilert. We used to be partners; I'm just taking care of you, okay?"

He was framing a comeback, but then the strangeness of this call from an off shift detective began to worry him. "What's wrong, Toni? Something bothering you?"

"Hell, I don't know. I don't want to prejudice you too much, but... I'm just sayin', it wouldn't hurt to keep an open mind about this one. I probably shouldn't have called, but I want you to be careful." She gave a humourless laugh. "God, listen to me. Look, Eilert, this is making for a dumb phone conversation. Why don't you just try to meet up with me tomorrow afternoon. Can you do that? Check with dispatch in the morning; they'll tell you where I'm working. We can talk then. Paranoia sounds less embarrassing in person. At least I'm hoping it will."

Toni waited a beat, as though expecting Weiss to press her, then without another word, she took his hesitation as an opportunity to end the call. Weiss looked at the stonework of the bridge for a few moments, and then looked over his shoulder at the wretched bundle on the pier. Still thoughtful, he pocketed his phone and let his gaze float up to the inviting glow of the control room. A shape moved against its warm light; the bridgemaster probably—someone who might be able to tell him more about Bryan Maitland's "accidental" drowning.

CHAPTER FOUR

Behind the angled glass of the control room windows, all the sounds from around the bridge seemed as muted and distant as the colours of the lake. And Weiss, his face still ruddy from the cold, could look down at the reporters starting to arrive beneath the police lights. He could also see the tilted reflection of two women in the room behind him.

Elly Rainer, the bridgemaster who had snagged the body in the channel, was perched on her desk so she too could see the pier. She was a redhead, stocky, still youngish, and seemed unaffected by her somber night's work. In the dead of winter, she had freckles. Maybe she'd been travelling.

"Was it like this earlier when you spotted the body?" Weiss asked. "You know—grey, light snowfall on the lake?"

Rainer screwed an eye closed in thought. "It wasn't actually snowing then." She turned, looking for confirmation.

Gale Vanderlin, who wore a real estate company name tag, nodded, her winter coat open over a sweater. Her blond hair was a thatch of hat-headed curls, but she clearly worked hard at a suburban glamor, her makeup fresh. "The snow's been sort of on and off," Vanderlin said. "There's a nest of Peregrine falcons on top of one of the bridge's counterweight towers. See? Up where the strobe is flashing? Elly's been letting me use the control room for bird watching. She's got authority. So I had binoculars too, see?" She stuck out her knitted chest, offering the binoculars for inspection.

Rainer looked to be judging the angle of the snowfall with a professional eye. "And it wasn't so windy. Right, Gale?"

Weiss glanced at the bridgemaster's boots which were resting on her seat cushion, and then looked out at the coal-black water reaching off to an ill-defined horizon. From up here, you could still see the slush swept away by a late-season freighter that an hour before had passed beneath the road platform into the city harbour, a blacktop highway to nowhere. He could make out Joshi caught in the spill from the police work lights, clutching his flask and looking forlorn. A wedge of Canada geese went by below the window.

"Could you tell what it was right away—that it was a human body?"

Rainer seemed to enjoy trundling the chair out a couple of inches with her heels, then rolling it back. "Well, I could tell what it wasn't. I'm used to watching for flotsam, so I figured it wasn't a log or tackle off a boat. So then I went down with my binoculars and followed it until it drifted into the canal. It was probably drawn in by the wake of the freighter. I got the boat hook out when it came close enough under the bridge."

"What's your boat hook like? Kind of fish hook-shaped?"

"Nah. You know, a *boat* hook. With a chrome t-shape at the end for snagging the gunwale. *Without* damaging it? Not a real hook." She crooked her little finger. "You never been on a boat?"

"So you just snagged enough of the coat material to hold the body against the movement of the waves? Did the coat tear at all?"

Rainer looked at him out of the corner of her eye as though she was being accused of something. "Nah. I was real gentle."

Gale Vanderlin, trying to picture it, was wide-eyed with sympathy. "It must have been awful, seeing a dead body. Did it bother you much, Elly?"

"It wasn't that bad with him floating face down and all. I didn't have to drag him out or anything." Rainer put her weight back on her hands and looked up at a monitor suspended from the ceiling. Every few seconds it would show a different angle on the roadbed and on the chain-link fences around the pier and bridge towers. She looked at Weiss. "I just let him bob up and down against the pier and phoned 911 from my cell. Waiting for the police was creepy, though. You know, babysitting a corpse—freezing my bejeezus. Just me and my frigging imagination. The waves were rocking him up and down real good."

Weiss was reaching into an inside jacket pocket, but his hand came out empty. "I was wondering what he looked like before the EMS guys got their grapples into him. Did you get a good look? His face...anything in particular?"

"Not then, but I was still there when they dragged him out under the lights, remember. I got a good look at the clothes: lightweight car coat, expensive-looking jacket, black leather shoes. I guess I was trying to avoid looking right at the face. I mean, why give myself nightmares, right? Bodies aren't my job, thank God."

Weiss gave a sympathetic nod and turned his back to the windows. Rainer went back to sipping coffee from a Harbor Authority mug. Weiss watched her for a moment and wondered about the bridgemaster's duties. His question didn't come out exactly how he intended it when he asked, "So, mostly you just hit the switch to lift the bridge when the bigger vessels come through?"

She frowned, and he thought she was going to tell him about her engineering degree and certification from the Harbour Commission. "Well, yeah, but I'm in radio contact with the captain sometimes before I even see the ship. I tell him conditions, hit the traffic lights at the last minute and start the counterweights down in just enough time to get the bridge out of the way for the shipping. It's about minimizing traffic disruption on Eastport. The timing's critical, you know."

"And between times you keep a lookout?"

"Yeah, when I'm not being a glorified security guard for harbour property. I'm responsible for a lot of shit, actually. You get paid for the responsibility." She put down the mug. "Is this going in your report? The stuff about my job?"

Weiss was preoccupied, and the question had been idle. He nodded slowly. "Yeah, maybe. Would that be okay?"

She appeared pleased. "Sure."

"There was a floater last year..." The words were barely out when Weiss realized he was talking to himself. The pleasant heat of the room was making his snow-wet coat steam and his thought processes fog up with stray associations, but Vanderlin, the bird watcher, picked up on it right away.

"What? Another body near here? Last year? No shit."

"Well, not *that* near. Over by Coote's Paradise."

"That's pretty near." Her half real, half pencilled eyebrow, went up.

"Yes. I guess. Anything else you remember?" Weiss said.

"Sure," Rainer said. "Sawdust. I could see sawdust caught in the folds of the guy's clothes. The coarse corn-flakey kind, you get from a chainsaw. Yeah, I noticed that when they were searching the body."

"Sawdust—that's interesting, don't you think?"

"Interesting? I suppose. Why? Does it mean something?"

"Something. I guess."

"Come on Detective. I'm being helpful, right?"

"Sure."

"So what about the sawdust? It's a picture stuck in my mind.

What would a detective say about sawdust? Or a coroner maybe…"

"A coroner? Haven't a clue. That's why they get paid more than me."

"Detective…"

The thin skin around Weiss's eyes crinkled and he unwound his long scarf. He wasn't sure why he was talking. "I don't know. How about a guy working with a chainsaw near the shore? But then again, our floater, he wasn't dressed for working, right? Not dressed for the weather at all. More the way you'd look walking from your car to a nice, shovelled doorstep."

Cocking an ear in anticipation and leaning forward, Elly Rainer put her mug down slowly on the desktop. Weiss followed the movement. There was still coffee in the mug—cold and covered by a dull film of grease from Rainer's sour cream donut. Talking as much to himself as the others, Weiss went on: "So, how about this: sawdust on top of ice." He reached over and picked up the bridgemaster's mug, raising it to eye level and carefully moving it so that the coffee continued to orbit within. "Sawdust—the kind you're describing—is more flake than dust, right?—it's lightweight, floats, and it could hide thin ice completely, maybe even open water if the surface was still enough." He held his hand above Rainer's mug. "It'd make the ice surface appear to be solid ground. Maybe the guy stepped onto a surface that looked solid. Bam! He goes right through."

Rainer narrowed her eyes. "Okay, yeah, maybe."

"But it's those shoes, you see…" Weiss turned to look down at the snow sparkling through the pool of halogen lighting on the pier. He wondered if it was just the call from Toni that was making him wary. Was she right about prejudicing him? Once suspicion was sown, it was too easy to let your imagination wander.

On the other hand, what did he expect? He was a detective. That's what he was here for: to intuit the presence of evil, or whatever the hell it was his instincts were worrying over right now.

"What about the guy's shoes?" Rainer prompted.

"The shoes. Yes. You know—leather, smooth sole. The body wasn't dressed for the bayshore in winter." He paused, realizing that he'd made the case to these two women for a suspicious death. Trying to picture a guy in slick dress shoes getting close enough to the lake to slip in? It wasn't easy. There were plenty of those expensive mansions along the lakeshore road on the Northshore Boulevard side, but their waterfronts were either natural rock or artificial breakwaters made of boulders piled there to stop erosion—tricky to climb on even in rubber-soled boots. A tumble from an icy dock, maybe? Sawdust spread on it to prevent slipping?

The blond real estate lady, who had been staring at Rainer's coffee cup, flashed Weiss a look of distaste. "So what you're saying is, this guy was dressed to party, and somehow he fell through ice into Lake Ontario."

"Or off a boat? If it was a guy in a snowmobile suit I'd have an idea what happened, but those leather dress shoes? I wouldn't wear those if I expected to be anywhere *near* water— even on a fancy yacht."

Gale Vanderlin's pencilled eyes were wide, straying to the darkness beyond the police lights. Weiss followed her gaze. She shivered. "This time of year it wouldn't take long for someone to die of the cold, would it? I mean if they did fall in the water."

Weiss nodded. "A few minutes, maybe. But sometimes the shock is so great... Involuntary hyperventilation, they call it. The man's nails looked abraded; he probably died trying to climb out."

The blond looked queasy, moving closer to Rainer and touching her friend's arm. Both women stared at Weiss for a few seconds, and he realized they were imagining the horrific violence of that kind of cold, a cold that could rip your breath away.

What was the matter with him? He'd said far too much, and he knew better. The press might get to the two women and he'd wind up with a media brush fire. But it wasn't the first time he'd caught himself letting his guard down to strangers. It was the loneliness getting to him again. Lately, a lot of Weiss's evenings turned into muted conversations with anyone who'd listen. To stop his rambling he needed to get away, somewhere out in the dark. He'd drawn the women into the brutality of it all: a slip, or perhaps a loud crack, and then the plunge, the cold striking suddenly and without warning.

Vanderlin looked at her friend. "Jesus."

Elly Rainer had become quiet, looking out the window at the patterns on the partially frozen bay. Then the marine band squawked and she hopped down to pick up the microphone.

Vanderlin crowded into Weiss's field of view, her arms crossed and her shoulders narrowed. "Are you thinking... What do you people call it? Suspicious circumstances?"

Vanderlin's bird watching binoculars were looped around her neck. They were crooked, lying sideways across her chest. Weiss shook his head and raised a hand. "I have to write it up—think of it as a story I have to tell. Only, I have to start with the ending and work back. How did it start, what happened? We look for a narrative that fits the details. That's all."

Vanderlin stared at Weiss. The atmosphere in the little glass turret was becoming toxic, and Weiss was the one who had to look away.

He muttered his thanks to the women, touched his hat and walked to the door. He could sense them exchanging glances behind his back.

Weiss rolled the steel-framed door aside just wide enough and long enough to swing out onto the catwalk, and on the staircase, he grimaced, the wind slapping his cheek. He pulled his collar up and wound his scarf. Out here, looking down on darkness, it was easier to imagine the sheer black body cold of the lake. If he had been in the moment, he would have hurried down the metal steps seeking shelter, but Weiss found himself lingering in the darkness barely aware of the pain on his exposed brow and slitted eyes.

Instead, he was somewhere else, letting his mind's eye conjure a well-dressed man floating in the sheltered waters of the canal; it could happen in winter when the heat of decomposition warmed the gasses and a corpse could bob up amid the ice granules. Sure, you wondered how a guy with a light topcoat got himself into the freezing slush. But you knew it would be the story of a man dying quickly of hypothermia—a few last minutes to think about a wife and family, or maybe a lover if the agonizing shock of the cold let him think at all...

But maybe it wasn't the thought of Brian Maitland's last minutes that had derailed Weiss in there with the two women; maybe it was the memory of a single photograph. Weiss hadn't been there last year to watch the crew break a young woman free of the ice and driftwood along the shoreline clutter of Coote's Paradise. That had been Toni Beal and her new partner.

He'd seen all the pictures, but there had been one photo in particular that managed to capture the tragedy—and it had apparently taken up long term residence in his memory. It showed a girl's frozen body, still miming the hump-backed curve of a floater, dripping there on a tarp, a deep gash beneath her rib cage—as though the first responders had dragged her up the beach with the kind of hook you use to tow a car. As though they'd embedded it under her sternum and turned on a winch. Hell, for all he knew, maybe they had.

All he could recall of the case was that the poor kid had been a teaching assistant at Brock University, small and fashionably thin. *She* hadn't been dressed for the shore either. She wouldn't have lasted long in the water; not even as long as Maitland with his fancy shoes. He promised himself that he'd find out what kind of shoes the girl had been wearing for her plunge into the lake.

CHAPTER FIVE

The cruiser was dark blue and grimy with road salt, and Weiss drove it back to the station through largely empty streets. The smart ones were in for the night where it was warm.

The records office was closed, so he signed out a key from the uniform on the desk crew, and let himself in.

The station was new, and the records room still smelled of recent construction. Weiss fired up a single row of fluorescents that popped on without a flicker and sat at the nearest workstation. It was a local network isolated from the web to protect the files. He ran the cursor down the case numbers, counting back to last winter. His best recollection was that the girl found along the shore last year had been treated as a suspicious death, but he would have remembered if it had developed into a full-blown murder case. He figured it had petered out into a deferred result or had been filed as an accidental drowning. Tomorrow he'd track down his old partner Toni Beal and find out what she thought, but for now, he wanted to be up to speed before talking to her. Maybe he'd even spot the red flag that Toni was inferring was there *before* she had to tell him.

He stared at the screen, realizing he couldn't narrow his search down to the actual file name without more information.

He thought about some possible search parameters.

Weiss had already entered the word "drowning" when it came to him—the girl had possessed a distinctive name. Yes—something sweet and pathetic to go with the grainy newspaper shots of a slender figure drawn up on the strand, all willowy arms and legs against a dark tarp. The digital photo came back to him, and he marvelled again at the burden of pity and outrage he seemed to carry around in his head. Her last name was...roses or lilies or something. He started to run the alphabet in his mind, but before he got to J, he spotted the name halfway down the screen: Cherry. Therese Cherry.

Weiss called up the case file and ran the few, sparsely annotated forms, his eyes darting. There wouldn't be much help here.

As he guessed, the case had been deferred. The case officers had been suspicious of foul play, but in the end, hadn't been able to justify a lengthy investigation.

My God—the girl had been nineteen. She must have hit the books and burned through high school. He scrolled to the lead detective on the case. Yes, this was the one; the lead was Antonia Beal—Toni. She would have been as thorough as the evidence allowed, would have given the kid a chance at justice.

Weiss dug his car keys from his coat and sorted out a memory stick. As he jacked it into the USB slot and typed in an access code, the girl's name cycled in his head: Therese. Terry.

Terry Cherry.

Cute.

———

The desk officer was surrounded by a family of angry tourists. He and a young trainee had gone into rapid overload trying to calm them down after their rental condo had been tossed by a professional thief. Weiss wasn't going to take a chance and just leave the records room key in the middle of this, so he spent a few minutes seated beneath the staffing calendar, alongside a little girl who didn't understand what all the fuss was about. Eventually, the desk officer managed to open the sign-out book and formally accept the key from Weiss, all the while gesturing for calm with his left hand. "Jesus Eilert, couldn't it have waited until morning?"

"Wheels o' justice. What can I say?"

The officer rolled his eyes. "The wheels of justice ought to back up over Jimmy Luther's balls. The condo job has his name written all over it. How many times have we run him in on robbery charges?"

Weiss nodded his sympathy and began to amble toward the roaring warmth of the entryway. He was thinking how much he preferred Jimmy Luther's predictable stupidity to the cunning he was beginning to sense behind two drownings...almost a year apart.

Weiss's fully depreciated Dodge sat snow-covered under the glare of the floodlights in the station's empty parking lot. He turned the key and the V6 roared to life. While the interior began to warm he switched his hat for a wool toque and pulled it down over his ears. Then he began scraping ice from the windows.

His apartment was on a hillside, its view of the lake ruined by a big Best Western, and as he shed his coat in the hallway, the aura of solitary pathos that trailed him dissipated, and he felt the pleasure of being home. The apartment had been his home since the death of his wife had freed him from an unbearable marriage. Once, she had been beautiful and intense, full of charming contradictions—part free spirit and part social climber. But then the contradictions completely sundered and a whole new personality had flared its quills until he could hide her indiscrete infidelities and abusive denials from no one.

Weiss's apartment wasn't a part of that lifetime; it was the home of someone resigned to, if not content with, his own company, and, in an oddly selective way, a man of culture. Weiss wasn't keen on art in general, but he was a supporting member of Vernon Court and the Museum of American Illustration. His two-bedroom apartment, hung with cobalt blue Parrish posters and sweetly gay prints by the Leyendecker brothers, was the retreat of a man surprised, and troubled, at being handed one last chance at happiness, a chance to look at human suffering from a fresh perspective—from the outside.

He plugged the USB key into his laptop and brought the Cherry file up. It occurred to him even as he was skimming the text again that it was a bad idea to read this stuff just before sleep; he'd been having trouble with insomnia again, so he palmed the screen down on the keyboard and stood up to the window. Taking one last look at the snow swarming the light in the parking lot, Weiss switched off his lamp and went to bed.

A torn and frayed curtain rippled in the silent wind, free of any horizon, and there was a figure in the dream—idealized and graceful. Its lines were lean. Boyish?

No, it was female—and she floated in space, free of the curtain—now piercing it with an outstretched arm and trailing finger.

The nightmare worked itself out as a sort of ballet: cool, nerveless and elegant, but Weiss tossed anyway, one leg kicking free of the covers. He knew where this was going; the girl would be forced to dance, to flaunt her beauty in this vague and harmlessly tumbling space, until she would be executed before his eyes. Would it be his wife, her body lying on the deck of a police rescue boat, or would it be the girl on the tarp?

The reasoning part of Weiss's mind—not at all fooled by the stylized, Cirque du Soleil spectacle of the dream—caught on right away that he was thinking about either the girl from the university or his wife, and it made him want to turn away, or get up and shuffle off to the bathroom. The urge to pee was tempting him awake, but the urgency of the dream held him captive. He had no choice but to look on in horror as the fatal ballet began.

He watched the girl's arms break the surface, her limbs extrude jointless as her blue fingers cast off arcs of frigid water. Unlike Brian Maitland's pallor, the girl's porcelain face still gleamed in its innocence. Maybe Brian Maitland—beefy, prosperous and middle-aged, whose leather shoes had glistened on the pier in a grimy puddle—had lived a careless life and invited his own death; Weiss didn't know, but this child... She had done nothing that her youth wouldn't forgive. Weiss got it. Toni Beal was telling him the two deaths were connected.

CHAPTER SIX

The mansion, perched on the long slope from the escarpment to the lake, made Eilert Weiss think about his salary. Once, you could afford to live in Burlington looking down on the suburban sprawl in patrician respectability if you owned railroads or a shipping line. Nowadays, so Prem Joshi had told him, you could pull it off if you laundered drug money for the local biker gangs. The windows of the mansion were soaring mirrors concentrating the winter gray of the escarpment and the tinsel of the ice-laden trees. The roof tiles, made of a sculpted orange enamel too slick to hold the snow, would probably outlive the young police officers who shivered in the driveway.

Weiss and Joshi went in under an arch of police tape and stamped on the plastic sheeting covering the front hall. Joshi tossed his coat on a deacon's bench and started up the stairs. "All the action's downstairs in the garage," Joshi said, calling back over his shoulder. "I'll see you down there in a minute."

Weiss made an "excuse me?" gesture with his hands. Then he sighed, and draping his coat over one arm, he took the stairs to the underground garage.

The garage, filled with the glister of polished foreign cars, sprawled beneath the entire footprint of the house and probably undercut the back garden as well. Punctuated with decorative holes left by the pouring moulds, the walls down here were bare concrete, but their surface had some kind of polymer glaze. It might have been the garage of a hotel or high-rise condo; the dark corners had been angled off and the floor was pebbled with a flecked, sand-textured paint.

The lighting was spotty, several of the fluorescent fixtures having been damaged and replaced by police work lights on wheeled yellow stands. And then there was the smell, a mercifully faint mix of smoke and burnt flesh.

Two plain-clothed detectives were using the boxy hood of a car as an improvised table, sorting photographs. Tom Krosnow, the older of the two, split the wrapper of a chocolate bar by snapping it in half. The other, a lean and corporate woman wearing frameless glasses, a gray suit and low heeled boots, was holding an eight-by-ten glossy at arm's length, comparing it with the shocking reality of the nearest wall. Her straight hair might have been long, but was intricately pinned up against the back of her head.

"Hi, Toni."

Detective Antonia Beal lowered the photo and pushed her lenses back on her small nose.

Tom Krosnow broke off a square of chocolate. "Hey, Eilert. And by the way, what the fuck are you doing here? *We* get the glamour assignments. You can't have this one."

Weiss got it. Toni hadn't mentioned last night's phone call to her partner. "Yeah Tom, justice must be seen to be done, but with class. Heard you had quite a horror show down here."

"Hello, Eilert." Toni acknowledged him with affected boredom. "All the sweetmeats have been carted away, but we had two bodies, Mr. Ossie Christo and his wife. A third in the driveway. An employee. Security guard, most likely."

"Biker connection?"

"Well, Christo had a suspicious gardener with unpaid parkway tolls, but we can't overlook his business associates, seeing as how they distribute meth on Harleys wearing Nazi helmets. Can't rule anybody out."

Weiss tried to imagine a scenario that would produce the scarred diorama on the wall behind the two detectives. He bristled his mustache at it. "Why is it that we drive on parkways and park on driveways?"

Toni frowned at her partner. "See? Now that's why Eilert'll never get the glam cases. Short attention span. Mind wanders."

"I heard that Eilert gets all the weird shit," Tom Krosnow said.

Weiss shook his head. "They're shit when I get them. I *make* them weird. It's a gift. But right now I'm just a tourist."

Toni sagged against a car that seemed to deflate a little. "You're off season on this one. The wreckage has been bagged, and the place has been swabbed and photographed. All we can show you, besides a few dinged up cars, is nitro burns on the wall and splatter on the floor."

"This is just a detour for Prem and me. I came to see you."

"How nice."

"I was hoping you could help me with one of my cases."

Toni reached across the car hood to punch her partner in the arm, then smirked at Weiss. "It's your floater at the lift bridge, isn't it? I heard. Actually, Tom and I've been expecting you. Right, Tom?" The other detective rumbled and broke off another square of chocolate.

Weiss understood the disguised awkwardness of the moment. Over the last five years, Toni Beal had taken chances with her career to keep Weiss afloat when his wife's suicide pushed him over the edge.

Toni closed one eye and put her elbows on the hood of the car. "You got an unexplained drowning and so you're wondering about the one we handled. Shit. What was her name? Cherry…"

"Therese Cherry," Tom mumbled.

"Right. Last winter. It wasn't quite as cold then as this god-awful climate change crap we're getting, but we fished her out along an embankment near the botanical gardens. She was frozen, coated with ice like a bloody hailstone. And I bet you're wondering if there's a connection with your current floater, both vics being wet and frosty."

"It was a pretty thin file, Toni. I got the impression you guys hadn't a clue what happened to Cherry."

"Fuck you too, Eilert."

"No offense, Tom. We've all been handed files that lead nowhere. Young woman with no enemies, no past. What can you do? You catch on that you're wasting the taxpayer's dollar."

There was silence and Toni and Tom exchanged glances. Toni took her partner's scowl as permission and said, "Not as quickly as you think, Eilert. We put a lot of time into that case. It just doesn't show in the paperwork."

Weiss shrugged. "Thought so. You wrote it up as an accidental drowning, but I could almost see the quotation marks around 'accidental.'"

"You want to know why the Cherry file is so thin? It's because we had a good idea who was responsible for her death from about day two of the investigation. For her *murder*, I mean."

Weiss raised an eyebrow. Toni took a few steps towards the burned and spattered wall, folded her arms and tipped her chin at the long vertical stains caused by blood running down from the ceiling. "See here, Eilert; I want you to meet Ossie Christo, or at least the bits we haven't wiped up yet." She followed a gravity-drawn rivulet of blood with her eyes until it met the discoloured flooring. "The coroner may have bagged his remains, but it's going to take a power washer to evict Ossie

Christo from his home. Now Christo, here, and Therese Cherry have more in common than you might think."

"Come on, Toni. A white-collar drug fence and a university teaching assistant? Cherry was hardly more than a kid."

"Yeah, sure...and she had nothing evil or brutal in her personal life."

There was a note of sadness in Toni Beal's voice. What was it that she wouldn't talk to him about over the phone?

"Christo? He lived in this nice house with its view of Lake Ontario, and he collected funny old French cars. Wasn't a violent person either, just a grey-haired little dandy who served as secretary to the Joseph Brant Historic Preservation Group. Neat as a pin with a mid-Atlantic accent. But he had *associates*, guys who enjoyed tattooing people with an electric charcoal lighter. We figure Christo crossed them in some way. Probably a difference of opinion in bookkeeping—they didn't appreciate the way he seemed to be getting richer than they were. So they knifed a guard and Christo's wife, and then, to take advantage of the fine acoustics, they blew poor Ossie all over his garage."

"Sending a message to future business partners," Tom offered.

"Toni, what..."

She turned to face Weiss and he could see the worry. "Therese Cherry was a promising scholar with a gift for teaching, lived alone and charmingly chaste. So there we are: Tom and I. You know, just running down the background when Tom here checks out the Cherry family. And it seems that Therese Cherry's father was a widower. And Therese's late mother? Well, her maiden name was Andrade, the same as Marcella Cole's. Marcella was her sister."

Weiss froze. He wondered if Toni could read the cold shock that he felt, the sudden tightness in his face.

Toni stole a glance at Tom who looked puzzled. "And *there*

you have it: Christo's problem was his business associates. Therese Cherry's problem was her family."

Tom wouldn't let Weiss's silence go. "Come on, Eilert; you were there. *Marcella fucking Cole*, for God's sake. Don't you remember?"

The murder charge against Cole had fallen apart just as Weiss himself had been approaching a complete emotional collapse over his wife. The Police Board had been looking for someone to blame for the spectacular unravelling of the case against Cole, and Weiss with his festering marriage followed by his wife's leap from the Skyway would have been an easy target. In fact, he would have been perfect; someone in the department they could scapegoat for sloppy procedure and then quietly forgive, citing his personal problems.

But Weiss had been lucky. Toni had been there to help him cover his forgetfulness and inability to focus until he could manage again. She knew how close he had come to losing his job. In the end, the detachment head had given him sympathy for his wife's suicide, when what Weiss deserved was a psych ward. Cole's acquittal wasn't Weiss's fault—at least not his alone, but in his grief and self-loathing, Eilert Weiss would have been a willing martyr. The softness of Toni's thighs had spared him that.

Now, in the hollow-sounding space of the garage, Marcella Cole's name had gone off like the blast that had taken Christo.

Toni knew that the mention of Cole would shake her old partner. She'd been watching him for five years since the Marcella Cole trial, unsure of his stability. But the floater by the canal meant Weiss needed to know what she knew about Therese Cherry's drowning.

Tom continued to misread Weiss's silence. "Marcella Cole? The Jo Brant Hospital murder case?"

At last, Weiss nodded to Tom. "Of course. She was accused

of murdering her husband. But she was acquitted. Completely exonerated. That was five years ago."

"Yeah, that's right," Tom said. "She walked." He crumpled his chocolate wrapper. "Biggest goddamn travesty of…"

Toni hadn't taken her eyes off Weiss. "When we saw the connection between Therese's mother and Marcella Cole, it all came back. Tom worked the Marcella Cole investigation back then too. Seems the whole precinct did. He knew what the Cole woman was."

Tom stirred. "Cold as ice and guilty as hell. All due respect to the asshole on the bench who let her walk."

Toni didn't want Tom telling this. She cut in.

"Now get this, Eilert: we find out Cherry's mother was killed falling off the rocks along Northshore Boulevard about two years ago. And do you believe this shit? Nobody bothered to point a finger at sister Marcella for that one. After her acquittal, the bloody woman got an *immunity from suspicion* card."

"But you're guessing Marcella Cole murdered her own sister," Weiss said.

Tom snorted. "Killed her own husband, walked on that charge, then killed her sister."

"What we feared back then was that we were freeing Marcella to kill again. The murder of her husband was just the tip of the iceberg. We suspected even then that there were others. It wasn't our fault she got off, Eilert, but Marcella was found innocent five years ago—so her record was sanitized completely. It's what they do with an acquittal, right? The court even *apologized* to her."

Weiss said, "And the sister's death? Was there a motive for that? Anything at all you could use to point to Marcella as a suspect?"

Toni looked at her partner, but Tom just scowled at the hood of a car. She closed her eyes and let out a slow breath. "The accident hypothesis was plausible and there was no specific history of animosity between the sisters that we could uncover; Marcella was cool and indifferent towards *everybody*. But you *know* her, Eilert. She's a sociopath. Who knows what set her off. A word, a perceived slight... Look, at the trial we came close to proving Marcella Cole was a serial killer, but we lost. And one of the reasons that we lost is that the key witness in her murder trial drowned. *Drowned*. Fast forward, and her niece, Therese Cherry, is found drowned.

"What if Therese Cherry caught on to who killed her mother? What if she finally saw what *we* all saw five years ago, that her aunt was a murderer? She was a smart kid, Eilert. Marcella would have a reason to get rid of her. We have a hard connection from Marcella to Cherry. And now you've got yourself a whole new drowning."

"Well, yes, but there's nothing to connect..." Weiss began.

"Yeah, I know. Maybe yours is just another drowning. All I'm saying is, be watchful. If we were right about Marcella five years ago, if she *is* killing, what should we be looking for? Bullet-ridden corpses? Bloody smears in underground garages? No, of course not. That's not her style. But last year we dragged Marcella's niece out of the bay, and now you've got a new floater in the same vicinity. Maybe you've got nothing. But if anyone with a local badge starts to forget about Marcella Cole, he'd be as dumb as the judge who walked her."

Tom nodded. "You can't get warrants, can't spend taxpayer money harassing citizens with spotless records. We couldn't touch any of the old files on Cole. They probably shredded them. Christ, Eilert...what were we supposed to do?"

Tom answered his own question. "I'll tell you what you do. You don't write it up. You can't. You wind up with a *thin file*."

"But if you don't write it up," Weiss said, "it never happened. Your work is lost."

"What would *you* have done?" Tom growled.

Probably hidden in some very dark room, Weiss thought.

But all he said was, "Forget that. Maybe I'll have better luck with my floater. Maybe not. I'm inheriting a lot of shit here."

What had Brian Maitland just become? A thread leading back to Marcella Cole and his own lowest ebb as a human being?

Weiss looked down at his rubber-soled shoes which still glistened, wet from the melted snow. "How was the Cherry kid dressed when you found her?"

Toni answered. "Winter coat. Heavy sweater. Nothing unusual."

"Shoes?"

"Winter boots. She was dressed for cold weather. It was early March."

"Okay, but were they just parking lot boots, or were they serious snow boots?"

"They were fashionable. You know. From the car to the mall. They had heels—thick, but high."

"Anything out of the ordinary?"

"What are you looking for?"

"Sawdust, maybe?"

"Sawdust?" Toni looked at Tom, but he just shook his head. "Maybe. The coroner didn't *call* it sawdust, but the trace in her pockets included some cellulose fibre. She'd been in the water a long time; the fibre could have started out as flakes of sawdust, I suppose."

Tom shrugged. "How about this for unusual? Antifreeze."

"Yeah." Toni nodded. "That's right. Traces of antifreeze in her clothes. Even in her lungs."

Weiss nodded. "I noticed that in the file. So, at some point, Cherry was in water treated with antifreeze? Maybe it was just a local pollutant. The lake water around here can be a toxic soup at times."

"Maybe this is what you're looking for: The water in her lungs was saltwater."

Weiss narrowed his eyes. "Why would it be saltwater?"

"Wait for it, Eilert. They found traces of potassium iodide in her lungs too."

"Iodine?"

"Yeah, you know? The stuff they put in *table* salt? What if…" She shrugged. "What if the fluid in Cherry's lungs was freshwater treated with iodized salt and antifreeze?"

Weiss stared. "She drowned in saltwater and was dumped in lake water later?" For a moment, he let his eyes follow the discolouration in the concrete at his feet.

Toni Beal slumped against a car. "Hell, I know it's feeble. We came at it a million ways."

There was the distant sound of footsteps in the house above. Weiss looked up. "Our lift bridge body is in bad shape," he said. "They should have sent divers in to land it, but the water was too cold, so the corpse is pretty torn up with grappling hooks. Your report says Cherry's clothes and body had puncture marks too."

"Yeah. The rib cage tear was more of a gouge. Could have been waves and rocks. Could have been hook and drag marks."

"But Cherry was just washed up by the current, right? No dragging, no defensive or sexual assault wounds?"

"Still, there were these deep gashes," Toni said. "Ragged. Not knife wounds."

Weiss was trying to frame the follow-up question, but he saw Tom's eyes shift and he turned to follow his gaze.

Prem Joshi was nodding his greetings from the stairway

"Where have you been?" Weiss asked.

"In the upstairs washroom."

"I thought you went on the way over at the coffee shop. Had your prostate checked lately?"

"I wasn't *peeing* in the upstairs washroom. I was fighting crime."

"Find much crime in the en suite, did you?"

Joshi looked indignant. "Well, yeah. You should see the bathtub. It's made of acrylic or something—completely transparent. Clear as glass."

Weiss shot a glance at Toni. "The bathtub? Should I even ask?"

"So I went down a floor," Joshi was saying, "and there's the tub, hanging down into the downstairs bedroom as if it were some sort of porno skylight."

Tom Krosnow smirked. "Well, at least they'd never lose the soap."

Joshi nodded as though accepting the wisdom of this. "But mainly I was looking for dental floss."

Satisfied that he'd accounted for himself, Joshi looked around, ignoring the horrific mural of dried blood. "What's with the old cars?"

"The guy collected Citroën," Tom said.

Joshi was unimpressed. "Citroën? God, they even *sound* like lemons. Look at that red heap. It's a kid's toy."

"Guy was a gearhead." Tom leaned on the closest car, and it hissed under his weight. "Citroën had some sophisticated engineering in their day; pneumatic suspension, swivelling headlights. They were the first production cars to have front disk brakes. But most Citroën nuts are just into the Gallic style."

Joshi sniffed. "Gallic style? The white one must have been designed by nuns." He appeared to lose interest and looked up at the dull grey pipes of the sprinkler system.

"Prem?" Weiss waited.

"Hmm?"

Weiss hefted his coat to one side and made a sweeping gesture at the wall. "This is Ossie Christo."

Joshi nodded and finally took in the wall, as though thirty

feet of blackened and abraded concrete could easily be missed. Except for the vertical blood drips caused by gravity after the initial explosion, the lower part of the wall was a blotchy, charred smear. Starting about a meter from the wall, they could make out the directional streaking of blast and spatter on the floor.

"Pretty much what they told us at the station," Joshi said. "So I was expecting this." He took a plastic box of dental floss from his jacket and handed Weiss the loose filament. "Here, hold this." Tugging at his arm, he led Weiss away from the wall. "We're going to line up with the spatter lines on the floor, okay?"

Weiss caught on. He squatted and pressed his end of the twine to the marks on the floor.

Walking the box end of the floss over to the wall, Joshi beckoned to Tom, who looked like he'd just been offered a panty liner. Joshi gave him the little plastic reel so that Tom could kneel painfully and put his thumb on the floss against the base of the wall.

"Right. Now we get the other angle." Joshi commandeered Toni, and the two of them stretched another reel of floss from the floor to the wall following the directional markings.

For a moment, they were all silent, their shadows looming large against the wall.

Weiss was the first to catch on. "The two angles don't meet at the base of the wall."

Joshi nodded. "So, Toni and Eilert, you keep your ends out there on the floor, and Tom and I will lift up our ends against the wall. Reel out some more twine, but remember—keep the floss in line with the spatter."

It took Tom a few minutes to overcome his conviction that he was being set up for a gag, but as they raised the threads—and the ends slowly converged, even he could see what the two lines of twine were telling them. He pouted his approval. "So the blast originated from, what, four feet up the wall? Nice trick, Joshi. Where'd you learn that?"

Joshi grinned. "This is how we improvise in the streets of Islamabad."

Weiss got up, taking his coat off his shoulder. "I bet you've never been to Pakistan in your life."

Joshi looked hurt. "Careful, Kraut. You're talking about my cultural heritage."

Toni was staring at the bloom of soot on the wall. "I don't get it. What does it mean? How could the blast have originated up off the floor?"

Joshi put his arm around her shoulders and squeezed. "It's all right, Toni. Just another example of boys at play. My guess is that Christo was tied up, sitting on the floor, had the explosive in his mouth—taped there probably—and it was set off with a cell phone from a safe distance. It's how these biker guys have fun at work."

Toni Beal stood her ground, but she stared at the wall as though it had become a snuff film.

Joshi gestured at the nearest car which had been t-boned by the blast. There were black marks at each tire as though the compact sedan had been dragged sideways across the floor. "From the layout, I'd say they wanted to paint the guy all over his Citrus here. You'd have to be a Harley man to understand."

"Citroën," Weiss said.

Tom backed away from the photographs spread out on the hood of a boxy roadster and looked down at its grill. It seemed to return his expression of disgust.

"Citroën. Whatever." Joshi walked off to the stairs, his self-satisfaction glowing on his back. "You're welcome, Toni. Tom. Come on Eilert, we have to wrap up the Maitland drowning."

A look passed between Weiss and Toni. He gave her the smallest of nods and turned to follow Joshi.

CHAPTER SEVEN

The big Ford was freezing and the heater was taking its time warming the interior. Weiss was driving, turning onto Dundas for the run back across the escarpment. "Don't you think that was a bit sexist?" he said, the mustache muting his grin.

Joshi frowned as he peered out at the snowbanks. "Oh. Maybe. I was just trying to help. Think I should apologize to Toni?"

"Just don't send her a bottle of scotch. That might be misinterpreted."

"I'm telling you, I didn't give you the damn scotch, okay?" The frown was gone and he was staring off into the gray distance. "Do you think maybe my sexism is a cultural heritage thing too? In the old country, my grandmother always had to walk behind my grandfather. That was until land mines became an issue. Then she had to walk in front of him."

"You're not supposed to be proud of your sexism, Prem. You're supposed to root it out." They drove in silence for a few minutes, descending the grade to Appleby Line. Weiss checked his mirrors and gave a small chuckle. "You know, I've never been to Germany either."

"Get out of here. I can hear it in your accent."

"Ha! My accent. My father was a German prisoner of war in Scotland. They kept him in a camp outside Brechin, a little town in county Angus. They would ship the low-risk prisoners up there. Security was a joke because no one at that camp wanted to escape back to the fighting. My father was in uniform, but he wasn't a soldier. He was an attaché who happened to find himself on the wrong side of the front, so they put him up there with the Italians and the interned British civilians.

"My mother was a Scot with an accent you could cut with a knife. What you're hearing is what's left of a lowland *Scottish* accent, with maybe a touch of High German from my dad."

"My God. You're a fucking Scotsman? That explains so much. I always pictured you cycling in the Alps or something."

"The Alps?" Weiss frowned. "You can't cycle in the Alps. They're mountains, for God's sake." He slowed for a light. "Picture me tossing a caber, why don't you."

"What's a caber?"

Weiss shook his head. He briefly considered trying to explain to Joshi why someone would try to throw a telephone pole end over end, but didn't feel up to it.

Joshi didn't seem to mind. He was looking out towards the lake reading the gray horizon again. "You know, my grandfather used to carry this big, really big, knife with him all the time. Kept it with him to his dying day. It was a religious thing."

Weiss glanced at him. "Sure. A kukri."

Joshi glanced sideways in surprise. "Yeah. A kukri. So anyway, Gramps would never show the blade to me. Said that whenever the blade was uncovered, it had to draw blood. He told me that when he took it out to clean it, he'd have to nick his thumb just to feed the blade. You could tell from the scabbard it was way bigger than a bowie knife though, and kinda curved. I mean you could've cleared sugar cane with the thing."

"I've seen one. Scary."

"Okay, then you can picture my grandfather, hunkered down watching TV with his Depends leaking, and, tucked in his wheelchair with his Kleenex and his channel guide, he's got this big fucking cleaver. They couldn't take it away from him because it was religious, so they just crazy-glued it into the scabbard."

"I bet he felt that he kept his manhood until the end."

"I guess. Must be tough keeping your manhood watching *Jeopardy* in a diaper."

They were quiet for a moment, then Weiss said "Remember the big murder case involving Jo Brant Hospital? It was five years back."

"Yeah. Some nurse got off on a technicality."

Weiss nodded. "The prosecution's star witness died. He drowned."

"Drowned?"

"That's right. The nurse—the head nurse, actually—more of a supervisor, was supposed to have poisoned her wealthy husband. A pharmacologist from the hospital, who was going to testify against her, drowned at his cottage, and the nurse's lawyer got her off. She had hubby's money to hire a Bay Street pinstriper. I did some background work on the case myself. Anyway, the nurse's name was Cole. Marcella Cole."

"Sure. I remember. I was up in Orillia then, but the scandal got a lot of ink."

"The trial was a worse mess than even the press knew. We thought for a while we could tie the Cole woman to some earlier murders too. In the end, we couldn't prove any of it, and she was dismissed with apologies."

"Must've been hard."

"God, yes. Here we had this emerging picture of a dangerous sociopath…and then one day, we realized we'd built a house of cards. Couldn't prove any of it."

"Why are we talking about Marcella Cole?"

"Because we're interested in unexplained drownings in the Hamilton—Burlington area. One of them is Marcella Cole's niece, Therese Cherry."

Joshi crossed his arms and was silent for a minute. Then he said, "Cole's niece? Hmm. You've started another house of cards."

Weiss watched the road, lost in thought.

Blaming yourself. That's what emotional collapse does to you, making you feel forever vulnerable. For days after, you're aware of the cramp, waiting for it to spasm again. With a breakdown, you've been right over the edge, and even after you know exactly where the edge is and you cower when you feel yourself veering towards it. That's what had happened in the garage with Toni and Tom. He'd felt it—he'd felt the tug on the wheel towards the abyss. Brian Maitland's corpse on the pier being the work of Marcella Cole? The thought horrified him, but it occurred to him that he was being given a second chance, a chance to make things right.

CHAPTER EIGHT

A flight of white geese, each bird as slender as a dragon, flew into the darkness over Burlington Bay. Down near the shore, a single swan floated with its neck straight up from the frost-rimed flotsam and slush. Looming behind a stand of trees furred with lichen, a row of three attached houses ran in a single sweep of grey brick facing the waterfront park.

When Carly Rouhl got to her father's house, an elegant façade forming the right wing of the block, she found a short loop of police tape draped carelessly over a bush, and two police Fords in the driveway. One was unmarked, but it had the little ashtray hubcaps of a police vehicle and she could see a computer screen low on the dashboard.

The yellow plastic tape struck her as odd—the sort of thing you'd see at a crime scene—but there was an informality to the way that it had been wound around a couple of branches that made her dismiss it.

Even the police presence didn't register as it should have; her father was a celebrity and his passing would mean there would be press to manage.

A white van was parked at the side of the road against the

snowbank. She skirted the tape and mounted the stairs to her father's doorway, a richly burled portal in dark oak, bracketed with slender leaded panes. The brass digits of the address—number 124, residence C—smouldered in the porch light, impossibly warm and mellow on a night of brittle cold.

Carly wiped her eyes, red and glistening with tears, and she was fumbling for her key when the door opened. A young police officer, about a foot taller than she was, frowned at her.

It took her a moment to catch up. "I'm Carly Rouhl. I got the message...about my father."

The officer's constabulary frown was replaced by concern. "Uh, yes, Mr. Rouhl's daughter. You, ah, *know* then. My sympathies about your father. He must have been a great man." For all his deference, Officer—Eberhardt the name plate said—held his ground in the doorway. "I, uh...I think the office would have cautioned you about coming to the house directly. You see, there are investigators coming. Soon after they're done, your father will be... They'll release the... to the coroner."

"I want to see him. I've been preparing myself for this for months and, well, here it is and I still can't believe he's gone."

"I understand your feelings, Miss, but believe me, it would be better if you didn't come in right now."

"Investigators? Did you say investigators? Don't they know about his health? He's been very fragile for months now. I can explain everything. I can tell them." Carly was looking past the officer, but there was nothing to see in the entrance way. "Doesn't somebody have to... I... The message said someone would want to talk to me."

"Yes, well that would be Detective Weiss, but he can't talk to you here. He's conferring with the site team. Here..." The policeman unbuttoned a pocket on his shirt and pulled out a business card. "He gave me this. Can you tell me where you'll be in the morning?"

"Detective? I don't understand why a detective needs to be concerned with this. Have you spoken to my father's nurse?"

"The nurse? Yes. Mrs. Crowther has been sent home. It would be best if you... There's nothing you can do right now."

Carly looked at his discomfort, and then at her boots in frustration. She thought about being a pain in the ass about this, but there didn't seem any point in arguing with the young officer. She took the card. "Well, normally after 8:00 a.m. I go into my office—the *Escarpment* office on Pearl. It's a magazine. It's not far from here. Should I go there now? Tonight?"

"I know where that is. It's in the plaza, right? There's no need for you to be anywhere but home right now. Why don't you just go to your office in the morning and someone will contact you there. Things will be clearer then." The officer pulled back and had begun to swing the door shut when something occurred to him. "Oh, uh, could you wait here just a moment, Ms. Rouhl?"

He shut the door but didn't close it properly as though that would be less of an affront, and Carly was left on the little porch. Her long hair was pulled back in a dark knot and her skin was pink with the wind. Her ivy league imagination took over and now the night was a shroud, draped close about the white columns and black ironwork, but then she trashed the idea as romantic crap. This was death. The one she had foreseen and prepared for. It wasn't playing out the way she had expected, but she was smart and mature, the one everybody depended on to know what to do. Unflappable...

But she was on her own now. She wasn't the daughter of a famous man anymore. Not really. And whatever she did, that unique distinction had defined her as much as her independence and efficiency.

She turned with short, stamping steps and looked across the road. This time of year, there was almost no-one on the beach strip, but a few buffleheads and gulls still skimmed the ragged stretches of open water.

It wasn't right. Didn't the world know that A.L. Rouhl had died tonight? There should be silent crowds, mournful music, the press awed into respectful behaviour. The hell with mundane reality.

But then, she knew her father and there was no doubt in Carly's mind that her father had chosen his time, and a thought seemed to flit in from the darkness under the trees—that everyone, the police and the investigators, were here to play out A.L.'s last script, even the writer's only daughter. Even she.

The cold made her grimace, and on her face, the only legacy of the old man's drooping mouth was the line of her own full lips.

There was time for a single car to go by over the sanded street. Kind of peaceful. And then the door reopened. Indy burst out, straining at his leash to sniff Carly's boots. Carly looked up, but the young officer had remained back in the hallway. Instead, a stocky man in a brown microfibre jacket had the leash. His skin was dark, slightly mottled, and he had large, heavy-lidded eyes. He offered his condolences quickly, but the sentiment never reached those appraising eyes. "Ms. Rouhl? I'm Detective Joshi. I wonder," he said, "if you'd take your father's dog," and he held out the leash. "You'll have to decide what to do with him."

It wasn't easy to break eye contact with the detective, but at last, the commotion around her knees made Carly stare down at the dog. When she did, she realized with amazement that she'd not thought of Indy at all. Another wave of pain caught her off guard, a near sob rising in her throat. She took the leash and, to be sure of her voice, she whispered. "Yes. Sure. Of course. I'll take care of him," was all she could manage to say.

It had started. Life after A.L. Rouhl. She tugged off a glove and then crouched down to rub Indy's right ear—the one that never drooped. To her surprise, the dog cowered. Just a little, but it was out of character for Indy.

Carly looked up and realized that the detective in the brown jacket had missed none of this. By the time she got to her feet her father's familiar front door was closing in her face with a polite and sympathetic slowness. Through the diminishing crack, she caught a glimpse of the young officer staring at the floor, and behind Joshi, the silent heart of the house.

Carly walked Indy to her car. When she opened the car door he didn't leap in. She stooped onto a half kneel above the mounded snow and tried to engage his eyes.

"How did it happen, Indy? Was he in pain? Was it hard for you to watch? It should have been me, shouldn't it? I should have been the one there to help him go. But no one called me... not until it was over. Why is that, Indy? You would have called me if you could, wouldn't you?"

Indy didn't share, but he did make a half-hearted attempt at getting in the back seat and made a couple of careless circles before slumping down. Carly went round and got in.

She turned the key so that the dash would light and placed her hands on the steering wheel. The night was so damn black. She sat staring out at the row of houses with their pinprick porch lights until an odd, uneasy thought came to her: they shouldn't let her drive. Not an emotional twelve-year-old. At last her brow dropped to the wheel and she began to cry with the anger and incomprehension of a child. There was a movement in the back seat and then she heard Indy's breathing in her ear.

CHAPTER NINE

It had been dark since five. Now it was just past nine on Thursday evening. Detective Weiss wasn't aware that Carly was outside in the dark, weeping in her car; he was listening to music. After a couple of minutes, he realized he knew the piece; it was by Edward Elgar. He closed his eyes and listened as the woodwinds did a slow elegiac march beneath a surge of strings. The sounds filled the small room with a prideful dignity. He had to remember what this was called.

A few more seconds and the music ebbed, allowing a single flute to colour its heartbreaking farewell. The name of the music came to him and his eyes opened and crinkled in a smile. He waited until the music settled on a resolving silence, looked at his watch, poked a couple of fingers into the right hand of a set of leather driving gloves to prevent fingerprints, and pressed the pause button on the CD player.

Returning the glove to his jacket pocket, he turned around to take one more look at the room.

Backlit by the evening gloom over Burlington Bay, the body of an old man was sprawled in a leather desk chair, his gray, balding head sagging to one side, in front of him an open laptop computer. On a curve of braided rug sat an antique pistol: a derringer. Weiss's smile faded. He began to pick his way through the clutter of the small office, past an untidy wall of books and a laced leather umbrella stand packed with every manner of rod, cane and stick, except, perhaps, for an umbrella —and went out into the corridor.

Reaching the kitchen, he pushed aside the door and took in the aroma of double roast coffee.

"I bring it from home," Mrs. Crowther was saying to a young police officer. Crowther's tidy nurse's jacket was protected by a blue apron. "I need a good strong coffee to stay awake in the evenings, but old Mr. Rouhl—he's a tea drinker." There was a painful silence and then she corrected herself. "He *was* a tea drinker. Always Earl Grey. Always black. No lemon or sugar."

Now Mrs. Crowther was offering biscuits to Prem Joshi who had returned, cold and red-faced, from a careful walk around the outside of the house. She didn't offer one to Weiss who lingered in the doorway; in fact, she barely acknowledged him.

He understood. It was the death on him, still clinging to his clothes, mirrored in his eyes. "I baked these myself," she said to the uniform, putting a loaded white plate in front of him. "Mr. Rouhl would sometimes have one with his tea." Officer Eberhardt, looking slick and upholstered in his winter jacket, his head shaved to a fine military stubble to hide a receding hairline, thanked her, but politely refused because Joshi had.

Weiss approved. It didn't seem right to eat biscuits, not with the great man dead at the end of the corridor.

Weiss tried to catch Mrs. Crowther's eye long enough to smile with sympathy, but she hid her face in busywork, rattling the utensil tray of the dishwasher with studied seriousness. The detective's smile turned patient and he beckoned to Joshi with a movement of his head.

Joshi, his coat and jacket open, slid out along the bench of the breakfast nook. Mrs. Crowther offered him coffee. "Ah, thank you, no ma'am."

She shot a resentful glance that just missed Weiss and then turned her back on them all.

The detectives stepped into the corridor, Joshi partially closing the door behind him. Weiss walked a few steps down the corridor, and then eased back against the wall.

Under a gray suit jacket, he wore a three-button vest. He tucked his thumbs in its pockets and looked at the floor. Joshi waited, staring at the detective's bristling hair. At last, prodded by the silence, Joshi said, "There's nothing outside. Nothing unusual. Oh, and the daughter was here. Showed up at the door. I told her you'd contact her tomorrow."

"You sent her home?"

"Yes. They must have warned her."

Detective Weiss nodded and then cocked his head down the corridor towards the little office. "This was called in as a straight-forward suicide."

It was getting late. Behind the office door, A.L. Rouhl's body was still in the desk chair. "You say the CD player was still playing at just after 8:30?"

"Yeah." Joshi nodded. "The music seemed irreverent somehow. I turned it off. I was careful about prints, though."

"Actually, you paused it," Weiss said. "That let me roughly time the tracks back to when Mrs. Crowther says she heard the shot."

"That's what you've been doing in there?"

"I can't do much else until the lab crew has been over the scene."

"You've called in the crime lab? Coroner won't do it for you?"

"Well, you know, at first glance it was just this sad, typical little suicide scene. A mouth shot into the back of the throat. Pretty straight forward. But then, well—the Enigma Variations."

"Oh God. Don't."

"Elgar—on the CD player. Interesting choice, hmm? I mean, what would *you* want playing? The last thing you would ever hear—the soundtrack for your departure from the world. I just listened to it: there's this sort of grand crescendo in the ninth sketch followed by a quiet bit. Anyway, that's exactly the moment I'd choose. I can see the old man holding the gun—waiting for it."

"Christ, Eilert. It's just a piece of music."

"Hmm? Oh. Yes," Weiss said. "Just music." He nodded and looked at the floor. He studied the narrow carpet for a moment. "Old guy in terminal decline decides to end it quickly. Bullet discharged in the mouth. What else could it be but suicide, right?"

"Simple."

Weiss nodded again and was silent. "Thing is, I started noticing the problems. Two problems actually...and one of them's a honey. Anyway, I figure I need a forensics team. They have to come over from Toronto, so in the meantime, we can make a prelim."

"Two problems." Joshi sighed and closed his eyes. "So, let's hear them."

"Well, there's this shadow on the wall..."

"Shadow?"

"A void in the blood on the window and window ledge—in the splash pattern. What it amounts to is there's no blood spatter on the window behind the corpse, and of course there should be—lots of it—because there's a very messy exit wound."

"You got all this in five minutes?"

"Just a quick look around. The arithmetic slowed me down —adding up track timings from the liner notes. Had to use my notebook. I hate fucking arithmetic. Of course, if the window behind Rouhl's chair was wide open when he fired..."

Joshi had to think. It had been half an hour since he'd been in the room. "But the window *wasn't* open."

"Well, you were on the scene first, and that's what you told me. Nobody's been opening and closing windows have they?" Weiss raised his eyebrows, and made as if to peer back into the kitchen where Nurse Crowther was trying to deal with either grief or boredom by shifting dishes about. "Could our Mrs. Crowther have closed it—after she found Rouhl?"

"Mrs. Crowther *said* she hadn't touched anything." Joshi hadn't asked too many questions, but he'd made sure to establish *that*. "You think she was lying to me?"

"I don't know. This is a scene that desperately wants to be taken seriously as a suicide, but here I am after a first glance…"

Joshi just stared. "Anyway, there's nothing on the snow outside the window. There's a hard crust over about three inches of undisturbed snow. Pure as the driven, as they say."

"We're not working with much yet, but I mean, right away, I can't help thinking about who we're dealing with here: this is *A.L. Rouhl*. The man was a famous writer, Prem. Spent most of his adult life writing books. I read one in college. Okay, I was *supposed* to read one in college. Point is, Rouhl was a respected literary figure. I can't see him being arbitrary about anything—far less his big death scene.

"Seems to me he'd want everything just right. Window, desktop, computer… Rouhl could've anticipated everything—right down to you and me standing over his remains."

Joshi straightened uncomfortably as though a reporter had just peered down the hallway. "Was he a mystery writer or something?"

"No. He was sort of… Well, a travel writer. But very successful and very popular; the governor-general called him a national treasure. I guess I'm going to have to study up on him a bit."

Weiss turned to face the door of the little office and appeared to be stroking a stiff left shoulder. "Indulge me for a minute. I have to be careful what I ask the lab people for."

Joshi snorted. "You got that right. They're going to take one look and say, 'Suicide. What are *we* doing here?' So just ask them to help you with your problems. Say: here's number one and here's number two."

"Yes. My problems." A tight smile that was mostly lost under the mustache, and then he was following the carpet pattern again. "You see, I was just considering the possibility. I mean, what if the old gent had staged a bit of a tableau for us? He knew he could count on being ignored for five or ten minutes around the time our Mrs. Crowther was taking over from the afternoon nurse. This is around eight o'clock. And he's sitting there listening to the music, holding his pistol. Could be he's thought it all through, how it's all going to look. Maybe he doesn't want us to rush his last scene—doesn't want the investigation to be nothing more than a bureaucratic formality. He wants us running about with bewildered expressions for a bit. Clearly a suicide and yet…"

Joshi nodded. "No blood behind his head wound. Okay, but there's no way he could control that."

"What if something had been behind him when the shot was fired?"

Joshi's eyes widened. "Or someone?"

Weiss smiled. "Ah, well, of course, that won't fly, because if there *had* been a real live person standing squarely behind Rouhl when the old boy fired, we'd probably have two corpses instead of one, the second body slumped on the floor behind the first, with a bullet lodged somewhere around the level of its heart. A deep throat shot at that angle would pass under the old guy's skull with plenty of penetration left."

Joshi frowned. "Let me think this through: you're talking

about some kind of object standing there behind him... Something that's no longer there. Then it follows that someone must have taken it away after Rouhl's death." Joshi raised an eyebrow. "The murderer?"

Weiss shrugged. "A murderer, or... Mrs. Crowther. She *says* she heard the shot from the front hall. She'd been watching the day nurse drive away, still had her coat on. On the other hand, she seems a little too composed for someone who's had the shock of hearing a shot and rushing in to find her employer's body."

Joshi nodded. "Then you're talking about *assisted* suicide. You're saying Rouhl got Nurse Crowther to help him."

"It's possible. She's a nurse who knows Rouhl's prognosis is hopeless; she sees the great man suffering every day."

Joshi shot a glance towards the kitchen doorway. Officer Eberhardt was accepting a biscuit. "Of course, with the entry wound in the mouth, it's unlikely she held the gun herself."

Weiss ignored the muffled conversation. "Truth is, none of this is very likely, is it—a nurse risking her career, her livelihood for a client? But, there you *are*, see? Do you see what I mean? Rouhl's puzzle, his *enigma*, makes us run around in circles. We're forced to consider, what, three...four? possible scenarios —suicide, mercy killing, assisted suicide? And murder, of course; an angry, determined killer might even stage-manage a mouth shot."

"Christ, slow down, Eilert. Let's take them one at a time. It's too late to check Mrs. Crowther for powder right? She's been rinsing dishes."

"I'll get forensics to check her clothes. If she was even close by when the gun was fired, they'll know. Soon as they've done their stuff in Rouhl's office, we'll have a proper look in there."

"All right," Joshi said, "the forensics people can try and find out if there was a second person in the room when Rouhl died. You said there were *two* problems."

"Yes. You got it so far? A clearly visible exit wound and no blood on the window."

"You think I need chart paper and coloured markers? Let me have it."

"Okay, the second problem is the bullet."

"What about the bullet?"

Looking pained, Weiss rubbed the back of his neck. "There isn't one."

The great man's wide lips were parted as though in mouth-breathing exertion, his heavy brows low in one last great, absorbing thought. Now at eighty-two, a workhorse hanging dead in its harness, Alistair Landseer Rouhl, in place, had stopped being.

The site team was getting ready to leave. He could hear them putting on winter coats in the living room. Down the corridor, Weiss was back at the office doorway, a gloved hand resting on the frame. Mrs. Crowther was gone, and the house was beginning to feel lifeless and official; a sanctified crime scene.

Joshi walked down the corridor and stood beside Weiss. The detective handed Joshi a small digital recorder. "This is just for my notes," he said. "It's on already. Just hold it up a bit..."

If the forensics people had told Weiss anything useful it didn't show on his face. He looked and sounded as though he'd been abandoned.

Joshi stayed near the wooden door, looking at the red light on Weiss's tiny recorder while the detective made his way into the cramped space around the office desk. Joshi wished he could have watched the site team in here with all their equipment, but the space was too crowded. It must have been similar to the stateroom scene in *A Night at the Opera*. Weiss was wearing latex gloves, but as yet hadn't actually touched the body. He circled around the old man and squatted in the narrow space behind his desk chair.

"The chair is low backed, so I can see the exit wound quite clearly." His voice was loud for the benefit of the recorder, and for the hundredth time, Joshi wondered at Weiss's slight, vaguely Germanic accent revealed in precise, clipped consonants. It didn't sound remotely Scottish. "Big. Messy. More or less what you'd expect from a mouth shot.

"There are two possibilities. The first... Well, I guess the bullet could have gone out the window if it had been opened all the way. An open window would have made it extremely cold in this small space. But it wasn't when you came in, right Prem?"

Startled, Joshi looked up from the recorder and shook his head. Weiss smiled. "First on scene detective says it wasn't cold."

He straightened up and turned to the window. "There's some blood here and here—at the very edges of the window pane and at the top, see? And the blood is misted; there's no directional smear suggesting the spatter hitting at an extreme angle, the way it would if the window was open. The main thing, though, is that there's no blood on the central and lower pane and none at all down here on the window ledge. Looks to me as if the bullet *should* have hit either the lower window pane or the painted wood of the window ledge about...here."

"Depends on how the old guy held his head at the last second," Joshi said.

"Yeah, but for the slug to have hit any lower than that—way down here on the wall—Rouhl would have had to be leaning back."

"Either way, though... Well, see for yourself. No bullet hole. No impact point. Nada. Nowhere."

"I don't get it," Joshi began, then took a moment to hold the recorder out to one side. "The window was closed. The glass is intact, but..."

"Told you the problem was a honey. There's no fucking

bullet. Site team couldn't find it either. It wasn't a happy symposium, I can tell you. They thought I was trying to test them or something."

Weiss looked down at the shrivelled old body.

A. L. Rouhl, grey of face, emaciated by his illness, lay slumped in his writing chair, an expensive piece of furniture in well worn black leather. His balding, age-spotted head lolled back at an unnatural angle over the chair back. "A great man, Prem. You'll be telling your biographer about this. There will be people making pilgrimages to Rouhl's grave."

"My biographer," Joshi said. "I hate to bother him again," and he looked morosely at the red light on the recorder.

Weiss let his gaze drift. "Look at this: these three framed pictures on the window ledge. The centre frame has been laid down on its face." He picked it up and tested the hinged stand on the ledge. "Seems unlikely it could have fallen forward, so it was put that way for some reason, or possibly knocked down." He made a sweeping gesture, imagining the kind of blow or scrape that would be required to pull the photograph forward on its face. "The site team took prints. The right and left photos show what you'd expect—family: Rouhl with his late wife I expect, Rouhl with a twelve-year-old girl...the only daughter. But the centre picture, the one lying down, shows Rouhl standing alone." Weiss angled it for Joshi. "And see, he's in front of some kind of monument or gravestone."

He laid the frame flat, precisely where it had been. "As for the window itself: tallish and relatively narrow. Folding push bar which demounts, allowing the window to be swung outward." Weiss carefully lifted the bar from its peg and drew it out so he could use it to press open the window. At the same time, he leaned gently against the glass with his glove.

"Hmm." Weiss sagged slightly towards the pane. "Well, that settles that. This window hasn't been opened for some time."

Joshi nodded. "Looks way too stiff for old Rouhl, at any rate."

Weiss put the bar back on its pin and drew a horizontal line in the air with his gloved hand. The line passed above the corpse's shoulder and ended just above the chair back. "With Rouhl sitting normally, the bullet would have exited about this high, just below the base of his skull." Weiss cradled Rouhl's head with two hands, one supporting the neck, the other the cranium.

He shifted the head carefully on the chairback. The motion was tiny, but even from where Joshi stood, the head appeared to move independently of the shoulders and made a muffled, grinding sound. Mercifully, from where Joshi stood he couldn't see any of the damage at the back of the old man's head. There was little visible on Rouhl's face except for a couple of reddish-blue welts in the cheek.

"At the back of the head—a large circular wound, the penetration at the edge of the skull clearly marked by swelling brain tissue beginning to protrude. The round should have taken a fair bit of blood, bone, and tissue with it."

Joshi stole a glance at the carpet. "Anything about the derringer? Make? Model?"

Weiss looked pained, as though annoyed at the digression. "Jesus, Prem, are you kidding? I only know it's a derringer from a Mel Gibson movie about riverboat gamblers. We'll look it up." He tipped his chin in the direction of the window. "The position of the exit wound itself is atypical. It suggests..." Weiss frowned. "...that Rouhl lifted his elbows before pulling the trigger." He was talking to Joshi now. "The most natural thing for a suicide to do with a pistol is rest his arms on the desk for support, right?—you know, lean forward a bit. Or to lie right back in the chair, deliberately shooting up into the cranium through the roof of the mouth."

Joshi rubbed the back of his head. "Either way, you get an exit wound in the scalp or high up on the back of the head. Or maybe it doesn't penetrate the skull at all and stays inside."

"Exactly. But this shot…this shot went straight back." Weiss raised his chin and mimed the pistol with his finger. "The trajectory here was probably more or less parallel to the floor."

Weiss was quiet for a moment, visualizing and thinking it through. At last he said, "You know, I admire the old gent, sitting up straight. No dejected, despairing stoop for A.L. Rouhl. It was a straight-backed, assertive act, with his head held high. A 'Let's do this' sort of boldness."

Weiss shook his head, turned to square himself in front of the window and, putting his weight on the ledge, looked through the glass at the snow-bright night.

He watched the streetlights for a moment then itemized: "There's a driveway immediately beneath the window. The roadway, then a strip of parkland, a beach—mostly snow-covered at the moment. Offset to the left, a public pier, with outbuildings; kind of a pavilion."

"No convenient walls with gaping bullet holes in them," Joshi added.

Holding the little recorder out to the side, finger and thumb, as though it was a small dead thing, Joshi half-whispered, "Didn't the forensics people say *anything* about the bullet?"

"Oh, yes. Got quite snippy about it, in fact, as though it was my fault. They kept asking how the scene could have been contaminated. Fuck."

Joshi shrugged off the sense of grievance. "Anyway, ball's in our court. For now at least, we say, what—that the damn bullet was intercepted somehow and removed from the room? Sounds ridiculous, doesn't it?"

Weiss let his head sag to one side, his eyes making an accounting. "When I write it up, I'll work on the wording.

"Anyway, you still have to wonder about the void back here: just plain not enough blood behind the chair. I asked the unit to look for a secondary blood source on the carpet, just in case a Very Stupid Person stood here while Rouhl was about to blast away, but there's nothing, of course."

"Best bet is to search the house again..." Joshi sighed. "...see if there's some object that might have been placed there. Who knows, I might have missed something at least four feet high with a massive, smoking shell hole in it."

Weiss's mustache furred upward, the way it did when he smiled. "Then finally we have the laptop: a Sony Vaio, business model." Weiss followed its power cord down to an extension and then to the wall. He bent to look at the screen and, with his gloved ring finger, he gently touched a key. Joshi could see the sudden pall of blue light as the screen lit Weiss's face.

"The thing is on standby just the way he left it. The keyboard's got a fingerprint reader and probably won't let us log back in without the correct fingerprint. But then, we've still got the finger, don't we."

Weiss took Rouhl's arm and hand and shifted the corpse forward. He splayed the right hand and dragged Rouhl's dead index finger across the window of the print reader. The screen flickered, turned a light grey.

"The computer doesn't seem to mind that the finger is dead. Very democratic, don't you think?" The light turned white. "And yes, we have a suicide note."

Joshi sagged back against the door. "A note? That's a relief. That clinches it, doesn't it?"

"Listen, Prem. Nobody's going to let us off the hook until we can explain where the damn bullet went, suicide note or no. That's why I'm going to have to write in 'cause of death —deferred.'"

"But the note—doesn't it... What does it say?"

"Well, it fits in nicely with the Enigma theme: short and not in the least helpful. Fresh page, new file. It's addressed to 'Dear Carly' and it's signed 'love, Dad.' As for what it says…" Weiss looked at the text with his head cocked to one side as though he were appreciating an abstract painting and then gave a tiny humourless laugh. "Actually, it's not a bad exit line for a writer."

CHAPTER TEN

Around 10:30 Friday morning, Carly was at the door of her magazine's office looking out through her reflection in the glass. Beyond the mirrored image of a pretty, dark-haired woman with a barrette above her left ear, a tall man with a longish brush cut unfolded himself from the driver's seat of a big Ford; it was the unmarked cruiser she'd seen outside her father's house. The man stood up and looked about, his gaze coming to rest on the glass door where Carly stood. "That's got to be him," Carly said, wrapping up an idle game of Spot the Detective she'd been playing since the call from Weiss's cell phone. The plaza was busy and Eilert Weiss began picking his way through rows of salt-encrusted cars.

Behind Carly, Peggy Goss was trying her best to rub Indy's head, but the lab kept ducking away. "What's the matter with Indy?" she said.

Carly stepped away from the door. "He was there when Dad died. The poor dog's going to need years of therapy. But hey, maybe that's not so bad. He's always wanting up on the couch."

"You know, I'd be happy to watch him until after…"

"Thanks, Peg."

The office was large and empty looking, as it always was right after the quarterly was wrapped up. For the next week or so, writers and photographers would come and go or would submit their copy online, leaving Peggy, retired and working mostly for the pleasure of it, to manage the office practically by herself. Peggy had picked up her computer skills as a travel agent, but her real value lay in a cheerful common sense that everyone relied on. Carly couldn't pay her enough and tried to make up for it in bonuses, which could be balanced against the cash flow. Since Peggy was one of the most self-motivated women she'd ever known, it was an odd system, and perhaps a little demeaning, but Peggy actually seemed to enjoy the recognition.

"Peggy, you've got Dad's last installment on the office system, right?" She heard herself say it and thought, *Well, look at me. Carly Rouhl is carrying on. Not much of a writer, no genius, but a hell of a plugger.*

"You're talking about the file you e-mailed from your dad's house on Monday?" Peggy tapped slowly and deliberately at the keyboard for a few seconds before confirming, "Yep, it's there." She wore her short, frosted hair in a Dutch bob, her tailored jacket and jade brooch looking tidy and business-like. When she looked up Carly could see the sympathy in Peggy's eyes. "It won't be quite complete though, will it? Did he add much this week?"

Realizing she had strayed perilously close to the subject of A.L.'s suicide, Peggy looked away.

"There won't be much more. Dad worked so slowly. There are a couple of pages still on his laptop, but nothing thrilling. We've got enough. After we polish up the last bit of the memoir for the magazine, we have to send the whole thing on to A.L.'s old publisher in New York. I guess they'll be looking for it now."

"Even as a complete piece, it'll make a pretty thin book."

"The version they put out will be a picture book heavy with

photos, part of an 'Illustrated Lives' series. I already couriered them most of the photographic materials, except for the few I kept back for us to use."

"How are you feeling about all this, Car?"

"I'm okay. Although... I feel cheated of something—of knowing more about him, more about him than the rest of the world, I mean. I don't remember feeling that way when he was alive."

"He didn't give this autobiography to the world, or even to the magazine. He gave it to you."

"I know."

"And you were there helping him. Have you read the latest pages?"

"I *typed* most of it, although I haven't had a chance to absorb what he was saying yet. I'll tell you what's going to be hard, though—editing it. Fixing it up, knowing he won't be there to okay the changes. That's going to be tough because I know how exacting he was. I don't think I'll ever be as discriminating."

Weiss came in with a commotion of gloves and snow boots, stamping his feet on the rubber mat and unwinding a long blue and white scarf.

Carly did the introductions and waited.

Shaking his coat off, Weiss sat down. Every now and then some of the people coming out of the Lee Valley store at the far end of the plaza would pass the office window on their way to their cars; they'd glance at the public service announcements and event posters in the window, or peer in at the potted plants that seemed to be everywhere in the office.

While Carly was rolling a chair over, Weiss tried to renew his acquaintance with Indy, but the dog kept his distance and didn't seem to know who to trust. At last, the detective rubbed his hands and gave Carly a sympathetic smile. She picked up on it—the hesitation. They were finally going to tell her something. Even then she had to tilt her head and wait.

"I don't think anyone has told you... It appears your father took his own life."

She sat bolt upright as though surprised. But no... Who was she kidding? If he could find a way, that's *exactly* what A.L. Rouhl would do. *You're so naive, Carly.* At least she understood now why the police were being guarded.

"How... how could he possibly *do* it?"

Weiss spread his hands. "His illness..."

"No, I mean, *how*? Did he use the drugs? Sleeping pills?"

Weiss nodded that he understood. He sat back. "Were you aware your father had a gun? A small derringer?"

Carly's eyes were wide and fixed on Weiss. After a second of silence, her gaze strayed to the near distance and finally, she looked down at the floor. "My God. My God, he shot himself." A dozen thoughts ran through her mind, but after a few more seconds passed she whispered, "Good for you, A.L. You got the ending right."

Weiss seemed to understand and gave what might have been a nod. "It was a comfortable little room. Your father must have been happy there."

Carly slouched in a non-committal way. Happiness was one of the harder concepts she had had to deal with.

"There was a glass of sherry on his desk," Weiss said.

"It would've been port. Yes."

"Well, why don't we start there? Please don't take offense, I know very little about your father, and I have to ask about his state of mind. Under the circumstances..."

"What? You're wondering about whether he had been drinking?" Once again Carly was a bit taken aback, but this was suicide, so it was an obvious question. "Dad actually used to be a fairly heavy drinker. Most of the writers of his generation were. Whiskey was his favourite. He *used* to be a drinker, until his medications made it dangerous for him to touch alcohol. He never gave it up entirely, but I think he was down to a glass of port or two a day.

"By the way, his giving up hard liquor more or less corresponds with the end of his life as a writer. The alcohol seemed to help him. I know that's not conventional wisdom, but when he drank he never seemed to get beyond a sort of boozy languor, and he seemed able to function that way...to write at any rate."

"Depression?"

"He got more reclusive and sullen as he got older, but he stayed productive until his health began to fail. Some critics said that his last book, *Meridian*, was 'more serious,' and, by their criteria, better. I think it was downright macabre. A friend said it should have been called *Profiles in Psychosis*. For all the critical acclaim, it also didn't sell that well. Not by his usual standards anyway."

"How did he work? The laptop?"

"Yeah. He kept up." Carly frowned. This must have seemed an orderly approach to Weiss, but she couldn't follow the logic yet. "Is this significant?"

"Probably not. I've always wondered how creative people do it. I'm an observer, not a doer."

Carly nodded and sounded bitter. "So, it seems, am I." She'd pictured this interview in her mind, imagining what direction it would take. This wasn't it. "In the last few years, he even got into voice recognition software, so he could dictate through a microphone. He probably couldn't have finished the last article without it."

"Because his hands weren't steady?"

Carly cradled her own right hand in her palm, staring down at it. "His hands were...steady enough to hold a gun. He just had no stamina. It was an effort of will for him to even dictate a paragraph."

"So, did you know he had a small derringer?"

Carly understood the implied criticism. "Yes, I guess I did. It was one of the hundreds of objects he hoarded. You have to understand that he was a collector of things—little tokens of humanity. If I'd remembered the derringer at all, I'd have assumed he had no ammunition for it. The gun would have been hidden in plain sight. Just another memento of a rich life."

Weiss nodded but took no notes. "There was a photograph behind him on the window ledge. It showed him standing in front of a memorial of some sort. Do you know the one?"

Carly frowned at the digression. "Photograph? Yes, I know it. It has a pewter frame."

"That's it. It seems a morbid photo to keep close at hand. Family crypt, maybe? The picture can't have been there all that long. He looks old in the picture and drawn, as though his illness had already begun to affect him."

"You're thinking the picture suggests despair? Don't try so hard, Mr. Weiss. You're right—he was capable of suicide, and it's in character."

"Just like that?"

"Come on, Detective Weiss; my father was about to enter a care facility. They would have lowered him into bed with a winch and showered him on a plastic chair—and he would have died there within the year. In his position, I might have done the same thing." *No,* she thought. *I wouldn't have had the imagination.*

"I see." Weiss reached inside his jacket and pulled out a small notepad. "Your father left a short note on the screen of his laptop. May I read it to you?"

Carly winced. "Jesus. A suicide note, you mean? Why didn't you say so right away?"

"Sorry. I'm a bit of a plodder with these things. I need to handle one thing at a time. Compartmental, I call it. But no real harm done, is there?"

Carly straightened in her chair. "Okay. Okay, give it to me."

"Here it is: 'Dear Carly, No answers. Only questions as usual.'"

Weiss's reading was flat and without feeling. Glancing at Carly's face, Weiss waited. All Carly gave him for his trouble was a puzzled frown.

After a nicely calculated pause, Weiss added softly, "It was signed, 'Love, Dad.'"

Carly's façade cracked. "Shit." Her face creased in pain and her eyes filled.

Weiss nodded, "I understand how you feel. Your father's note has no comfort in it, does it? After what he did, well, you must feel hurt by that."

Carly looked out the window, breathing, giving herself time. She kept her chin high so the tears wouldn't run. A few seconds later, her voice under steely control, she answered, "You're wrong there, Detective. He left me the longest fucking suicide note I've ever heard of. I was just a little slow recognizing it as such. I was publishing a three-part article in my magazine. It was sort of an autobiography, a memoir, and I had already printed two of the pieces in my magazine. The last one was on the laptop in front of him when he died. The whole thing was his swan song, his summing up at the end."

"I see. Then you must be eager to see the last part—the part still on his laptop."

"I helped him write it, Detective Weiss. I sat with him almost every other night, proofing, taking dictation. I pretty much know what's in it. In fact, I emailed a partial draft of part three to our office computer too."

"Ah, and it seemed just about finished to you?"

"With a bit of editing, it's publishable."

"But...finished?"

Carly realized that this was an important question—to the police and to her. She thought for a moment. "I would have expected a little...I don't know...poetry? in the last pages?

Instead, it just went on, in a matter of fact way. On the other hand, I don't know what the hell else he could have said. I had a sense that he was thrashing about looking for an ending. If you ask me, he wrote his ending with that preposterous little gun."

Weiss looked skeptical.

"No. I'm serious. I know the way he thought and he would look at his life as an unfinished story in need of a climax. Hell, he probably even anticipated the denouement."

"Remind me about denouement."

"Sorry. In a story, it's the little wrap up at the end after the climax. The loose ends."

"Do you mind telling me where you're going with that?"

"The denouement? That's us, Detective. You and me. Obliged to write the final word on his passing."

"I see. And you think I should sign off on his suicide and tell the world it was…what did you say? 'In character?'"

Carly didn't answer, puzzled by the question. She probably meant just what Weiss had said, but there was something about the way Weiss put it. The detective didn't want to be a rubber stamp on a death certificate.

All the same, Weiss's expression remained mild, his manner unhurried. "I'll have to hold on to his laptop as part of the investigation. We bagged it and, honestly, I haven't had time to even unwrap it yet. I take it I won't find anything there anticipating his suicide."

"All three parts of his memoir were mostly about the people he'd met and borrowed from in his writing career. There was surprisingly little about himself. It was… it was as though his whole life had been lived vicariously through them, while he sat alone in that little room of his, writing it all down from memory. The truth is, that was his style all along. He seldom worked from notes and I have no idea how he remembered so much, or with such intimate clarity, but it made him famous."

Weiss nodded, looking around the *Escarpment* office. "Perhaps you'll let me continue this chat another time. When all the...uh, usual little tests are done." He took his time getting up and retrieving his coat and scarf. As he passed Carly, he squeezed her shoulder. "Thanks," he said. "I'll get the laptop back to you in a few days. "By the way, I'll be pulling his medical records."

Weiss was looking back over his shoulder as though anticipating a reaction.

He didn't get one. Carly was alone somewhere with her thoughts. If she'd been paying attention, Carly herself would have recognized this little bit of questioning technique. She was supposed to notice Weiss's silence nudging her with an unseen elbow.

And she did get it at last. She stood, managing a breathy mutter. "It was his immune system. The doctors couldn't seem to agree on what caused it to weaken. Things started to go wrong..." She thought for a second. "...about three years ago."

CHAPTER ELEVEN

An hour before the Sunday service for A.L. Rouhl, Weiss introduced himself to the bereavement director at the Talbot Funeral Gardens. Weiss hadn't intended to question the funeral director, just let him know he would be observing from one of the side aisles and that he might need to take some discrete photographs with his phone. All the same, the director seemed determined to unload his anxieties on Weiss as the service got closer.

"I have a problem. Judging from the crowd in the hall and in the parking lot, the main chapel's benches aren't going to be adequate. I'll get one of my ushers to set up an audio-video feed to one of the smaller chapels. If that doesn't do it, we'll have to set up yet another monitor in the front foyer. I haven't seen such a large service since the mayor.

"Knowing full well that A.L. Rouhl was one of the few people in the city with an international reputation, faded though it might be, I arranged for our largest venue to be available, but the turnout is impressive. Ah well, I'll just send our staff out front. They'll direct people to park up the hill at the golf club, or along the shore at the marina.

"Here's a sad thing, though—Rouhl's daughter, Carly,

requested only a single pew be reserved for the immediate family. The service is about to start, and it's clear that even that won't be filled."

Weiss nodded. "It seems A. L. Rouhl left a big footprint on the literary world, but a small mark on his family."

Weiss was well-read himself, and when the service got started at last, he was impressed by several of the distinguished figures who rose to speak in front of the closed casket. A former premier spoke eloquently, sparking tears even in the eyes of people who had never personally met Rouhl. Then there was the tall Hispanic man, a recognized famous voice on public radio. He stood up in a black cloak, similar to what an opera impresario might wear and purported to speak for admiring readers yet unborn, and remembered Rouhl as an anointed demigod of the literary pantheon.

As he spoke, a slide show of Rouhl's life lit up the wall above the altar. It was dramatically framed by the arch of the ceiling and there were decorative sconces on either side. Weiss recognized the symbols: alpha and omega, the beginning and end of the Greek alphabet. As one slide dissolved into another, unfolding Rouhl's life—the young journalist, the new bestseller, the literary lion—Weiss mused that his own life was focussed mostly on omega. The funeral director and the detective's job began at the moment of death.

Weiss squeezed his eyes shut—it was happening again: beneath the looming bridge, his wife on the deck of a police rescue boat, his own suit and tie absurdly loose on her broken body, her face a massive bruise from the impact on the water. He shook his head with enough force to attract one or two stares, then the vision ebbed and he could follow the current speaker again.

The tall man in the cloak was good. He somehow managed to use the word genius, not once but three times, without making it sound fulsome.

The parade of speakers went on for over an hour, and all the while Carly, sitting with an elderly aunt and a few cousins, would rise each time to shake hands and acknowledge the condolences of these distinguished strangers. Weiss pictured the speakers lined up out the door, checking their notes, each one eager to show how important they had been in the great man's career.

Towards the end, Weiss went out to the foyer. Most of the latecomers were still wearing their coats, probably because the cloakroom was overwhelmed. Everyone here was watching a large screen television. On screen, the unmoving camera angle took in both the lectern and casket. Most of the time Carly's dark head and shoulders were a still presence at the bottom left of the screen.

Looking just as distinguished in his sleek, black suit as any dignitary rising to the lectern, a tall, conspicuously handsome man watched the monitor, an expensive-looking teal coat draped over his arm. Weiss took up a spot under the main entrance arch and tried to get comfortable against a stone column.

When it was Carly's turn to rise, she stood at the podium looking tired and dispirited. "I'm going to read a passage," she said, "from my father's work." Weiss watched her tug a worn paperback from her jacket pocket in an unpracticed way that seemed out of keeping with the formal mood. Weiss noted the stoop and hesitation and thought of Julia Roberts playing a librarian.

Carly began to read from the paperback in a flat, undramatic tone that contrasted with the praise of the polished public admirers of Rouhl the storyteller.

"My father wrote: 'The ancients had long believed that there were monsters beyond the far horizon. There must have been some who were disappointed to learn that it wasn't true—that there was just more of the same. There must have been some who refused altogether to believe the cartographers of reason. I have never been a religious man in the conventional sense of the word,' he writes, 'but I too refuse to believe that the world is limited to what we can readily see and understand. The truth is that I only found my voice as a writer when I learned to trust my heart. It brought me more insight into the lives of others than a man of my small accomplishment and skill deserves.'"

Carly stopped reading her father's words and looked out over the heads of the congregation. "I always wondered about this passage," she said in her own tired voice, "because it's one of the few places where Dad talked about his gifts as a writer. Since I went on to study writing myself, I naturally tried to get him to talk about the passage, but he wouldn't. I think that's because he was a modest man—and that whole passage is, after all, nothing more than modesty describing what several of you have called 'genius.'

"For all of his reluctance to talk about it, my father was enthralled by the power of storytelling and..." Carly paused searching for a word. "...full of...*wonder* at the gifts his muses brought to him. It awed him that he could write the details of a man or woman's life, and that it would become the truth itself."

Weiss listened as this soft-spoken woman went on for a few short minutes, trying to be honest and rooted in her memory of a real and vital person, while all around her public mourners were paying tribute to her father's reputation and stature. Weiss watched her finish, and go to sit down, but she stopped and reached back to retrieve the old paperback from the podium, nodding her apologies. She held it in her hand for a moment, looking at it as though acknowledging an old friend, then she fumbled it back inside her jacket pocket and sat down in a hall that was silent and reflective. Weiss was left with the firm conviction that that old paperback had travelled a long way in Carly's pocket.

Joshi had downloaded Carly's plate number and located her car. Then he had managed to park nearby in Weiss's unmarked cruiser. Weiss joined him after the service, slipping into the passenger seat, and waited. There were fans who wished to shake the hand of the film actor who had played one of Rouhl's characters, intellectuals who sought out the author's famous academic and literary friends, even a few colleagues who knew his editors, but of the large audience, few seemed to owe condolences to Carly, local girl, publisher of a regional magazine, the *Escarpment*.

Weiss and Joshi watched through the frost-starred windshield. Weiss noticed the good-looking man with the expensive teal coat; he looked as remarkable out here under the tall light standards as he had in front of the foyer's television monitor. It looked to Weiss as if he were waiting a pace or two behind Carly while she shook a few hands, falling in behind her as she stepped down off the steps of the chapel. Despite this, Carly hadn't noticed him.

Weiss was a little surprised to see the news teams ignore the daughter, focusing instead on the distinguished New Yorkers and nearly famous Londoners who had flown in for the service. They were content to let Carly and her small family group disperse to the parking lot.

Weiss ran down his window and found that as the group drew closer to Carly's car he could make out snatches of conversation here and there.

The cousins, a matronly woman with hair dyed as black as her Persian lamb coat, and two heavyset middle-aged men who appeared to be twins, were subdued, undemonstrative. Weiss suspected that Carly's Scottish-English background explained the family's social reticence and reserve. They clearly weren't used to expressing emotion.

"What are you going to do with the house?" asked a twin.

"I hear Cornell is after his papers," said the other.

"Papers?" Carly said, mystified. "You mean the junk in his desk drawers?"

A stooped man from A.L.'s generation whose walk suggested a bad hip, and who hadn't been seated with the family, waited his turn with Carly. When Carly saw him, she embraced the elderly man warmly. "I'm sorry about you losing Paulette," Weiss heard Carly say. "She was a good friend to Dad. Always doing him favours, helping with research..."

One of the twins turned at this. "I hadn't heard, Mike. When did it happen?"

Old Mike, fragile and careworn, managed a brave smile. "Just over a year ago."

"I didn't even know she was sick," the other twin said.

"She wasn't," Mike said. He was clasping Carly's hand so hard it shook a little, as though he were imploring condolences rather than giving them, and Weiss sensed the old man was reliving the injustice of his Paulette's passing.

"She was happy and fit. We were just back from a holiday. It just...happened. None of us were prepared. Blood poisoning they called it, whatever that means." Mike's smile was intact but his eyes were creasing with pain. Weiss realized that as a surreptitious watcher he himself was being drawn into private grief, and he turned away momentarily, missing Carly's reaction.

The parking lot was at the top of the gentle slope of the memorial gardens, a slope that took the plowed pathways and snow-drifted memorials all the way down to the shore of Burlington Bay, and Weiss could just make out an enterprising videographer set up between two large monuments, getting a wide shot of the event for the evening news.

Well outside the family circle, a well-dressed woman with a long grey scarf stood in attendance, as though she too might be waiting her turn to approach Carly. She looked to be in her late forties, and although her hair and lower face were swathed against the cold, she still managed to seem discreetly attractive, even allowing for the unflattering gloom of a mid-winter overcast though the woman's brow was pale. Weiss watched her for a moment, riveted by her quiet poise, wondering if the woman was feeling slighted, ignored by people who should recognize and acknowledge her. But as Weiss watched, those strangely familiar, perfectly defined eyes creased into the briefest of smiles and she turned, walking away with an abruptness and proud self-sufficiency that asked for no sympathy.

Weiss lost her in the shadows between the parking lot standards and he frowned in thought, allowing his head to sag until he was staring down at his feet.

When he looked up the young man with the teal coat had turned away from the family group and had begun to walk slowly—right towards the unmarked cruiser.

At his side, Joshi muttered, "Uh, oh."

Weiss turned briefly to Joshi.

"Okay," Joshi said. "I parked too close. You're such a nag, Eilert."

Weiss slouched as though in conversation with Joshi, but the man in the teal coat had no reason to take an interest in the two men, and he brushed right by the open window.

Just behind the cruiser now, he began dusting away snow with his glove so he could sit on one of the icy parapets that separated the parking lot from the snow-covered lawns. Weiss turned the ignition key so he could use the power mirrors. The dashboard glowed. With a faintly audible whir, he angled the mirror on his side until he could see the man cross his shiny, heeled boots. The pose was perfect, as though he were professionally conscious of the picture he made in his expensive suit and pristine coat. Weiss thought of the classic Arrow shirt ads by Leyendecker.

Carly turned in the direction of her car and it was obvious she saw the man seated there on the parapet. She was so absorbed in the men's fashion shoot tableau that she didn't give the detectives a glance. The blue unmarked cruiser was begrimed with salt and the windows partially obscured with frost. In Weiss's mirror, the man seemed pleased with Carly's look of sudden pleasure.

Moving past them with an awkward shuffle, Carly Rouhl stood in front of the man and said, "That wall can't be comfortable."

"I wanted to make sure you saw me."

She was nodding. "Good of you to come, Evan. You're not a devoted Rouhl reader, are you?"

"Not really, although I've read one whole, entire book of his now."

"Bet you I know which one."

"*Meridian,* the one you read from." Evan gave a weary smile. "Well, it's the easiest to get hold of without resorting to Amazon."

"You know, it's too bad I never had a chance to introduce you to him. The fans weren't exactly camping out on the lawn towards the end. He would have liked talking to you. Especially since you read a whole, entire book of his."

"Actually, I..."

Carly's back was to Weiss. She seemed to be waiting for the good-looking man to go on.

"...I did. Meet him, I mean. Just this last Tuesday, in fact."

"Tuesday? Really? He died on Thursday!" A gust of wind swept away a couple of her words but Weiss could hear the disbelief in Carly's voice. "Where would that have been? He almost never went anywhere."

"At his house. We talked."

"You *talked*? What, just the two of you? How did that happen?"

"Simple. He called me."

"Oh, so now he used the *phone*? Christ. This gets better and better. Why did he do that? I mean, no offense, but in the first place, he'd turned into a virtual hermit, and in the second..."

"He was dying. Yes. I didn't know about his illness then, and it took me a while to catch on just how serious his condition was, but in a roundabout way, I think that's what it was all about, why he called me. It was about his dying."

Carly looked away from him and Weiss, steering the mirror, briefly caught the astonishment in her face. "Tuesday. He had, what—forty-eight hours to live? Why didn't you call me then? Let me know that you were going to see him... No, wait. You would have, wouldn't you? He *asked* you not to."

"Did you know he read all your articles? The major pieces anyway; he said..."

"He didn't like most of it."

"That's not true. We made a little small talk. He respected your writing. He said so."

Carly considered that for a moment, wanting to hear more, but that thought was overtaken by another: "Wait a minute. The only way he could have even known you... Are you saying he called you because of the *profile* I wrote on you?"

Evan nodded. "That was how he introduced himself. He was pretty slick at breaking the ice with a stranger. I guess a lifetime of research makes you good at approaching people."

"You're describing a man I thought had ceased to exist years ago."

"Why? He was still writing. You must've known that."

"Of course. For the magazine..."

"He said it was a sort of brief autobiography he was doing for you. A memoir."

"For *me*? Did he say that? He gave me first serial rights, but the memoir was always intended for his New York publishers too. He knew the bastards in New York would keep it on a shelf to run as an obituary. And he knew my magazine was the only way he was going to get an audience for it while he was alive."

"My God, you didn't actually say that stuff to him, did you? Your father?"

"It's a style he taught me—a kind of no bullshit journalese. It didn't seem to bother him. I loved the old guy and he knew it, but we never talked about stuff like that. 'Just make sure you get *your* version out right away,' he said. Well, I sort of kept my promise. I got parts one and two out last month. Of course, part three doesn't count. He didn't give me a chance to get part three out before he shot himself."

Evan looked away and tugged his coat tight, as though bothered by the cold for the first time.

"God, Evan, I'm sorry. I forgot that the press hadn't released that—that it was suicide. I didn't mean to shock you."

"It's all right. I'm fine."

She turned in discomfort, and for a moment seemed to be studying the rear bumper of the cruiser. Then, without actually making eye contact, she said, "Look, I don't know if this is seemly or dignified or whatever in the circumstances. But the truth is, I don't want to be alone right now. I need, I think, an hour or so to just keep moving and talking and... Would you... Would you let me take you off that wall for an hour or so? I don't know, maybe a quiet drink at Benny's?"

"Benny's? That's where we wound up doing most of the interview, isn't it? The place with the window thing? Sorta nice."

He gave her the kind of perfect smile that casting directors put on their contacts lists, and she shuffled in embarrassment. "Or if you're attached to it," she said, "I could put up a tent, right here around your wall. Hell, bring the wall with you, or..."

He spared her. "Benny's, please." Then frowned. "What's the matter, Carly? Do I make you nervous? I seem to remember we were kinda getting past that."

"I don't know. I have this thing about TV people. I'm afraid of them the way some people are afraid of clowns."

"Oh, come on."

"My mother told me that when I was an adorable toddler she let me do a turn as an extra in a TV show. All I had to do was cling to this actress who was supposed to be my mother, see? I had no problems with that. The actress was cheerful, and she smelled nice. But in the scene, she was being given tragic news by the police, so every now and then they'd do a take, and this actress would have to break down in tears. One minute she'd be smiling, chucking me under the chin, the next she'd be freaking, wailing her heart out. After every take, she'd have to break character real fast and calm me down with big smiles and all. Screwed me up good."

Weiss was distracted by Joshi in the driver's seat sniffing in derision. "When did this become a goddamn stake out?" he asked. Weiss made a tiny shushing sound. Joshi muttered anyway. "You want me to back up a few feet so you don't miss the big kissing scene?"

"I see," Evan was saying. "Was any part of that story even remotely true?"

"I come from a family of storytellers, but they tell me I *was* a child once."

"I'm not sure I buy that. I want to see the pictures." He got up and touched her arm, still smiling, but then his expression changed, becoming guarded and uncertain. "But first I do need to talk to you."

"I think you do too. My father had no interest in television."

"We didn't talk about television."

"Okay. So I have no idea why it would enter his mind to call you."

"Okay. Benny's then?" he said.

The lot was almost empty as Carly and Evan made their way together, and then to separate cars. By this time, only a few vehicles remained in the back lot, one a blue Lincoln tucked up against the snow banks left by the parking lot plows. Its windows were dark and the engine was off despite the bitter cold. Weiss noticed Carly glance without interest at the driver seated behind the wheel as she passed by. It was impossible to say if Carly made eye contact because the impassive woman behind the Lincoln's steering wheel was motionless in the harsh shadow engraved by the light standard. Weiss knew it was the same woman he had seen lingering close to Carly earlier; the long scarf was gone, replaced by obscuring gloom.

And she remained that way for several minutes after Carly's car followed Evan's out into the evergreen alley of Northshore Boulevard. The parking lot had almost emptied into the busy, snow-narrowed boulevard, and the circles of floodlit tarmac, made more desolate by the snow-banked memorials nearby, were deserted. Only now did the driver of the Lincoln lean forward to turn the key in the ignition. The blue Lincoln pulled forward creaking snow until it was passing directly under a tall standard. For less than a second, the Lincoln's interior was awash in reflected light and then there were just the receding points of her tail lights.

Joshi turned to Weiss who was staring. "What's the matter, Eilert? The blue car? You know the driver?"

"I didn't get a great look at her. But..."

"How about the plates? We could run them."

"Covered in snow."

Joshi started the car and was about to follow, but Weiss touched his arm. "Look at the traffic."

"So, what's going on here? Is this important? The woman in the Lincoln?"

"Maybe, but I don't see..." Weiss put his arm on the seat back, turning to face Joshi. "I saw her watching the family earlier. Damned if it didn't... It's been five years."

Weiss's voice was flat, and he knew he wasn't making sense. The confusion, the inability to think was happening again, the way it did during the nurse's trial—and when his wife was picked up roaming the streets by a black and white from the harbour division. That time she'd been wearing one of his work jackets over her slip. He'd lost all focus and suffered constant anxiety when he had to leave for work, worried about the next dangerous episode in her decline.

The hotshot professional detective was losing it, paralyzed by indecision.

"Hey, easy guy," Joshi said. "Maybe if we do it like charades. I know all the hand signals."

"Prem, the driver of the Lincoln, I think it was...." Weiss, looking a little sick, turned away. "It was Marcella Cole."

CHAPTER TWELVE

Carly had to circle until she found a spot on Locust Street but Evan Favaro had been luckier; he'd found parking right outside Benny's. When she came in, he was waiting for her in a booth opposite the lakeward view. He'd avoided getting too close to the cold windows. Beyond the bar's forlorn outdoor patio with its row of bistro tables glazed with ice, a snowplow scoured its way around parked cars. Beyond that, the harbour moved with a long swell that looked more oil slick than slush. A coast guard rescue vessel with its red maple leaf rode at anchor.

They smiled, but as she slipped onto the seat, it was as if the table between them was a mile wide. The weeks since their last evening together seemed to sit there, right beside the malt vinegar and the pepper mill. She couldn't shake her first impression of him—that there was something obvious and uncomplicated about his good looks, and she found herself wondering how he would look in later life when he would wear the face he had earned. Growing up with a father whose every expression was a weave of brooding contradictions made her wary of openness. Maybe her greatest fear was that an aging Evan would look much the same as he did now.

She'd doubted then—and she wondered now—whether the daughter of A.L. Rouhl could wind up with someone so...shallow? No, that was unfair. She didn't know him well enough to lay that on him.

Still, he'd made love the way she expected—politely, his passion sensitive and considerate. She'd been moody and petulant in return, for reasons she didn't fully understand. Why had he been so damned forgiving? He should have kicked her sullen ass out of bed then and there.

"Classy, huh? I just buried my father, and here I am in a bar."

Evan crossed his wrists on the tabletop and smiled. "It's supposed to be a deli. When is the burial?"

"His ashes will be kept in the central mausoleum until his own plot is ready. Do you mind if we don't..."

"God, of course. I'm sorry. What can I get you from the bar?"

They talked about drinks, Carly deciding that all she wanted was some hot tea. Evan placed their orders asking for coffee and a slice of coffee cake for himself. Carly wondered all the while if she should try to explain how these last few weeks had been for her, her father's failing strength drawing her in, the responsibility for the memoir shifting more and more to herself. Responsibility for the nursing staff, for his long term care, for the eventual celebrity funeral... Oh, and she was expected to have a *life* while this was going on. Some things had to give—Evan had been one of them.

She thought about his calls, missed and left unanswered, but it wasn't her feelings of guilt that broke the silence, it was her curiosity. "My father called you up. I still can't get past that. A.L. phoned a man I dated twice?"

"We dated once. The first time doesn't count. All those hours of talking we did, technically it was all for the article—Evan Favaro's little bit of home town celebrity, courtesy of *Escarpment Magazine*. You were interviewing me, remember?"

"It's easy to forget that. I seem to recall you asked as many questions as I did." The man from behind the bar showed up with their plates and put the forks down slowly so he could steal a glance at Carly. He turned to go, giving Evan a quick smile of envy that Carly caught. It blew her train of thought. "Evan, I..."

She shook her head, trying to regroup. Evan had come to her; that had to mean something--that he still thought about her. But for all that, she felt that this impromptu date, or wake— or whatever the hell it was, wasn't going well. She screwed her eyes shut, trying to focus. "What did you mean when you said your talk was about his death?"

"Not exactly about his death, about dying. I'd say it was about tidying up loose ends." He sighed and centered his wedge of coffee cake on its plate. "He called because in the article you wrote about me you mentioned my, uh, sideline. 'Sideline' is *your* word, by the way."

Carly frowned at him, straining to follow over the noise around them. "I don't recall..."

"Mostly you were interested in my TV work, but you did mention that I've done handwriting analysis for the police. Document comparison and graphology. I'm not surprised you don't remember. In the article, you kind of touched on the forensic side of things in passing. I think you threw it in because you wanted to show how 'surprising' I was or something. You treated it as an amusing aside. But your dad sure picked up on it."

Carly looked uncomfortable. "I remember you telling me you served as an expert witness in a few trials." She stopped in mid squirm, as the notion sank in. "Wait, and the old man wanted to talk to you about *that*? About handwriting?"

"He told me it was background for something he was writing."

Carly sniffed and rotated the handle of her mug of tea so she could warm her hands against the green enamel. "I can see him working that line in his sixties even. For the past five years, though, it isn't even remotely in character. What was he up to? Did he want to know about *me*?"

"You came up, but no. He kept leading the conversation back to the handwriting thing." He shrugged. "No, this was deliberate. There was something he genuinely needed to know from me."

She watched him sip coffee. "The only thing he was writing was the memoir for the magazine. It called for no research, no interviews. It was just a few musings on his life. To be honest, if it wasn't for his skill as a writer, it would have come across as the ramblings of an old man. I'm not faulting him—if you understood how weak he was. It's all he could handle. Even writing that… He was painfully slow with it, so I'd help him in the evenings. He hated dictating, but I think he longed to get this job over with. The point is, I more or less know what's in there, and I can't think why…" She fished out her teabag and let it puddle on a paper coaster. "Why'd you agree to see him, anyway? Did you do it for me?"

"I wasn't even supposed to tell you we'd talked."

"Now there, see? Why would he even *care* if I knew?" She struggled with the idea that her father had taken an unexpected interest in someone she knew and then tried to keep it from her. Maybe she was giving her father too much credit, but it did seem pure A.L. to care about her and yet be too reserved to let her know.

Evan closed his eyes, remembering. "It was just a talk. I remember a nurse was there making tea and moving around the kitchen the whole time."

"What happened? What did he ask you?"

"Well, he was polite, earnest, interested…"

"It must have made you uncomfortable. His frailty… He'd gotten slow, his speech was labored."

Evan made a smoothing gesture, sweeping a crumb from the

table. "We were talking about how serious handwriting analysis works—the way I can usually get a sense of a person from affectations of style—so he handed me a sort of vinyl bound notebook, a diary maybe. And he asked me to demonstrate.

"Of course, I began to protest. People are always doing that kind of thing to me because of what I do on TV. I explained that what he asked wasn't something that I could just do in an instant; that what I got from a specimen hand was usually vague, and that I relied a lot on context to help make sense of whatever I could discern…"

"So, did he buy into the graphology thing, or was he skeptical?"

"Not skeptical. No. That's the thing. He needed it to work. I found myself holding this notebook, the one he'd handed me, leafing through it. Honestly, I was mainly just trying to find a way to politely return it. But he just sat back and wouldn't take the hint. I found myself glancing at a few pages, looking for something that I could say without playing him. When I do this stuff on TV, half my attention is on the subject, picking up body language, facial expressions. I didn't want to play that game with him. I don't know what it was he wanted, what he *needed*, but if I was going to tell him anything, it would have to be from the page of that diary and nothing else."

"He wouldn't get the message? That you weren't going to do magic tricks for him?"

"Your father knew how to use silence. There I was, turning pages, unsure what to say or do. That's when the diary…" He looked at the table and made the same odd smoothing motion on its surface. There were no crumbs. "It…"

"Evan, look, you don't have to tell me anything. Who the hell am I to cross-examine you? What happened was between you and him. It had nothing to do with me."

"Maybe it *wasn't* about you, but it is *now*. I've got to tell you this. It's been weighing on me. I can't change anything by bringing the meeting up at this point, but *your father* thought it was important, and now he's not here to tell you why. Maybe you can figure it out."

Carly looked bewildered. "Wait, are we still talking about his diary?"

"*His* diary? Ah, see, I considered the possibility it *was* his, that he wanted me to tell him something about himself. After all, that's what I do on TV most of the time—you know, read people's personalities, relate their handwriting to their lives. Honestly, that stuff's not very scientific. Some of it is just telling people what they want to hear, flattering them and reading their reactions, but people seem to love it. They think I'm doing magic.

"Anyway, at first I handled the book, reluctantly, with that premise—that it was his own hand. I guess I thought I might pay him a few honest compliments and warn him that any serious study of the writing would take time. Perhaps he would be satisfied with that.

"Getting information from a text requires me to study it carefully, but with experience, you get so that certain things leap out at you, at least some of the time. Well, the first thing that hit me was that the diary was absolutely full—the margins, the fly leaves. The writer had ignored all the conventional margins and white space and written into every corner of the pages. There were a few business cards in pockets on the inside cover. I turned one over and even the back of the card was covered in writing: tiny, perfectly uniform writing. This wasn't subtle. This was psychosis writ large.

"When I was still marvelling at this, wondering where he had come across something so bizarre, I realized something else that made the hairs on my neck stand up: the diary had been used, written in, way beyond normal wear and tear, okay? But despite that, *every surface* in it and on it was clean and unblemished except for the writing. No edge abrasion, as though it had been handled only by a gloved conservator.

"I knew right away it couldn't be his handwriting. Everything was telling me the writer of that diary was narrow, prosaic, and utterly, utterly compulsive. By this point, I couldn't help being curious, so I came right out and asked him who it belonged to."

"Did he tell you?"

"He said the diary belonged to a nurse. That he had used it to research a story he'd written. He said he'd tried to return it once but lost his nerve."

"Lost his nerve? That's a funny thing for him to say. He wasn't overly concerned about other people's feelings."

"Anyway, that's what he said. And he said it was a *nurse*, Carly."

Carly was quiet for a moment, frowning at the gray horizon beyond the windows. Then she gave a small chuckle. "Storytelling," she said. "In the end with him, it always came back to that. He was playing *you*. Entertaining you. He was a genius at that."

"No, it was more than that, Carly. Your father had this same intense look on his face the whole time—he was refusing to feed me any suggestions. If anything he was trying to keep something *from* me. Making sure that what I told him was my own reading of the diary. Do you know the diary I'm talking about? Did he ever show it to you?"

Carly did a rapid inventory. Life with A.L. was all about clutter, but nothing helpful came to mind. If she could miss a pistol and ammunition, a vinyl bound diary would hardly stand out. She shook her head. "He had all his stuff, this whole world of experience, that he never shared with people, except through his writing."

"Carly, I'm so sorry, but I think you should look at that diary again. Get hold of it, and take it seriously."

"Why? What did you tell him about the diary?"

"I didn't have to *say much* of anything about the diary to him. He saw the way I'd reacted to it. The diary gave me a shock. He was getting the confirmation he needed just by watching my face and my body language, playing me at my own game, I suppose. I can't remember how I put it, but I told him to *be careful* around the writer of the diary, that, nurse or no nurse, her reactions would be abnormal. After that, we both just sat there for a few minutes. Then he seemed to let it go, and it was just polite conversation. I asked him about his writing. I guess I sounded a little star-struck."

"So the diary, was it just a test of your skill?"

"Don't dismiss it, Carly. Your dad's face gave nothing away, but he'd kept that notebook close to hand for a reason. It was the reason I was there. He was interested in that diary." Evan shifted uneasily, and Carly wondered if the awkwardness she'd been picking up in the deli wasn't about their relationship after all. Her father had set up this little deli get-together days ago. He was stage managing her life from beyond the grave. She was still acting out A.L.'s denouement.

"I spent an hour in that room, Car. Touching the arms of that chair, taking in the scent of musty books and shaving lotion. It took me a while to sort it out, but for me, that whole room was imbued with his unease. It's not that he was afraid exactly. Not about dying. I think he was even resigned to his own death. But there was something troubling him, troubling him a lot. You must have been aware of that."

Carly thought about that—A.L.'s moodiness had been as constant as the wallpaper, not something Carly thought of as having a single source. "And he thought *you* could help?"

"I've been wondering... maybe he was trying to tell *me* something. And I just wasn't getting it. What if the nurse—the one taking care of him. Her name is Crowther, isn't it?"

Carly laughed. "Mrs. Crowther? You think he gave you Nurse *Crowther's* diary? She was there *with* you, wasn't she?"

"No, not in the room with us, I hardly saw her. Anyway, how else would he get his hands on a diary belonging to a nurse? What if she was the one he was afraid of? Showing the diary to me with the woman in the house would have been foolhardy —*or* an act of desperation. What do you know about Crowther?"

"Not a lot. She's sort of the boss, scheduling the shifts of the other two nurses. Checked their references and so on."

"How long had she been taking care of him?"

"About a year. Evan, I'm not sure where you're going with this, but my father was sick long before Mrs. Crowther came along, and despite her stuffy manner, she took good care of him. I could say the same thing about the day nurses too."

"Okay," Evan dunked a corner of his coffee cake, swallowed it and then just sort of picked away at the rest. "Only—something about that diary was compelling him, and two days after he showed it to me, he was gone. I've been turning that over in my mind, trying to make sense of it. And now you tell me he took his own life."

Carly reached across the table, her hand stopping just short of his. "Look, Evan, there's no reason for you to feel guilt over any of this. Despite his sickness, Dad was clear-headed, thank God. There's no reason to think his death was more than a very sick man choosing his time."

Evan sat back, watching her face, searching for the shock and pain she felt. It reminded her what a good job she was doing of hiding it. For a minute they were both quiet, finishing their cake, listening to the odd beeping sound from some kitchen gadget and the buzz of businessmen in rubber shoe coverings comparing tablets.

When they finished their cups, Carly picked her hand bag off the bench and swung her legs out.

Evan grabbed his coat. It looked expensive, but he wasn't treating it that way. "Car, I'm glad that your mind's at peace about your father's passing. It's what I wish for you, and maybe it was stupid of me venting my...confusion. We can end it here. I just needed you to know."

She stood up beside him. "I'm sorry, Evan. For some reason, Dad laid a burden on you. It wasn't like him to do that. I don't know what to say except there's nothing you could've said or done to change the outcome."

Evan nodded. Carly took his hand and touched her cheek against his. They stood apart for a moment, then she said, "I'll try and find the diary, have a look at it." She looked at him, thinking that now she was going to politely allow Evan to walk away, and she couldn't think of a way to stop it from happening. "He'd been very sick for a long time, Evan."

Evan had reached out to her and she was letting him feel as though he'd made a fool of himself. That's not what she wanted. She watched helplessly as he put on his coat.

"All the same," he said at last, "if you change your mind—about anything—and if you can find the diary..." He pulled on his gloves. "What I do on TV is a sort of pop psychology act, but I *am* capable of looking at that diary professionally. Your article was good, but I think you missed that part of me."

There it was. Another act of generosity and caring extended to her; a nice person would pick up the offer gracefully, and thank him.

She gave him a small smile, but as they walked out into yet another February snowfall, her good intentions seemed to get lost in swinging doors, buttoning coats, and the crackling cold.

"Let me walk you to your car," he said.

"No, that's silly. Your car is right here. Just go." *No, wait. That's not the way she meant it...*

"Okay, then. I'm so sorry about your dad."

He took keys out of his coat pocket, sorting through them with care. For a moment they stood together looking down at the snow. And then he stooped, drew his perfectly tailored legs into the car, closed the door and drove away.

CHAPTER THIRTEEN

Mrs. Susan Crowther lived in a bungalow covered in frosted ivy runners that here and there trapped pockets of snow. She seemed to share it with a younger woman of Asian descent, whom she introduced as Li. After a few minutes, Li, round-faced and smiling, disappeared and Weiss could hear her moving about in the kitchen. Li's eavesdropping was obvious in every muted click of a dish and dribble of water.

Mrs. Crowther led him to an enclosed porch area that was two steps down from the living room. Most of the interior space seemed to be cushions, but Weiss managed to uncover a nice little nest where, for several seconds, he continued to sink down slowly.

"Now, I understand you heard the shot from the front hall."

"Yes. Unbelievably loud. And such a little pistol too."

"And then, when you went in, you saw the pistol on the floor?"

"Yes, I saw everything. I'm a good witness. I'm a professional, you know."

"Can you tell me how much time elapsed from when you

heard the shot and when you got to Mr. Rouhl's office. Did you rush in?"

"Rush? No. Honestly, I...I called out Mr. Rouhl's name several times, then I thought to catch Elena before she drove away. You know, the afternoon nurse."

"Yes, my colleague is probably talking to her now."

"Anyway, when I looked out, Elena's little car had already driven off. So, I closed the door and started towards the office, but I was thinking, you see. The possibilities...wondering if maybe a robber was in the house. One of those home invaders you see on the news—people threatened in their own living rooms by..."

"So you made your way to the office cautiously? Looking into other rooms along the way?"

"You have a gun, Mr. Weiss. You can kick your way into a room shouting 'police' and blaze away..."

Weiss raised an eyebrow trying to picture such a thing. Before he could stop himself, he was thinking how he'd write up "blazing away" in an occurrence report: *I identified myself and entered the room while discharging my weapon at various targets of opportunity as itemized in the subheading below.* "You've got the wrong idea about me, Mrs. Crowther. I'm cautious too." He moved his digital recorder on the satin cushions and watched its red light once again sink silently. "You're telling me it was... what...five minutes before you actually pushed the office door open?"

"I suppose. And there he was."

"Yes. I'm sorry. And the dog? Where was he?"

"Indy? I..." She frowned and tugged at the corner of a cushion. "Indy was... He was on the carpet. On his favourite spot. Yes, he looked at me when I came in, and then drooped back onto the carpet as if he was waiting for something else to happen. With one ear up, of course."

"Head down on his paws. Not cowering or distressed?"

"Not distressed? Well, of course the poor dog must have jumped out of his skin when that thing went off. He must have realized his master was dead. I'm just saying he had taken up his usual spot again. He was on the floor."

"That must have been near where the gun fell."

"Yes. Indy was lying on the carpet, Mr. Weiss. As he always did."

"In the time it took you to get to the office, did you hear anything? Any evidence that there might have been someone else there?"

"Nothing whatsoever. No one came my way and the only other exit was from the kitchen to the patio out back, and it was still locked. I checked."

"Of course, but that door can be unlocked from the inside or from the outside keypad."

"Well, yes. And it locks automatically when it's pulled shut; it has one of those push-button combination locks on the outside. All the windows were secured too, *including* the one in Mr. Rouhl's office." She added an indignant sniff to this, having been grilled on the subject before. Weiss looked out at the snow-sagging hedge and tried to recall Joshi's analysis of the patio and pathways outside number 124C. Someone could have gone out the back from the kitchen and made an escape from the small yard, but Joshi had found no marks in the snow to suggest that.

"Were you close to Mr. Rouhl? I mean, was he becoming a friend as well as a patient?"

"Mr. Rouhl was a very private sort of man. He spent a lot of time in his own head, you might say. Polite but distant, you see."

"And he had few visitors?" Weiss asked.

"Except for his daughter. Young Ms. Rouhl was there just about every other night. Usually late."

"It's unusual for a sick and elderly man to stay up late, isn't it?"

"Mr. Rouhl preferred to sleep in and stay up late. That's one of the privileges he would have lost going into a palliative care facility. There they dress you early for breakfast if you're mobile at all."

"You must have felt sorry for him, knowing that he was going to be institutionalized like that."

"I suppose." Crowther shrugged. Weiss watched Mrs. Crowther's body language carefully. She was compassionate but hardly distraught over her employer's prognosis. He couldn't envision her risking her career to aid a suicide. "His money wouldn't have been much use to him once he was bed-ridden," she said.

"Yes, Mr. Rouhl's success appears to have made him a wealthy man," Weiss said.

"In the work I do, Detective Weiss, I've often served as a transitional service for people who would eventually need assisted living facilities."

"You think the other nurses would feel the same way? Detached, I mean."

"Detached?" She considered the word, perhaps wondering if it was a sleight. "Why are you asking me this—about how I *felt*?"

"Well, frankly I'm wondering how Mr. Rouhl got access to a gun and ammunition and kept it from all three of you."

Mrs. Crowther sighed. "Mr. Weiss, that office was filled with...with Mr. Rouhl's things. He was a collector of *things*—and he wouldn't let anyone throw any of it out. He insisted that it all meant something to him. He could have had that little pistol in plain sight and it would have been utterly lost in the clutter. Then there were his desk drawers; I never went in there."

"Fair enough. Was there a housekeeper? You know—a cleaner?"

"No. We provided his meals and cleaned them away. Mr. Rouhl's daughter would do what little tidying had to be done."

"So it's entirely plausible to you that old Mr. Rouhl could plan and carry out his own suicide without help of any kind?"

"I'm sure you know more about guns than I do, Mr. Weiss." She began in weary resignation but stopped, and Weiss looked up from his recorder to see her staring at him in puzzlement. "When I *think* about it…"

"Yes?"

"Well, Mr. Rouhl was a very clever man, and as far as I could tell, his thought processes weren't greatly diminished by age. It would have been *so* much easier for him to manipulate his medications to cause his death, and so much more dignified if you know what I mean. He must have chosen the gun because… well, because he knew it was there, I suppose, or because death by violence was, you know—dramatic."

"Suicides with guns are sometimes a resentful message to the living," Weiss informed her.

"Mr. Rouhl got along well with his daughter, as far I could see. Oh, that reminds me—there *was* one visitor. A handsome young man, in fact. He spent about an hour with Mr. Rouhl on Tuesday evening."

"That was two days before Mr. Rouhl died. Tell me about this visitor."

"Well, they sat in the living room. I made some tea."

"What did they talk about?"

"I left them alone, but I heard the greetings, and I got the impression he was a friend of young Ms. Carly. He was someone she'd written about." Mrs. Crowther gave a sly smile. "But I could tell from his embarrassment that their relationship was more than that."

"You think he was Carly Rouhl's boyfriend or lover, you mean?"

"It was an impression, Mr. Weiss. I was only in the room long enough to serve tea, then I stayed in the kitchen until he left."

"Did you see him when he was leaving?"

"Briefly. I thought he seemed a bit troubled, perhaps. You know, polite, but preoccupied—as though something had upset him."

"Do you remember his name, Mrs. Crowther?"

"I made a point of respecting Mr. Rouhl's privacy."

Weiss smiled in understanding. Figuring perhaps she didn't remember and was invoking her professional discretion as an excuse. Ah well, another question for Carly Rouhl.

CHAPTER FOURTEEN

Carly was used to making the walk from the magazine office down Brant to Lakeshore and along to her father's house. This time it was a mistake. She hadn't given the cold snap its due and was soon suffering from the onshore breeze angling across the waterfront park. She tugged at her collar, trying to deform her hood so that it protected the windward side of her face. She'd always thought of her hip-length coat as warm, and she had a lined cotton jacket underneath, but her slacks weren't thick enough. The front of her legs was becoming numb and her forehead was smarting.

She considered going all the way back to the plaza to get her car, but the thought passed, and she took comfort in the idea that she could get another layer of clothes at her father's place for the walk back. Besides, the wind at her back wouldn't be nearly as bad. There was no car at the house. A.L. hadn't driven himself in years.

It was dark already, and the lights in the park made neat ovals on the snow. Up ahead, the pier, slippery and chained off in this kind of weather, jutted into the gloom of the lake. When she made it that far—to the pavilion with its shuttered snack bar and padlocked shower stalls—she felt that she was almost there.

She noticed that a vandal had spray-painted something rude on the snack bar sign in fluorescent orange. It looked vivid, fresh, and sickly at the same time, and Carly thought it odd that someone would choose to idle outside long enough to deface a sign at this time of year. The cold gave the idea of homelessness a painful edge.

She made her way to a sharp cut in the snow wall along the street which had been burrowed out by a city worker with a shovel. The gap was narrow and, in her winter boots, Carly had to step in line as a runway model would putting one foot in front of the other. She wiggled her hips a bit for balance and then took her time to cross the salted muck of the street.

A.L.'s house wasn't welcoming. On the sidewalk, path, and driveway, the snow was trampled, rutted and dirty. At least the police tape had been removed and Carly had sanded the front steps the day before.

Inside, she shook the slush off her boots and rummaged in the front hall cupboard for the slippers she kept there. Recently she'd spent more evenings here than at her apartment, but the place felt different now—hollow and bruised as though the report from her father's little derringer were still echoing through the rooms.

The sitting room, with its expensive furniture, startlingly orange and redolent of the 1970s, seemed somehow wan. The room was organized around the glass doors of a fireplace set in cultured stone. The mantle was a single block of oiled pine. It was here she had sat, taking dictation on the laptop when the old man grew tired and couldn't type anymore.

She remembered Evan calling her cell phone a couple of times, leaving brief, non-committal messages. If it hadn't been for those long nights coaxing episode three of the memoir to completion, maybe she would have answered or returned his calls, fishing for a meeting, instead of waiting so long that it would have been embarrassing to phone him at all. Or maybe that was a rationalization. She had let so many friends and connections slip away out of nothing more than a paralyzing reserve. Carly was an introvert and letting people get close wasn't easy for her.

And then Evan getting that peculiar call from her father that drew him into her life again.

It would have been here, in the sitting room, that A.L. had entertained Evan while Carly was working late at the *Escarpment* office.

She pictured them there: the night nurse, Mrs. Crowther, hovering in the kitchen, bringing in tea. Her father would have sat over there, head bowed as though he could no longer support its weight, but smiling up at Evan through those wiry, drooping brows so that he seemed to be frowning too. Evan over here—here on this straight-backed couch which her mother had once tried to soften with little cushions. And, let's see... Evan would have taken the diary from A.L., held it briefly, and put it down...there, on the end table to his left. Yes.

The diary wasn't there now, of course. Mrs. Crowther wasn't a housekeeper, but she had chosen to keep the place tidy, thinking it would reflect on her in some way. She would have asked the old man where he wanted it.

What would he have said to her? It was a piece of unwanted junk, surely. Put it away in some drawer?

Of course, if it was important to him in some way—or if, as Evan surmised, it had been Nurse Crowther's own. Well, then A.L. would have buried it under his chair blanket and hidden it as soon as he could. Carly imagined him shuffling over to the bookshelves in his office and pushing it, seemingly at random, among the clutter of souvenirs that fronted each and every row of books: old pipes with faces and stubby legs, a mahogany cylinder packed with poker chips, an old gillie stick that leaned against the front edge of a shelf. To anyone but A.L. the diary would be effectively lost in the clutter—hidden—but the old man would remember exactly where it was and think of it as safe.

That would be the test, then. If her father actually valued the diary, if it wasn't just a piece of junk he'd dug up to test Evan, it would be there on the precious wall of books—the wall A.L. would stare at all day from his desk chair.

Carly took her coat off, even though it was cool in the rooms, and she went into the short hallway that led to her father's office. She came to a stop, hands at her sides, fists opening and closing slowly. The thought of the violence that had soaked into the lath and plaster of the little office ahead of her made her hesitate. Death had filled her father's room as suddenly as the sound of the gunshot, and as much as she tried not to think about it, she had to wonder how long his heart had continued to beat, how long his body faltered on after that unique and intricate mind was shattered. Borrowing strength from the memory of A.L.'s tough stoicism, Carly closed her fingers on the door handle and turned it.

Nothing happened.

She leaned in against the door, forcing it, and her mind seemed to sweep on through, projecting her three paces inside the room.

But, in fact, the door seemed to be locked. She was still in the hallway, frowning at her blanched knuckles.

That was impossible, of course. The door was never locked. Carly doubted that A.L. would have remembered where the key to the office was. She shook her head once and leaned into the door, this time setting her shoulder against the panels.

At last, the jamb yielded with a slight squeak as though the door had been swollen in its frame. The knob still in her hand, Carly's eyes traced the door frame in puzzlement. She went in, turning back to examine the jamb and the lock.

While she still had her back to the room, the first thing Carly noticed was the familiar smell of her father's port. But that thought was supplanted immediately by the realization that the scent came to her on warm air—stuffy even. The office, unaccountably, was a good ten degrees warmer than the rest of the house. That would account for the stiff door. There was only one thermostat in the house and the office should have been as cold as the rest of the main floor rooms. But, unlike the rest of the house, this room, which should have had the bitter pall of recent death about it, didn't feel chilly and abandoned at all.

On the contrary, it felt...

Without knowing why, she was suddenly filled with alarm, and she spun about, taking in the room with a series of hurried glances. She realized her heart rate had gone up, and she was backing defensively against the door frame.

Bloody silly, of course. What was she afraid of? The room was lit and comfortable as it had always been, the three lights pooling where they should, the shelves dominating the wall to her right, with the minutia of a lifetime strewn along them. And there, right at eye level, easy to reach and easy to see...not hidden at all, was a black diary.

A.L. had kept it close, all right. It was slipped in with the books, but the old man had let it protrude an inch, as though ready to be pinched out again. Pushing aside a tiny brass incense bowl and a wedge of driftwood, Carly drew out the book with its featureless vinyl binding. She looked at it, opening it in her hands to verify that it contained the tidy illegible lines Evan had described.

Without thinking about it, Carly had continued to step further into the room—had turned toward the window—before she actually looked up and saw the laptop computer on the old man's desk. It froze her. Stopped her dead in her tracks.

It was there: A.L.'s laptop—her father's laptop. The one the police claimed to have tightly wrapped and neatly labelled.

Her grey-blue eyes wide now, she approached it, as though the open computer was the biggest soap bubble she'd ever seen, teetering there on the green desk blotter. She inched around the desk, her mind laying rubber but getting nowhere. She wanted to leap forward and look at the screen, but at first, her eyes were fixed on the tiny scratches A. L. had made on the keyboard with his watch strap. If this was a hallucination, it was impressively authentic.

She was ready for the screen now. Let's see: would it be her father's face frowning out at her from a little blue window? A chummy note from Detective Weiss thanking her for the brief... very brief loan of the computer?

Then she actually became aware of the screen; it showed her dad's odd but familiar screen saver, a tangle of carved ivy incised into polished red granite.

She touched the keypad. The word processor leapt up on a largely blank page. There, in the large serif font A.L. used to help his failing vision, were her father's last words.

Sorry Carly, No answers—only questions as usual. Love, Dad.

The first rational thought that came to Carly, after a slow thaw in her frontal cortex, was that the computer hadn't put itself in standby mode. That would happen if it was left idle for...how long? She couldn't remember what it was set up for. Ten? Fifteen minutes? A half dozen improbable explanations tumbled through her head, seemingly all at once, but she still felt as though someone had just done a clever magic trick, and she had no idea how it had been done. Her neck hairs began to tingle.

Well, Weiss had *said* he would return the laptop. All the same, she wasn't ready for the idea that Weiss had gotten in here and deliberately set it up on the desk just as it had been that day...

She got the sudden notion that the police were playing with her mind to get her to betray guilt. Was there a hidden camera or mic? Did those site investigator people keep copies of the house keys so they could return at will? Was this standard forensic procedure—clean up the scene and return the impounded evidence unannounced while people were out at work? She took a step back.

Dear God, she felt an awful spasm in her belly. Hell, this is how people shit themselves—those fuckers had even put a full glass of port back beside the computer.

She spent a moment listening to her own breathing, trying to determine whether she was frightened or angry. Fingering through the tiny pockets of her jacket—an action that made her jut her elbows—she eventually found Weiss's business card. Carly picked up the old landline desk phone and tapped in his number. Fired by what she now recognized as indignation, she scowled while the phone purred.

Then it just stopped, to be replaced with an unfamiliar silence.

"Hello?"

No, it wasn't complete silence. It wasn't the static hiss of distant circuits either. It was the echo of a very large and very empty room. It was as though she were listening to someone's polite cough swill around in a cavernous seashell. She stared at the receiver, and then ran her eyes from the ebony cradle down the cord, noting the outlet low on the wall behind the desk. The phone was still plugged in. Giving up on the roomy silence, Carly put the handset back.

She went out, through the cold living room, all the way to the front hall cupboard, rummaging in the pockets of her coat for her cell phone. She juggled the cell for a few seconds until she was able to thumb in the number she had just called.

Weiss picked up right away.

"Hello, Detective Weiss? Carly Rouhl." Carly could feel her anger draining away, eroded by doubts. "I'm at my father's house."

Weiss's end was a tumble of noise for a second as though the detective were switching hands. "Just a minute, I'm walking to a quieter room." Then he was back. "Okay."

"I wanted to ask you about Dad's laptop," Carly said.

"Sure." Weiss waited for the question. To Carly, it sounded as though someone was moving furniture about in the background.

"I was wondering…if you got what you wanted from the memoir file—from the…uh…autobiography."

Weiss hesitated. "I wish I had something to tell you, Ms. Rouhl…" The detective was speaking slowly, making little delaying sounds, "…but I need more time with it. You did say that wouldn't be a problem." A pause. "Or was there something else?"

Now Weiss would be wondering about the dogged silence on Carly's end. "Ms. Rouhl? Was there something you needed to know?"

"I was in my father's office," Carly said.

"Ah. The office. Yes?"

"I'm wondering…" A long pause. "You know where the laptop is, then."

"Of course, safe at our Hampton Road offices for now. Are you all right, Ms. Rouhl?"

This was absurd. Carly was stumbling like a guilty woman. If they had cameras in here they'd zoom in on her face and months later the jury would be able to watch her stunned expression on a big monitor right beside the witness box. "Yes. Yes, I…I'm a little rattled being here alone, I guess."

"I understand. It must be hard. Take your time."

"No, actually. I shouldn't have called. Not now. I'll call back later when I'm...feeling more myself."

"You haven't come across the diary you mentioned, have you? You said you'd take a look."

The question took Carly off guard. She'd had the diary in her hands of course, but couldn't even remember putting it down; she must have dropped it somewhere in the office.

She didn't know why she lied to Weiss, except that it was an easy lie. "No. I haven't spotted it yet." She could call Weiss later when her mind wasn't whirling, when she'd had a chance to look at the diary herself.

Now, again, it was Weiss's turn to hang silence on the line, a silence that was broken when they both started to speak at once.

"You're sure you don't need..."

"No. I'll call...another time. Thanks. I have to go now." Carly hung up with a sharp poke at the phone.

She'd sounded shaken, just what the police wanted maybe, but her priority now was time to think.

What if someone had returned her father's laptop without Weiss's knowledge? That had to be it. The computer was right there in the office. She'd seen it. No point in arguing with Weiss. It was there and the final words of her father's life were on it, making the memoir as complete as it would ever be. She'd look at it one more time, and then she'd let Weiss have it back.

Of course, this could be a deliberate ploy by the investigators. Maybe they were hoping she'd try to change the files on the hard drive in some way, then they'd show her the copy they'd made, confronting her. This was insane. She hadn't anything to hide, hadn't done anything.

She went back to the office through the open door, marveling again at the warmth within, and sat down in the desk chair...the chair in which her father had died. She hadn't even thought of that, gothic imaginings swept aside by a need to understand.

She brought up the memoir article, scrolled to the last paragraph she could actually remember from their evening collaborations and began to read. It only took her a few minutes of scrolling back and forth to realize that little had changed from their last session. That was it then—this represented their last time together. That would have been Monday night.

On Tuesday, A.L.'s last companion had been Evan Favaro, not her—not his only daughter.

Carly's gaze shifted to the CD player for a moment, her glance drawn by a tiny red light that indicated the machine was playing. If she'd thought of it at all, she would have assumed the police had left it that way, the volume turned right down. But her mind had found its way back to Evan and his offer to examine the diary professionally: the diary that had been her father's last obsession.

Evan's story about the diary had taken on a grudging significance in her mind. Now it seemed a bridge to her father's last hours. Although she couldn't remember putting it down, the diary was on the desk beside the glass of port, the light projecting the port's ruby whorl across its cover. With all the baggage of a rich but ragged life about him, at the end, A.L.'s mind had dwelt on that damned book. Her father had gone to his death talking to a stranger, thinking about a stranger.

Carly was far from sure that calling Evan was the sensible thing to do, and she was struck with the same debilitating reticence that had kept her from calling before, but she needed someone to listen to her, and whatever his motives, somewhere along the way, Evan had counted himself in.

She stood, digging for her cell once more. Turning towards the window, she opened the phone and put in the area code. With a mix of annoyance and surprise, she realized she didn't remember his number and it wasn't on her phone. It would be on her own laptop at the magazine office, or she could look it up.

REQUIEM FOR THURSDAY

Palming the phone, she rested her hands on the window ledge and let her brow rest against the cool glass. Below, on the ledge, the pewter picture frame lay flat, face down. The office window behind the desk chair had a double pane, but its glass was still pleasantly cold against the heat of her forehead. Outside the sealed argon insulation of the pane, Lake Ontario seemed motionless beyond the park lights.

Although she knew the sky had been clear for two days, the snowfall looked impossibly fresh, an illusion of the light, no doubt. It was a steady, shadowless light, filtered through a deep cloud layer, and brighter than it had seemed when she was out there in the cold.

She kept looking, her thoughts at last beginning to idle. Perhaps she was waiting for a car to speed by, but none did. Quiet...followed by quiet.

And then the quietude passed some statistical norm, and she began to wonder where everyone *was* tonight.

There wasn't a soul in the park, not surprising considering the cold perhaps, but she couldn't see a Canada goose or a gull anywhere either, not even in the lee of the pavilion snack bar, where they would ride out the onshore winds. But then, the breeze itself seemed to have stopped, and a preternatural stillness had settled everywhere. Even the lights of Hamilton, far across the narrowing end of the bay, didn't twinkle, as though the great arc of frigid sky over the warmer lake had ceased to shimmer.

That's when she noticed the sign above the snack bar.

It took her a minute to realize what was wrong with the sign —what was utterly and unavoidably wrong with what she was seeing there. It took her another long, clenched minute to understand that what her eyes were telling her mattered, and that if she was to go on living her life with the usual convictions and assumptions, she would have to go out into the cold right now. She'd have to stand outside there at the pavilion again and read the pathetic, fluorescent orange scrawl that, hardly more than *an hour ago*, had seemed to smoulder on the cold wooden sign. She needed those vulgar, spray-painted words to be there, and she needed to reach up and feel the slick texture of the paint. That would be a trick, though. Right now, looking out from the window of her father's office, her eyes were telling her the words simply *weren't there* any longer.

CHAPTER FIFTEEN

Weiss ended the call, frowned at the screen of his cell phone for a moment, then tucked it away in his coat. Prem Joshi stood looking at him from the doorway of the empty lecture room while in the hallway behind him a noisy flow of university students passed by.

"That was Carly Rouhl, A.L.'s kid," Weiss said.

"What did she want?"

"To tell you the truth, I'm not sure. It was a pointless call. She asked about her father's computer—the laptop from the old man's office."

"The suicide note."

"Yeah, the *apparent* suicide note. And then there's A.L.'s memoir. That's on there too—the one that's going in the daughter's magazine."

"Anxious to get it all back, is she? Maybe young Ms. Rouhl doesn't want you looking at what else might be on the laptop."

"Hmm. Things are just trundling along, aren't they? I haven't even unwrapped the damn thing yet. Maybe I *should* be looking closely."

"So are we talking to this psych prof now?"

"Right. I just had to get out of the madding crowds to hear what Rouhl was saying. The shrink should be at the end of this corridor."

"Maddening crowds, you mean."

"Actually, it's... Never mind."

Professor Deanna Leung received them in her small office and offered tiny bowls of tea from an elegant little chrome machine. They both accepted and Joshi took to studying his cup, which was filled with a perfumed green liquid, turning it carefully as though searching for a handle that he knew must be there somewhere.

Deanna Leung was a small Asian woman with a short geometrical hairstyle that Weiss thought might be a wig. She was wearing a satin shift that was the most marvelous shade of grey, a shade that might have been borrowed from the overcast outside her window. "As part of the assessment," she was saying, her voice too precise for a native speaker, "we talked to Cole's family, of course.

"No love lost there," Leung said and settled into her desk chair. "And they let me into her house, with all the proper warrants and such. Curious how much you can tell about a person by looking at her living space." Weiss looked about him at the office occupied by Leung herself. It was mostly window broken up by vertical blinds. The bookshelf behind them was curtained with grey felt and a single yellow HB pencil lay on her empty desk.

"So, you were in her house—the one up near the Rockchapel Sanctuary? What can you tell us?"

"Well, the first thing you'd notice, of course, is that it's a house made possible by her late husband's wealth and Marcella's own inherited sense of upper middle-class privilege. Marcella sees herself as entitled, you see, to some degree of wealth, but more than that—to gentility." Leung glanced out her window at the gray sweep of the campus. "She doesn't mind living alone in a slowly diminishing world; it makes it easier to avoid the little breaches of etiquette that threaten her poise as a privileged lady."

"If she's wealthy, why does she work?" Joshi asked.

"Well, you see, there are two dynamics in Marcella's personality: the need to protect herself and her dignity, and the need to control—to control just about everything in her environment. Her career, at least before the scandal, gave her influence; and as head nurse, she'd achieved a degree of control over others."

Weiss nodded. "She's still working, you know, but her ability to control people? Well, diminished."

"That I find interesting. Perhaps her job still serves her need for decorum. Respectability."

"Anything else about the house?" Weiss asked.

Leung leaned back in a chair that was entirely invisible even behind her narrow shoulders. "In her house, there's this high vaulted great room in which she obviously spends most of her time, and it's dominated not by the expanse of windows that look down on the city and the lake, but by the rich wall of curtains that shut them *out*. Classic defense mechanism."

Weiss frowned trying to follow along. Leung's speaking voice reminded him of a narrator in a documentary. "Above the stone mantle of the fireplace, I remember she had a print in a lacquered, Art Deco frame. It made quite an impression on me."

"Because her choice of art told you something about her, you mean?"

"I wish you could have seen it, Detective Weiss. Absolute textbook. The print was of an oil by Edward Hopper in which a woman, smartly dressed in a blue tailored suit, is sitting in a New York automat. She's wearing a neat hat with a tiny feather, and behind her are the little glass doors which in those days were used to display slices of cake, sandwiches, bowls of chili and so on. You must have seen pictures…"

"Sure, an automat. 1930s and 40s, right? They were cafeterias built like big vending machines."

"Yes, but you see, in the painting, none of the foods are actually visible; only the many rectangular panes with their identical coin slots."

Joshi's eyes turned slowly to Weiss, as if Leung was babbling about her abduction by aliens.

"Marcella Cole was an intelligent woman," Leung said. "She probably knew perfectly well that she identified with that woman's isolation, the woman in the painting. That the empty chairs and tables, hinted at in a few orderly brushstrokes, represented a relentless and bitter desolation. I'll bet Cole could have told you about the cool, muted colours, and the pallor of the woman's expressionless face beneath the harsh, artificial light of the automat."

Weiss ignored Joshi, who had taken to moving restlessly in his chair. Joshi was probably worried the academic was going to itemize Marcella's CD collection too, but he continued to devote most of his skepticism to the tea.

Leung didn't pick up on Joshi's discomfort either. "What Cole might have missed," she said, "what she might have been *incapable* of recognizing—was that the real spell the painting cast over her was in none of these things. Oh no. I'm sure that in Marcella's case, the real power of the image was discreetly suggested behind the woman. It was those rows of identical boxes, you see—those blank windows—neat, orderly, each with its coin slot, each with its handle, each forever closed."

Weiss frowned, doing his best. "The row of boxes?"

"Don't you see? All that food: pies, cakes, soup... Reduced to a series of blank pigeon holes. It's the perfect paradigm for an obsessive—the messy variety of the world reduced to simple order. Everything in rows. Everything in its place. I even wrote up the painting in my report."

"The report you submitted to the prosecutor's office."

REQUIEM FOR THURSDAY

"Of course. My other great find was her diaries. They were on a set of bookshelves in the main room."

Weiss straightened in his chair. "You read her diaries?"

"Actually, no. It would have taken a team of people to do that, and there was so little time. I find it amusing that the sheer tedium of her writings is her last line of defense. It's legible but tediously bleak and repetitive. Anyway, I didn't need to read much. You see, for Marcella Cole, entering something in her diary would have made it real. The family told me they'd made her keep a diary as a child back in Johannesburg, and that it had become part of the way she lived. I suspect the power of it had appealed to her—the way those externalized memories assumed permanence and authority through the written word: so it is written, so it was done."

Leung's eyes widened. "You should see them, Detective—the shelves, I mean: tall, austere, and done in Chinese lacquer. There's a sort of telephone table in front that has an uncomfortably angular matching chair. She uses an 01 needlepoint Rotring drafting pen that lies conveniently at hand."

Leung steepled her fingers. "And the text inside the diaries? Well, the words are tiny and even. Each sentence she adds to these journals matches the others so that they must seem like a shadow moving down the page."

"I don't see the importance..."

"Detective Weiss, you came here for my opinion. I assume that includes what I was *not* permitted to include in my report. Having read the testimony from the trial, and having followed the trial in the press, I believe Marcella Cole was nothing less than a practical and practiced killer. She had taken her first victim at the age of nine, you know, and had never forgotten how easy it was."

"She killed someone? At nine?"

"Well, that's what it amounts to. That piece of information came from the family. I found out that when she was growing up in South Africa she had watched her mother discipline the black servants, and one day, in a fit of childish anger, she had accused an old black servant of touching her. She'd done this without tears or drama, simply by writing it down and manipulating her father into finding the words. Classic sociopaths are instinctive manipulators.

"So cool, so efficient—the power of the written word. She'd watched, probably amazed as the horror took root and ran its course," Leung continued. "At first, Marcella scarcely understood what it was she was implying, but when the Johannesburg police questioned her, she picked up on what they were after, and she fed their looks of anger and disgust with just enough detail that the old man was quietly taken away and hanged from a shade tree."

Leung went on: "Her sister told me that their parents hadn't tried to keep the outcome of the incident from Marcella. In fact, they made a point of telling her about the hanging. They told her so she would feel *safe*."

Leung sniffed her derision. "Safe? I suspect that the little girl felt *more* than safe. I expect the incident had made her feel *powerful*. I believe that thereafter she would kill again, not with passion, mind you, but with indignation—with that same hauteur of a colonial landowner disciplining a domestic"

Joshi looked at his watch. "You're reading a lot into a shelf of diaries."

Leung shook her head in pitying patience. "Shelves, Detective Joshi. Shelves. In all, there were seven shelves. Each was neatly and perfectly packed with books and—stunningly—each book was identical in every way. When she had finished aligning each diary with its neighbours, smoothing spine after spine, the diaries formed seven perfectly even, delicately corrugated walls, each diary probably representing a year of her life, each one with an identical black vinyl cover. Would you care to guess how many diaries were on those shelves?"

REQUIEM FOR THURSDAY

Joshi opened his mouth to say something, and Weiss closed his eyes in dread, but mercifully Leung went on. "I counted sixty."

"Wait a minute," Weiss said, "Even if she started at the age of nine, Marcella's not that old."

"Very good, Detective Weiss. When I looked, the top shelf was full of more or less empty books."

"So she bought enough books to keep her going into old age. What do you mean they were more or less empty?"

"Yes. Intriguing detail, isn't it? Even these diaries, the empty ones—the ones representing her own future—they had a few scattered notations in them. These later diaries were set aside for a life not yet lived, empty, blank and clean, ready to receive the minutiae of days and years to come. And yet, page after page, they were sprinkled with... Well, I couldn't tell: promises, goals, reminders, and anniversaries pending? One wonders..."

She shrugged. "And then, of course, unless you were as meticulous as Marcella herself, you'd fail to notice one other subtlety. For all its apparent perfection, the pattern was broken."

Joshi rumbled and shifted uncomfortably, but Leung ignored him. "Naturally, the police would have been most interested in the current diary—the one covering the year leading up to the murder of her husband and the trial. So I looked for it, but it was missing from the shelf. It wasn't obvious at first, because the missing book had been replaced with a cleverly crafted spacer that kept the gap open. A thin vinyl spine mounted on a hollow metal frame covered the gap. She must have had it custom made."

"It makes sense," Weiss said, "that she'd remove the diary for the current year—the year of the trial. She probably kept it with her, so she could be sure no one would read it."

"Yes, I suppose. But, that spacer also guaranteed that the perfect pattern of the diaries wouldn't look disturbed...even by the little gap left by a missing book."

"And this diary may still be missing?"

Leung laughed. "Oh, I suspect it's back where it belongs now, but how would we know that, Detective Weiss? After all, Marcella Cole is a respectable citizen again, with a right to privacy." Obviously amused by her own gift for irony, Leung grinned, her teeth long, white and symmetrical. After a moment she glanced at Joshi who was still clutching his little cup and saucer, and said, "More tea, Detective Joshi?"

Joshi sat up, suddenly apprehensive and ready to do battle. He looked at Weiss as though the question might have been a slight of some kind that he had missed, then he gave a simple, "No." Then, as a pointed afterthought, "Thanks."

Weiss shifted forward in his chair as if getting ready to leave. "One last question, professor. You said Cole was a killer without passion. Suppose I were to tell you she drowned her victims. Does that suggest anything to you? Any pictures pop into your head?"

"Drowning. Well, as I said, passionless. An execution, perhaps. You know I visited an old prison museum in the course of my studies. They used to use a version of waterboarding to discipline prisoners back in the thirties. The prisoner was strapped in a chair with his head enclosed in a sort of small barrel. They'd fill it with water and bring the prisoner to the point of drowning before opening a spigot to drain the water. You asked me if a picture popped into my head. Well, there's my picture." Leung took a delicate sip of her tea, cradling the tiny bowl in her hand. "Although, of course, Marcella Cole would never open the spigot."

CHAPTER SIXTEEN

The office window Detective Weiss shared with Prem Joshi was in north Burlington, within sight of the escarpment. On the eastern side of the building, it looked out towards Headon Road and the traffic streaming down from Lowe's and the Wal-Mart plaza.

There was construction tape and drywall dust on the inside of the window. The office was brand new and utterly without character. They hadn't even delivered Weiss's files from the old station, the building they had torn down to make way for the new performing arts centre; the file cabinet was trapped in some halfway storage hell up in Waterdown. Real estate in downtown Burlington had become too expensive for the police; only well-off types like the Rouhls could afford to live down there near the lake.

Prem Joshi sat looking morosely at a spread of open files on his desk. He picked one up and frowned at it. "You wanna tell me how your Marcella Cole got from Toni Beal's floater over to our famous author suicide file? What's she doing showing up at the Rouhl funeral?"

Across the room, Eilert Weiss was stroking a touchpad,

watching a screen of text scroll upward. "I haven't any idea. Welcome to Marcella's neighbourhood, Prem."

"She's contaminated my blotter. She a literary groupie or something? Did she know A.L. Rouhl or someone in the family?"

Weiss stifled a yawn. "Well, okay, here's a starting point: I remember hearing that A.L. Rouhl was at her trial. He took an interest in the hospital murder. That's like five years ago, okay? It's hardly surprising that Rouhl would be curious about Marcella; Rouhl was a nonfiction writer and he got most of his material from his travels, but there was a juicy story developing in his own home town. It must have seemed irresistible even to an elderly man nearing the end of his writing career."

"So did he actually write about her?"

"I don't know Rouhl's books that well, but if he did write about her, it would have been a few years back—around the time of the trial, I guess. I gather he's been too sick to write for the last couple of years."

"Marcella attending the old guy's funeral though; that's gotta be a mark of respect—right?"

"Gloating, wouldn't you think? Rouhl was one of the press covering her trial, recording her humiliation. Then of course murderers sometimes choose to attend the burial of their victims."

Joshi twisted in his chair. "Jesus, Eilert. Victim? Rouhl? Where the hell did *that* come from? When you're going to make grand leaps, at least arrange for a drum roll. You're talking about tossing out our neat suicide and dragging in a wild card murderer?"

The pale skin around Weiss's eyes crinkled. "Yeah, I know. Do me a favour, will you Prem?

Keep an eye on me. When I think about that Cole woman I'm apt to get a little crazy. Still, we haven't completely written off Rouhl's death as a suicide, and now here's Marcella goddamn fucking Cole mincing around the fringes of our case like the angel of death. Then there's that teaching assistant, Therese Cherry, floating in the bay—who, it turns out, was related to Marcella."

Joshi shifted uncomfortably and made a sort of what-the-hell gesture. "You hear stuff around the coffee station. Most of it's crap of course. I don't pay much attention. But I'm thinking now it's on my blotter and maybe I should be hearing it from you."

Weiss kept looking at his desktop computer screen, but he seemed to deflate slightly. There was a silence filled only by the creaking of Joshi's chair, then Weiss cleared his throat, trying to be sure of his voice. "The Cole trial five years ago. It was... It was a perfect storm for me. I was going through some personal stuff and I let some things slide at work. I probably should've taken a leave, but it was an all hands on deck time at the detachment and I wasn't thinking too clearly back then anyway."

"I heard about your wife. I'm sorry."

Weiss nodded at the screen. "Should make me kind of an expert on suicide, don't you think? I can tell you what a blunt instrument suicide is, how personal it is."

"So now we're back to Rouhl?"

"I don't know, Prem. In Rouhl's case, his death all seems so tidy. The daughter seems actually proud of him—for 'writing a good ending' if you can believe it. She'd be just fine if we call it suicide."

"Doesn't want us looking too closely, you mean?"

"Maybe. I don't get her. Either the old man was using her, making her co-write his farewell to the world, or *she* was writing the ending for him. I can't tell."

Joshi creaked back in the chair, doing inventory on his thoughts. Weiss appeared motionless, but the cursor on the screen in front of him was slipping up and down in a steady rhythm. "I guess you heard the bit about my wife wearing my clothes. Makes for a good story, huh? Freakish…"

Joshi stopped creaking, aware that Weiss had drifted back to his wife's suicide.

"A woman'll put a guy's shirt on. Cute, right? But no. She was dressed up as me. Tie, even raided my sock drawer. How's that for personal, Prem? She was taking me with her when she jumped off the bridge. Nice touch, don't you think? How's that for writing an ending to your life? I couldn't get her to get help, get on some meds, so we fought a lot. She must have come to hate me, and she orchestrated her suicide to get as much attention as she could. And she wanted it clear to everyone that she blamed me for…hell, for everything."

Joshi sat up and tried to cover his embarrassment by taking a stapled document from the largest file and pretending to study it. After a few seconds of creaking chairs and rustling papers, he decided to change the subject. "So, we've got to understand where Marcella's coming from."

Weiss finally shifted and gave his eyes a quick rub. "I can help with that. I wasn't lead on the Jo Brant murder, but I helped do background on Marcella for the prosecution."

Joshi put down the file and swivelled to listen.

"We were making the case that Marcella was a genuine sociopath—one of that four percent of society that has no moral instinct, no scruples or capacity for guilt."

"Yeah like the senate. So, *did* she murder her husband?"

"Hell, yes. Probably did the crown's star witness too. I'm telling you, Prem, the trial was this crazy dance. Even the jurors knew she was guilty, but when the judge did his compulsory caution at the end, they knew what he was saying—'the crown has failed to make its case.' He was saying, 'Reasonable doubt,' so they let her walk. But for anyone who was involved in the prosecution, Marcella Cole will always remain unfinished business."

"Okay, so you figure we've got ourselves a textbook sociopath?"

"The crown managed to convince the jury Marcella was obsessive compulsive—the kind of obsessive compulsive who doesn't acknowledge her condition. That's why she managed to rise to head nurse in her department, you see. The woman's ego is solid, unassailable. To this day, she sees herself as entirely rational. And, of course, there are no laws against her kind of careful, anal behaviour.

"Not surprisingly, she's had no honest relationships in her life, but it'd be wrong to describe Marcella Cole as lonely. She's mistrustful and uninterested in other people, and she's chosen her solitary life deliberately. She's got no real friends, and her marriages? Well, they served only to make her financially independent, and ruin the lives and families of two men in passing."

Weiss swivelled, staring out the window. "Funny thing is, Marcella's isolation gives her an inner stillness that some people back then recognized and even admired. I remember it showed mostly in her face: she had an unlined brow and these perfectly symmetrical, expressionless lips. It's a kind of Botox of the heart. I remember looking at her in court, watching for a reaction to all those people getting up and saying how odd she was.

"One of the tricks you learn is to watch for differences between the right and left side of the face. Someone will smile with the left side and betray something else, some other emotion with the right. That's when it hit me—Cole's face is perfect. Perfect symmetry, right and left, perfect features. That's uncommon; in fact, I don't think I've ever seen it before and it's what makes her beautiful. But to me, it's a dull, unmemorable beauty—and then there's her fashion sense; she's immaculate, but somehow about twenty years out of date."

"Some guys actually get off on that," Joshi said. "Retro kinky."

"Yeah, I know what you mean. If a woman's taste is far

enough out of whack, it becomes a kind of fetish thing, like Madonna. Marcella definitely had that going for her."

"So? Did she react to what she was hearing from the witnesses?"

Weiss shook his head. "If there was anything going on behind those eyes, I didn't see it. We all have a sense of self, but the psych file says Marcella's self-talk was 'spare and uncritical;' mostly it was strategic, aimed at preserving her dignity in the face of a 'carping and intrusive world.' I think I'm quoting."

"Nicely put. Who are you quoting?"

"Actually, that may have been our friend Professor Leung."

"Good. Anything else?"

"Marcella's career path was smoothed by race and privilege in South Africa and she eventually found her niche in administration. She ran a nursing staff in Johannesburg with enough efficiency to avoid drawing negative attention, and when South African society changed and the hostility of her co-workers threatened her stability, she immigrated here—to a country in dire need of people with nursing qualifications.

"You know, in the context of Marcella Cole's life and the violence she's probably gotten away with, that trial for murder was a rather limited affair. The whole thing hinged on her having obtained an untraceable and dangerous drug immediately before her second husband's death. All the evidence was circumstantial."

"So an expensive lawyer had no difficulty getting Cole bail?"

Weiss nodded. "The prosecution fell apart when the key witness, a young pharmacologist, had a tragic accident. The family said he was a strong swimmer, but this young guy somehow managed to drown at his family's cottage while his wife was away taking in a local studio tour."

Joshi sat up, staring in disbelief. "Oh, come on. The key witness against her conveniently drowns and no one *wonders*?"

"Of course they wondered. There were suspicion and questions, but no-one could imagine how Marcella might've pulled it off."

"No one?"

"Well... I remember a conversation I had with a girl at the coroner's office. Cute kid, an assistant or intern or something. She said something off the record: it was the kind of irresponsible, speculative comment you can make when you've got no official standing. She suggested that the pharmacologist might have drowned 'somewhere else' before being put in the lake. If I'd been...up to speed, I should have followed that up." Weiss shrugged and ran his fingers along the window ledge, studying the white plaster dust he had disturbed. "It started me thinking —that we should have been running a second murder investigation. The body might have been dumped—but in the end, it probably wouldn't have made any difference—at least that's what I tell myself. That I'd never have been able to prove anything. Cole has survived by being careful and preternaturally clever."

Joshi turned back to the files and started to read. "You make her out as some freak of nature, but I bet there are more people like her out there than you'd believe, day by day, year by year successfully screwing the rest of us."

"Yeah. She's kind of a circus tightrope walker, never missing a step, and all the while she's dropping water balloons on our heads."

"Water balloons?" Joshi smirked.

"Yeah. Water. Because we're, you know, the clowns."

CHAPTER SEVENTEEN

Eilert Weiss noted the material of Evan Favaro's suit wondering what it must have cost. It was as though television people bought their clothes from a warehouse the public could never enter—a place where all the shop assistants were fashionistas. The show's director, a flamboyant refugee from the BBC, Allyn Hache, turned to Willie Canmore, a script assistant with a red barrette in her short hair, and gestured to the monitor. "Where'd they get him anyway? He's too big for a fashion show. Who is he? He a regular?"

"Are you blind? He's not just *big*. He's a hunk. Jesus, you hate real men, don't you?"

Hache raised a brow and said, "Shut up?" making it sound like a casual question.

Willie ignored him. "What's the matter? You're usually a pretty good judge of beefcake. Don't you think he's hot?"

"Maybe. Yeah, sure. Not hunky, mind you."

Weiss stood in the darkness behind the sound man. "Is he in a relationship, do you know?" he asked.

Willie shrugged. "Evan? Nah. Not that I've heard about. Divorced. Stays with his brother- and sister-in-law when he's in

Toronto, owns a condo in Burlington. The producer says one of the advertisers asked for him. He was in the last spot they bought."

"A commercial?" Hache swung back and forth in his director's chair making it creak in the cramped space of the control room. "Maybe that's why he looks familiar." He looked up at the multiple images of Evan on the set, appraising the line of his arm against the chair. Evan wore a dark suit, the jacket hanging open to disclose a cream-coloured shirt and mauve tie, and the long angle of his legs did wonders for the negative space.

Evan appeared to notice the camera trucking towards him. Weiss expected a quick smile from him, but Evan picked up a clipboard and let it stand up defensively on his knees.

Willie moved a headphone forward over her left ear and leaned closer to the director. "You've seen him around, Allyn. He shows up on TV here and there. Talks about relationships and stuff."

Allyn Hache closed one eye. "Yeah. That's it. I've seen him. He reads people's personalities from their handwriting." He plucked at his mutton chops thoughtfully. "Okay, so I can see how he'd be perfect for *that* kind of thing. Woman's man and all that. He's got authority. Women would trust him." Hache took a fresh look at Evan, was quiet for a moment and then, without taking his eyes from the screen, half-turned to the script assistant. "Wrong for this show, though."

Willie sighed. "He who pays the piper."

Hache wasn't giving up. "Look at him. He's not getting enough sleep or something."

Weiss shifted his attention up to Evan's warmly lit face. His sandy-coloured hair had some height but it plunged straight down his long neck almost to his shoulders. The effect made Weiss think of an arch in a gothic cathedral.

Evan self-consciously went back to looking down and to the side, allowing his long hair to swing in, curtaining his ear. With an effort, Weiss forced himself to look past the compelling jut of the man's jaw and the hypnotic brow and caught what the director was noticing. Evan was either nervous or worried about something; his lower lip was deformed by a gentle bite.

Willie nodded. "Okay, so he's got something on his mind. Maybe he's afraid he knocked up the floor director. Now *she's* been looking heavy, let me tell you. Anyway, give the guy a chance. The sponsor thinks he appeals to widows with disposable income and you can't argue with Madison bloody Avenue."

The director rumbled in his woven chair. "Fine, fine. Tell everyone to get ready. Lighting just gave me the high sign."

Willie tugged her headphone mic into place and cupped it with her hand. "Okay, people." She gave some last-minute directions to the floor director below, then hurried aside to loom over the sound man. Seeing what she wanted on the digital soundboard, the script assistant nodded to the director.

Hache gave a single nod of his head and touched a button on the console. "Let the jacket hang straight, Evan. Very nice, everybody. Casual but energetic." Weiss could hear the boom of the director's voice beneath his feet.

On the monitor Evan nodded, straightening his tie and focusing. The studio lights warmed and softened Evan's features and a professional calm came over his face.

"Okay people, recording! And... " Hache twirled his index finger in warning and then jabbed it at the monitor. Willie barked into her microphone for the benefit of the floor director.

There was a beat and in that moment Evan was transformed. He smiled at the studio audience. It was a smile that kicked the warmth of the set up a notch or two and brightened the studio.

Hache stared at the monitors, his finger jabbing from one to another to direct the switcher. Softly, he said, "Holy shit," his eyes widening. Weiss glanced up from the soundboard across at the director and then up to the monitors.

Hache dropped his hand. He turned his head slightly, swallowing hard. "Willy dearest, tell number two to keep giving me close-ups of Evan. There's a good girl."

Willie spoke into her mic and sauntered over to Hache. "Well?" she said, looking smug.

The director nodded slowly. Below them, the show had begun and Evan was talking with charm and ease to the host.

"Yes, well," Hache sniffed, "He has presence."

Hache kept looking up at Evan, who was in close up once more. Without turning he said, "Years ago I had to interview an actor for this thing…this entertainment show. He was young then and already he was a minor movie star, right? So I'm looking at him thinking, what's this guy got that he gets paid ten times what I get? He's no Greek god—just this ordinary-looking guy. Anyway, at some point, I ask him some stupid question about nothing in particular, and he pulls this *look*. Kind of a surprised smile, you know? And suddenly, wham! I get it. And I think, 'Fuck me,' and I wrap up the interview, and I go home depressed."

Willie grinned. "What? The guy *had* it?"

"Jesus, yeah. Charisma. Had it in spades. At that moment, he could've had *me* for the asking. But he didn't ask, thank you very much."

"And Evan? He's got it?"

He glanced up, giving Willie a sullen pout.

"Oh, c'mon, Allyn."

"All right. All right." He patted his pockets. "I caught myself envying the fucking clipboard, all right? Does anyone have a cigarette?"

Weiss smiled and left the control room. He took a carpeted staircase to the studio floor and emerged behind a set of tubular bleachers that held the studio audience. Cautiously, he moved out into the light.

Down here, Weiss could see Evan's full television makeup; he looked as flawless as a mannequin, his cheeks and brow warm with the matte luster of a Lladro figurine. His tie dropped in a soft asymmetrical pattern from tight beneath his throat to a smoked nickel belt buckle. Beside him on the couch was a woman from the audience, a freckled redhead, juiced at being chosen to sit on camera with Evan and the female host. Her hands were flopping in her lap like a landed fish.

Evan held a clipboard on his knee, on it a sample of the woman's neat, child-like handwriting. He smiled at the redhead and the director, knowing where the power was, called for a close up on Evan. "You hold things together, don't you Fran?" Evan was saying. "All around you, your family is off doing important things, but they count on you to be level-headed and centered. You're the one they turn to when they need a sensible, practical opinion."

The red-headed woman tucked her long hair over her ear for the fourth time and laughed. The audience chuckled, taking this as a yes.

"Tell me, Fran, you handle the money a lot, don't you?" Evan frowned at the clipboard as though discerning subtle clues. Evan had been told he was talking to the mother of infant twins. "Bank account? Credit card bills?"

"Oh, yes. My husband's happy for me to take care of the boring stuff." Caught up in Evan's sex appeal and the woman's ingenuousness, the audience smiled in sympathy. Above in the control room, the video switcher was catching all of this. Here and there, the director would call up a rostrum image of the redhead's letter, shot earlier.

Weiss watched this go on for a few minutes. If, in his own analysis, Evan was missing the mark, he would pick up some body language or fleeting expression on the woman's face, skill-

REQUIEM FOR THURSDAY

fully steering the conversation in a more promising direction. By the end of the segment, he was ahead on points and over the top in charisma. The host, a lovely black woman, turned to commercial business, somehow managing to carry an undertone of delighted gratitude right into the break.

When the show was over, Detective Weiss couldn't get near Evan. He had stepped near the slowly moving line of audience members filing towards the exits, and some of the women had engaged him in a mixture of questions and adulation. Weiss watched from the end of the noisy line. Evan Favaro wasn't exactly a star, but up close, he looked and sounded like one.

There had only been three other men in the audience, each brought along by a wife; Weiss, who had eventually managed to squeeze in beside a busload of red-hatters from Scarborough, felt like a thorn in a long winter coat among so many freshly misted roses. Despite the demands on his attention, Evan had picked up on the tall incongruity of Weiss long before the last of the audience had ambled past him.

Weiss finally managed to introduce himself with a smile that was all about his eyes, the corners of his mouth being upstaged by his mustache. He managed to make a discrete gesture, displaying his credentials. "You called my precinct and volunteered some information, Mr. Favaro." He tapped the pocket of his jacket as though to suggest a notebook. "What I have is that you visited A.L. Rouhl at his home. That was...Tuesday? Two days before his apparent suicide? I was hoping you could give me an idea of Mr. Rouhl's state of mind at that time. Was it a social call?"

Evan sat down carefully on the aluminum bleacher. He'd been sparkling with adrenaline for the cameras, and now he was visibly settling down. His face relaxed, and it was as if some of the makeup had disappeared. Weiss realized that a part of Evan's charisma was a thing he could summon through an act of will. He looked up at Weiss with dark brown eyes made bright by the studio lighting.

"A social call? Not exactly. You see, I'd never met Mr. Rouhl before. It seems he had a specific reason for inviting me."

"But he did call you, asked you to come to his house?"

"Yes. He knew a little bit about me because I'd been out with his daughter, Carly. Carly and I met because she wanted to write a magazine profile about me." Evan tilted his head and his neck hair surfed his shoulder. "It sounds odd, but in the published piece that Carly did about me, she talked about my television work, barely mentioning my use of handwriting analysis. All the same, Mr. Rouhl seems to have picked up on that particular detail. He told me he actually watched one of my television appearances at home."

"You seem surprised."

"The program the great A.L. Rouhl saw was… Well, it was a lot like this show actually." Evan gestured at the set with its stainless steel kitchen and crescent of couches.

"It was a sort of woman's program—an afternoon show about fashion and decorating mostly. I did a little segment last week about relationships."

"As an expert?"

He smiled. "Don't judge me too harshly, Detective. I have a master's degree in psychology and training in handwriting analysis. What I do here is entertainment, but I can perch a pair of glasses on the end of my nose and do useful work too."

Weiss grinned. "And all that stuff you told that young mother today?"

"There's some real science even in that, but sure, I play it up for the audience. We get the audience volunteers to sign waivers, and I try to be positive and helpful."

"Does what you do on television make you uncomfortable?"

"Well, I hope none of my former professors ever watch it, if that's what you mean. Anyway, the handwriting thing is what caught Mr. Rouhl's interest. And that's why he went out of his way to find out about the show."

"And he felt he could do all this because you were seeing his daughter?"

Evan looked over at the big windows that gave the studio a cool blue panorama of Queen Street. "Car and I, well, we only dated...twice."

Weiss noted the ambivalence. He understood how Evan could be drawn to Carly Rouhl; she had an expressive beauty that was heightened by her cleverness. It wasn't as easy to imagine A.L.'s daughter involved with this chiselled mannequin, his studio makeup flawless under the light bars. "So you think it was the handwriting business, not your training in psychology that caused old Mr. Rouhl to call you?"

"Well, both really, but it was the oddest meeting—odd at the time, even odder in retrospect. I called the local police after his death because I just wanted someone to know..."

"So he—what, phoned you? And you agreed to visit? Was his daughter there?"

Evan mimed surprise. "No. I expected her to be, but it turns out Car knew nothing about all this until I told her at the funeral. There was a nurse in the house, but she never sat with us. I was actually alone with Carly's father the whole time."

"Time of day?"

"Evening. Eightish."

"So the nurse would have been Mrs. Crowther."

"Yes, that was it."

"Take me through this odd little meeting."

"Yes, well the gist of it was he produced this journal, a sort of diary, and asked me what I thought of it—what I could make of its owner."

"Yes, the diary." Weiss straightened.

Evan's eyes darted, as though shifting from Weiss's right eye to his left. "Yes. You know—a sort of personal journal thing."

"And he believed you could do that? Analyze people from their handwriting alone?"

"I've done some profiling for the Wentworth District Police, and I stand by handwriting analysis as a tool within a broader investigation. But it's not magic and it's certainly not infallible. To be asked to do a serious analysis on the spot? Well, that's not much more than a party trick, and yes, I suppose that's what these television appearances are."

"Do you know the term 'cold reading,' Mr. Favaro?"

Evan sighed. "Yes, of course I do, and you're quite right, Detective. I do use cues from the subject, I pose leading questions, and I make ambiguous statements—but only on television where I'm essentially putting on a show. I use my knowledge and my training as far as they'll take me, but I make a living in part by being a TV personality, and when I have that hat on, I'll admit I'm not being a very good scientist."

"And Mr. Rouhl? He wanted you to do your tricks on this diary?"

"He *said* he wanted to learn about handwriting analysis for something he was writing, but he was in much more of a hurry for that to be the case. I quickly caught on that he was genuinely interested in the writer of the diary. Anyway, I did my best to explain."

"What? That you couldn't *really* tell him anything definitive about the writer of the diary? But then you did look at it?"

"I turned it over in my hands as we talked. I riffled through a few pages. A few idle glances. It was more nervousness than anything else. I wasn't going to pretend…"

"What exactly did you tell him, Mr. Favaro? All said and done, you have scientific training, so when I ask this, you understand I need the answer of a professional."

"Yes, but you have to let me explain. This media work I do won't last. I've picked up some specialized training to prepare me for my work with the police. That's where I see my career going: forensic work. As part of my studies, I've had to familiarize myself with the writing of abnormal individuals."

"The writing of criminals?"

"Yes, and psychopaths. There's quite a body of literature on it, of course. I've seen facsimiles from all manner of sick and delusional individuals."

Weiss nodded. "I see."

"Then can you understand that there are some things that, to a trained eye, leap off the page?"

"Did it occur to you he might have been showing you his own writing?"

"He told me the diary had belonged to a nurse, a woman that he had known." Evan shook his head emphatically. "God, if it had been his... But no, it couldn't have been his," Evan went on. "It would shock me more than I can say if that were the case. From the context of that meeting, I think he was looking for confirmation of what he already knew about this woman: the writer of that diary."

"Any idea what he was doing with someone else's diary?"

"He said he had used it to research a story for one of his books."

"Did he say how he came by it?"

"No."

"And the name of the nurse?"

Evan looked away. Weiss could tell that he was thinking, being careful. In the end, all he said was, "He didn't give a name. In fact, I warned him about telling me her name. I told him that I might find myself in an awkward position if anything he told me had legal implications."

"Well, whether he told you more or not, you told *him* something. Otherwise, you wouldn't be trying so hard to rationalize it."

Evan nodded. "That...that book... It wasn't just the cursive, you know—the script. There were other things about the pages, the cover even..."

"What did you tell him?"

"He was a kindly old man. I was a guest in his home."

"Mr. Favaro..." Weiss looked at the polished concrete floor and waited. There was something soft and weak about Evan Favaro, but he couldn't help liking him which made Weiss wary.

Evan got up. "This is what I told him, Detective. I said I hoped he would have nothing to do with her. That the writer of that book was..." He closed his eyes. "I think... I think I may have used the word *dangerous*."

CHAPTER EIGHTEEN

"I'm Don Fucking Quixote." Eilert Weiss sat at his desk, scowling at a laptop computer surrounded by plastic wrap.

Detective Joshi—grey, tough as a goal post, and dark-eyed—toted his cup of coffee into the office and sat behind him. "Thank you for that Eilert, and a good morning to you too."

"It's not good for a detective to be thought of as quixotic, Prem. Not a career path signpost, if you catch my drift."

Joshi looked over Weiss's shoulder at the laptop. "What's bothering you? The Rouhl thing?"

"The Rouhl thing."

Joshi nodded. "It's the press, isn't it? Celebrity sensation and all." He grinned over the rim of his cup. "Your own damn fault of course."

"Jesus, Prem, not you too."

"Come on, Eilert. 'A spokesperson said there were points of interest?' Points of interest? What did you think the media were going to make of *that*? It's a suicide, for Christ's sake. 'Points of interest' is what you say for a fucking axe murder."

"It wasn't me. I never said that. They got to the kid, the

uniform. He probably heard the line on TV. It's not his fault; he thought he was being discreet."

"I hope you gave him a crash course in discrete, beginning with how to say 'no comment' in English, French, Middle Saxon, and Urdu."

"He's all right. I'm the one unjustly accused and hectored by his peers."

Joshi grimaced at his coffee. "Okay, I'm sorry. I'm having a bad day. I just wasted two minutes in the washroom trying to get hand sanitizer out of a carbon monoxide sensor. The world is getting way too complicated. I'm sorry you're Don Fucking Ho or whoever. What's with that anyway?"

"Forensics e-mailed Mercer over my head. They couldn't understand why I was requesting so many expensive tests, so of course, Mercer has to come in and lecture me on focused scenarios. Wanted me to prioritize. He accused me of being on a quixotic fishing expedition."

"Shit. Did you look it up?"

"I didn't have to look it up."

"So what kind of expedition *are* you on?"

"I'm on a non-quixotic expedition. I mean, I'm not on *anything*, okay? I'm just trying to model a scenario here. A situation where you get an exit wound and no bullet—and they're not going to let us move on until I do. Do you understand that?"

"Great. So, what you got?" He watched Weiss make stretching movements for a moment, then a thought crossed Joshi's mind. He winced. "Oh God, Eilert, not the Dick Tracy thing?"

Weiss looked hurt. "Of course not. The ice bullet idea doesn't work, it's been tried."

"So what then?"

"So I asked them to test the barrel of Rouhl's derringer for blood. For blood *inside* the barrel."

"In*side* the barrel? Jesus Christ. What for?"

"A burger bullet." Weiss waited, feeling Joshi's eyes on the back of his neck. He shrugged. "Okay, but it might actually work."

"What the fuck is a burger bullet?"

"You know, a bullet shaped out of frozen ground beef. Nobody's tried that. As the fat melts during percussion it would create its own lubricant. Unlike the ice, the plug might actually make it out of the barrel. On the wall, it would be more or less lost in the prevailing gore."

"Jesus, Eilert. Sounds pretty fucking quixotic to me."

"I know, it's ridiculous, but when no tidy solutions offer themselves, you get…"

"Desperate?"

"Look who we're dealing with here, Prem. You think it's a coincidence the deceased is one of the most ingenious writers of our time, and I can't find his damn kill shot?" Weiss swivelled around in his chair. "It even occurred to me that…"

Joshi leaned forward. "Omigod. Something even crazier than a burger bullet? Give it to me. I'm gonna love this."

"Don't enjoy it so much. Just listen: Rouhl was dying of an immune system failure. He was having his blood drawn regularly for tests." Weiss's voice became wistful. "Maybe somehow…"

Joshi's eyes widened. "What…" Then he gave a little gasp of delight and his face lit up. "No, wait, I'm way ahead of you." He spoke with slow relish. "A bullet moulded out of Rouhl's own frozen blood—a blood bank bullet. No! A clot cartridge, a hemoglobin howitzer, a…a…"

Weiss ignored him. "The burger bullet's not perfect. There are tests that could identify traces of animal tissue in the spatter. There are even tests that could identify different blood types in the residue—if you can get the buggers to *do* the tests, of course—but a bullet made of his own blood? Abso-lutely untraceable, *except* of course if you can find blood inside the gun barrel, where it's got no business being." He shrugged. "Anyway, I thought, what the hell; it was worth a shot, so to speak."

"Blood in the barrel. I can't believe you *actually* had the nerve to ask for the test. It's nice to know this investigation is going ahead on such a solid footing. Got anything else? Bullets made of supercooled helium that vaporize on impact?"

"Nothing actually sane that gives us a spent slug or even accounts for the anomalies in the blood trajectory."

"God, is the whole case like that?"

"Nah. The rest is neat enough; Rouhl had gunshot residue on his right hand and there are only his fingerprints on the gun. Motive, method, final note on the computer screen... It's suicide writ large on a bloody billboard. But how do *I* write it up? The void in the blood spatter is bad enough, but when you've got no ballistics, you at least need a theory that covers the facts."

"Okay, but wouldn't it be better if our theory didn't play well as comedy? We don't want laughs."

Weiss let out a slow sigh. "Remember the Enigma Variations?"

"The music that was playing at the scene."

"Yes. I looked it up. Seems there are two levels to Elgar's Enigma. Each variation in the piece was supposed to be a portrait of an individual—someone whose identity is never fully disclosed."

"Yeah. So?"

"Don't you see? It's easy. That's Rouhl's writing style: a series of real portraits with the identity masked—nonfiction fiction."

Joshi looked like he was washing his face without soap. "God, but you're sounding needy, Eilert. Can you leave my name off this report?"

"It's the second level of the Enigma that has me intrigued," Weiss grinned, enjoying Joshi's discomfort. "Each of Elgar's movements is a variation on a musical theme. Now, usually, the composer puts the passage that inspired him up front as a sort of introduction. You know; the theme, then the variations. But in the Enigma Variations, the theme on which everything else is based never actually appears. Some people think the original theme is something famous. Maybe 'God Save the Queen' or 'Auld Lang Syne.' Elgar wouldn't say."

Joshi stared at the ceiling. "Think how much overtime he could have saved the Halton Police Department if he'd only opened up."

"Makes me think of a character in a play who's talked about, but never actually appears on stage. Did you ever see *Waiting for Godot?*"

"I saw *Die Hard*. Yippee ki-yay."

"The point is, Prem, we're being jerked around by somebody damn clever."

"How about the daughter? She's as clever as her dad?"

At first, Weiss didn't answer, but he pursed his lips and drew an elongated question mark into the clean, white dust of the window ledge. "Forget the daughter for the moment. I want to tell you about my visit with her boyfriend, Evan Favaro—and his story about a certain dangerous nurse. It seems the infection on your blotter is spreading."

CHAPTER NINETEEN

"Sure you wouldn't enjoy a coffee?" Weiss said, gesturing with his own paper cup. "There's a machine downstairs."

Carly gave a polite smile. Her lips were as generous as her father's, the smile...interesting. She must have been wearing lipstick, but it was subtle. "Thank you, no. I'm fine." She had on a skirt suit with an open jacket which made her patterned blouse project in a curiously provocative way.

Weiss sat with Carly near the big window in the Hampton Road office. There was no desk between them and both were motionless in new fabric chairs that still had tape and white labels stuck to them—Weiss comfortable, Carly intent. Weiss discretely noted the silky material of her blouse pulled taut between her nipples and wondered if there was a name for the delicate and characteristic buckling of the material there. There was a word for cleavage; there should definitely be a word for this.

"That's my father's computer," Carly said, looking over Weiss's shoulder.

Weiss was holding a green paper cup; it said Starbucks on the side, but it was brewed tea, and the tea wasn't green and it wasn't from some damn digital samovar. The tea was hot and Weiss had been prying the lid with care to rescue the teabag. Then he looked up, recognizing that the computer comment was an odd thing for Carly to have said. It was the second time she had betrayed discomfort over the laptop. It wasn't as though Carly was just noticing the machine. They had taken their time getting settled, and it had been in clear view the whole time. He met Carly's eyes and took his time answering. "Yes. I can't hand it over just yet."

Carly seemed troubled by something, but she said, "There's no immediate hurry. Have you read my father's stuff before?"

"No, I'm afraid not. I made a point of phoning a teacher friend of mine who knows your father's work. I wanted a fast summary, you see. It reminded me a little of how we used to cheat in English Lit. And, of course, I did a simple web search. Wish we'd had *that* in college."

"And?"

"Well, let's see. I know your father wrote mostly non-fiction. He did some short stories early on but decided he had no gift for making things up. I gather what he did have was a real genius for making use of an anecdote, remembering what people told him. I find that endearing. It means he was a raconteur. His most successful books were sold as travel books, isn't that right? But what made them compelling reading were the characters he described and their stories. Fair enough?"

Carly nodded. "Dad had a way of weaving stuff together. Comic stuff; dark, distasteful stuff. Anything that had a story attached to it."

"All of this against the background of his travels, I gather."

"The places were always secondary to the people. All that stuff about the towns and countryside, the train rides and the taxis… It gave a kind of picaresque unity to it all, but travel was no more than a narrative gimmick to him. That's how I always saw it, anyway."

"What do you think, Ms. Rouhl? If I knew your father's work, would it help me understand the tragedy in that room?"

Carly shook her head. "There are books to be written about A.L. Rouhl, but in the end, suicide is an act of simple will."

"Any doubt in your mind about that?"

"What? That it was suicide? No, I believe you. My dad didn't have long to live, and his quality of life was declining fast. It caught me by surprise, but in retrospect..."

Weiss watched Carly's movements. Her fingers, long, winter pale, polished in a tone that was close to natural, were caressing the leaves of Joshi's South African Jade which spilled down beside her. It wasn't nervousness—A.L.'s daughter was a bit stiff, like a scholar at a sherry party, but for all that, she looked tough and wary. "You were asking me about a diary. Mr. Favaro tells me your father showed him a diary a couple of days before he died."

"Yes. He told me you'd spoken." Even so, Carly looked surprised that the detective had taken the trouble to follow it up.

Weiss's next question was elaborately casual, almost weary. "Still no luck finding this nurse's diary?"

"You actually think it's important then?"

"Perhaps when I see it, I'll be able to tell you more." Weiss could see that Carly was about to take the initiative, so he went back to the subject of Rouhl's books with enthusiasm. "My teacher friend said A.L. Rouhl's work is 'episodic and journalistic.'" Weiss savoured the words. "I'm quoting. I got the impression my friend enjoyed most of it, though. So, how about you? Did you read his books?"

It seemed a simple question to Weiss, but Carly frowned and steepled her fingers as though the answer was going to call for a lot of qualifications and caveats. "The later books got kind of dark and brooding. An old friend of Dad's told me she couldn't finish his last two books."

Weiss sipped some tea. "Neat trick he had, though—getting people to talk about their shame and sadness. My teacher friend says your father avoided lawsuits by changing people's names in his books, but that some people were still shocked to recognize themselves in his work. Perhaps some were even...offended?"

Carly raised an eyebrow. "Oh, I see where you're going. You're wondering if someone might have wanted to shoot him. Is that really worth..." Carly shook her head. "I mean, I guess you're right about his way of working, but..."

"Yes?"

"When he was home—and he was home most of the year—he was always sitting in that office of his, writing or reading. It's true he would travel now and then, much like your average tourist, I guess. Lots of Best Westerns and IHOPs. People find this hard to believe, but he was no man of the people. He could be charming when he wanted to, but frankly, it beats me how he managed to make so many connections or insinuate himself into so many private lives. Friends he bumped into overseas would tell me he seemed content to pass the time with them in a hotel lounge or bar."

"You've obviously thought a lot about this."

Carly looked out the window. "The truth is, it always bothered me that he was so damned good—with so little effort. I've been to the Cornell School of Journalism, Detective Weiss. I have an M.A. in English Literature, and when I write one of my little pieces of fluff for the local market, I go out and sit in people's parlours and ride around with them all day in their cars—as they say, a good journalist should."

"And your father?"

"God, it just looked so goddamn easy for him. I swear he made up half the stuff he wrote, non-fiction or not. And yet if you accused him of that, he'd just shrug and say he didn't have that much imagination. In fact, he said it so often that it became a point of pride with him. They even put it on his dust jackets.

People took the admission as proof of authenticity because he wrote utterly convincing stories.

"His books were just collections of that kind of character stuff, all woven together with a few nice descriptions of the setting. It worked for him. People would snap up his books in hardcover.

"If you ask me, Detective Weiss, that stuff about having no imagination—that he was just writing down what he knew, what he'd found out—it was a lie, pure and simple. A. L. wasn't just a journalist. There's no way he could have gotten into people's lives so deeply. He didn't have the geniality. He didn't have... He didn't have the *charm*.

"What he was, was a hell of a writer. He did a bit of research, but then? He embroidered, fabricated. He *must* have."

Weiss continued to watch her, his pupils searching her face in micro-movements, but when she stopped and seemed to appeal to him for understanding, his gaze dropped and he studied his tea. "Was he a well-educated man?"

Carly sighed. "Educated? No. Not by academic standards. He was just well-read. You know, self-taught. He was a man interested in other people's lives—in vicarious experience. Introspective, shy even, but for all that, he was a good listener. People who aren't keen on talking often do that. His only other interest was storytelling itself. He did love to talk about the craft. Saw it as some noble, semi-mystical calling going back to Anglo-Saxon 'shapers,' passing around the jug in a mead hall.

"I think he wanted me to believe that I could do it too—be a storyteller like him. But I couldn't, not the way he did it. Long ago I decided that being Alistair Rouhl's daughter was something special and enviable, but a damn sight less than fulfilling. The press talked about my father as being a great author; I, on the other hand, am a local magazine editor. Not even much of a writer anymore. Still, my eagerness to be A.L.'s daughter sustained me right through senior classes in journalism at the university. In the end, the realities of becoming financially independent of my father made me...what? An entrepreneur? Shepherding a glossy local magazine into the black after years of hustling and compromise."

She stopped for a moment and when she resumed Weiss had the impression she was addressing herself—not just as a rhetorical gesture—but in fact. "Wait a minute, Carly," she murmured. "A little journalistic detachment, please. It wasn't just that I had to make a living. No, the truth is, I don't have *it*—that creative spark that used to give everything my father wrote a life of its own. To almost anyone else, heading a successful magazine would have been a source of pride, but when your father is one of the pantheon gods of non-fiction prose, it's just not enough. And now he's dead, and I'm alone with my mediocrity. It seems I've inherited everything—money, the house, royalties—everything but the gift."

"You're too hard on yourself," Weiss said.

"Yeah, sure. You know, not so long ago the time came when my college coursework demanded that I study andYeah, I know. Do me a favour, will you Prem so I'd seen it coming. It had to be that damned book *Meridian*, of course. Even back then it was on curricula all over the English speaking world, and it probably will be for decades to come. Knowing that my fellow students were all waiting to hear what Rouhl's very own daughter had to say about their hero, I'd tried to keep my scholarly distance, but as I was writing I couldn't help thinking about all the times I'd been shooed out of his study so that he could get back to writing the damn book. I mean, secretly, I'd enjoyed the reflected celebrity everyone bestowed on me; it made me feel as though I was part of literary history myself. But in the end, I had no more insight into my old man's gift than my nerdy friends had. All I knew with conviction was that A.L. hadn't passed the gift on; that genius was going to skip a few generations, or as seems more likely for an unmarried only child me, it would die with him.

"I understand journalism, all right. And it's hard work—a lot like what you do, Detective. You ask questions, you look up facts. But I don't think I ever quite understood what *he* did. I swear A.L. had the gift of making a narrative out of next to nothing. He had no notes that I ever saw, just a few souvenirs from his travels. Sometimes, I would watch him work. It amazed me that he would spend so much time musing, chewing on some conversation he had in Savannah six months ago or something. He would meet someone once, write about them—and end up with pages full of a kind of…insight.

"You know something, Detective Weiss, if you're looking for the mystery of A.L. Rouhl, try to find out how the hell he *did* it."

Weiss's eyes widened. Carly had become centered; cold even. He waited while Carly crossed her arms and leaned back in her chair.

"I mean, shit. How do you become a world-famous storyteller without imagination or research?" Carly stood and looked across at her father's orphaned keyboard. "Now *that*," she said, "*that* I'd love to know."

CHAPTER TWENTY

When Carly called Evan, she caught him in his car on the way back from the Queen Street studio. His voice was straining to compensate for the roar of the car and it was impossible to read his reaction when she asked him to meet her.

"I'm still in makeup," he said. "I have to get home and change. I could meet you at the Lakeshore house at five, if that's okay."

She accepted gratefully, unable to express to him her growing edginess. However, by the time his expensive little hybrid pulled up beside her Mazda, the sense of urgency had gone. Instead, she felt muddled and directionless, and she found herself embarrassed at the story she would have to tell Evan.

Stepping out of his car, Evan was wearing a warm coat, quilted and hooded in a light grey material and casual street shoes, but he'd chosen to wear dress slacks instead of jeans. She wondered if, when he was finished calming her vague anxieties, he was going out somewhere. With someone. His skin looked scrubbed and the shadow of a sandy beard was beginning to show.

Although Carly had always found that sort of symmetrical,

Hollywood look uninteresting, she had to admit the man was gorgeous.

She touched her hair. It was tidy and had a natural sheen, but it was what she thought of as "default hair"—what a woman got if she did as little as possible to it. Okay, so he was prettier than she was, but she figured she beat the hell out of him in the "mysteriously unforgettable" department. A former lover had said her Celtic features "lived in the mind," whatever the hell that meant, and she'd adopted the notion as a compliment.

He took a few steps up the driveway to A.L.'s house, and then looked back at Carly. "Aren't we going into the house?"

"There's something I need to explain first." Carly pointed to the spot across the road where the public summer pavilion jutted from the icy hillocks of the shoreline.

In the insipid late afternoon light, they walked towards the pavilion, a modern grey building in vertical board and batten, its surface already distressed by the abrasion of time and abuse. The whole structure was perched on a timber dock, reinforced with a scaffold of doubled beams and the effect was curious, almost Elizabethan. Yet the building was covered with caged light blisters that aped the portholes of a yacht.

They approached the pavilion's hamburger stand, shuttered firmly against the winter cold, a Breyers Ice Cream sign standing out against its road salt-stained walls. The proprietor had hand-painted some prices neatly on the sign above the shutters: hamburger and fries $6.00, Slushy $2.50/$3.50. The lettering was amateurish but regular in an odd shade of yellowish-pink. Someone had taken the trouble to add "blow jobs free" in fluorescent orange spray-paint, the offending lettering still fresh and clean. The joke was spoiled somehow by the fact that the new letters were too large and bright.

When they drew closer, with Evan choosing his footing carefully, Carly touched the lettering—first the old, precise pricing, then the graffiti, confirming what she could already see.

"Do you see this? This graffiti? Can you see that it's new? Not more than a few days old, wouldn't you say?"

Evan caught up, tugging his coat's linen hood together beneath his chin. "Charming," he said, his lip curled in an expression of distaste bestowed equally on the graffiti and the ice-scoured shore.

Instantly losing interest, he looked around. Carly followed his gaze and noticed a green painted oil drum that would again serve as a garbage can when the spring melted its white cap. There was a sign from the medical officer of health warning swimmers that the lakewater hereabouts might be polluted. Further out onto the dock, past a row of doors marked "Men's, Women's, Men's, Women's", and a pedestal with a footrest that in the summer would have held a coin-operated set of binoculars, was a wall of showers looking uninviting in the bitter wind from the bay. Equally uninviting except to dogs, whose tracks frozen into the beach seemed to converge there, was a snow-clothed picnic table subsiding into the frozen sand.

"God," Evan said. "Why are we out here? You want me to look at *vandalism?*"

Carly nodded at the pavilion wall. "This is what I want you to understand: that you can see all this, the pavilion and the burger sign..." She turned to face the street. "...from the window of Dad's office. Over there, see?" She pointed.

"Okay." Evan turned away from the wind and squinted back at the house across the road. "You can see all this from his window. So?"

"From Dad's office window..." she repeated.

Evan frowned, his eyes going from Carly to the sign and then back to the distant window. Wondering if he'd missed something, he said, "Your dad's office is the small window to the left of the bay window? Jesus, it's freezing out here." Evan pulled his coat tighter and stamped his feet. "What are you getting at?"

Carly seemed to take in his discomfort for the first time. His coat paid homage to winter in a fashionable way, but wasn't nearly heavy enough. His shoes were leather. She winced in sympathy. "God, I'm sorry, Evan. Let's go into the house." She put her arm in his and they started for the steps that would take them back onto the snow-covered sidewalk. She helped him find footing for his inadequate shoes on the icy steps. "I just needed you to see the graffiti."

"The graffiti? What for?" Evan said, fully absorbed in staying upright.

"Well, the orange lettering..." She shook her head in exasperation, unsure how to put it. "Last night when I looked over here from the office...Well, it wasn't there."

Evan stopped suddenly and stumbled a little trying to turn around. Carly squeezed his shoulder, her other hand reaching up to support his wrist. Evan's first reaction was to search her eyes to see if she was serious—if she meant what she had said literally. Then he twisted a little further until he could see the defaced sign above the locked metal shutters.

"The graffiti wasn't there? What do you mean? Someone did it today?"

"No, Evan. The letters were there before I went into the house last night. I saw them as plainly as you did. But those words, the crude orange ones, they just plain weren't there when I looked out from Dad's office window. Same sign, same shutters. Got it?"

Evan stood still for a moment, grimaced, and then started back towards the road with a determination that Carly took for skepticism. "I'm sorry. I have no idea what you're getting at," he called without looking back.

"Okay, but I need you to hear what I said. I'm telling you, the bloody lettering wasn't there, and that's not possible, is it?"

Evan kept going and all Carly could see was the sheen of his coat and the back of his legs as he struggled along the sand-strewn path. They made it to the edge of the parkland and stopped on the lake side of the street. They both stood in the narrow gap cut in the snow cast off by the road plows. Evan checked for traffic before crossing the road.

When they were across, crunching up Rouhl's driveway through the gap Carly had shovelled for her car, Evan heard the scuffling of her boots stop and he turned to look at her. "What's the matter?"

For a moment, Carly just looked straight ahead at him, her eyes widening. Then she turned until she was looking back across the road at the narrow gap out of the park they had taken without thought.

"Car?" He followed her eyes, but even as she stared at the fresh cut scraped through the snow, it took her a moment to make the connection. Then she ran forward, grasped Evan's arms and made him look her in the eye. "Evan, what the hell is happening here? That gap in the snowbank on the far side of the road? The one we just used to cross the road. That wasn't there *either* when I looked from Dad's office window. I didn't see it last night."

"So it was shovelled out today sometime."

"No! I walked to my father's house. So, I must have *used* it crossing from the park. I wouldn't have been able to cross here without it. But I swear it wasn't there when I looked out maybe an hour later."

Evan looked at her, bewildered.

"It wasn't there when I looked *out* at it from Dad's office, Evan, and yet last night I *walked through it* on my way to the house."

Silent, Evan just turned and started back up the driveway.

Carly kept pace. From behind him, she spoke slowly, controlling her voice. "Can you at least acknowledge you understand what I'm saying?"

"No," Evan said with a helpless shrug. "I'm sorry, Car. I can't.

I hear the words, but you seem to be saying you've found a magic window or something."

Carly winced as though she'd been slapped. She suddenly realized how badly she needed someone on her side through all of this and for an awful moment she thought she was going to cry. When they managed to look at one another, Carly was hurt, despairing. A car blew by on the street, accelerating into the distance.

"Carly, I'm sorry."

Carly broke the moment, walking to the front doorsteps, brushing Evan's shoulder as she passed. She stopped on the top step and he waited for her to open the door. She rummaged in her pockets for a second and then looked at her keys. When she spoke, it was with an implied shrug. "So, Evan…care to have a look through my magic window?"

CHAPTER TWENTY-ONE

They were in the sitting room; coats hung in the cupboard, boots on the plastic mat. The furniture was cold to the touch and the fireplace exhaled the faint smell of ash as cold outside air settled down the chimney. Evan was pulling off his wet shoes when Carly produced the diary.

He stared at it. "Yes, that's it. That's the one he handed me that night."

"And looking at this book made you think he was in danger?"

Evan made eyes toward heaven and sighed. Carly had made him sound like a clairvoyant.

When Evan didn't reach for the diary, Carly turned the black book in her hands and opened its pages. The heavy vinyl cover had slots inside. There was a single business card arranged neatly in each slot. She took one out and flipped it over. "All these cards, they have tiny writing on them as though they were just extra pages from the diary."

Evan nodded. "I told you; she's used every possible surface. "Car, try and understand: handwriting is…it's a crude graph of a person's personality. Even with a glance, I can usually infer some simple aspect of a writer's character; that's what I rely on in my television work. *That* hand, though...is different. It brought to mind some ugly specimens I've studied in my forensics training. To someone trained in graphology, that book is eccentric in a dozen ways. The closer I allowed myself to look, the more my experience set off alarms."

Carly nodded. "Okay. Even *I* can see it's strange. For one thing, the book is full. I mean, *incredibly* full. Writing on every page: tiny, neat writing. "

She allowed the pages, one after another, to slip past her thumb so that she was leafing back towards the first page. "And, what the hell is this? The first pages have been scribbled over—the first twenty pages at least."

"I knew what that was right away." Evan angled his head to look. "It's called cross writing. Back in the days when paper was precious, people would write letters to one another this way: a normal page, and then you turn the page and carefully write a second page right on top of the other—at right angles to the first. It looks illegible at first glance, but surprisingly enough, your eye gets used to it, and, with a little practice, you can read the two pages quite easily. See? You just ignore the lines that are vertical."

"Why wouldn't this nurse person just start another diary? The book itself doesn't look expensive."

"It's another tip-off that the writer is obsessive. The diary represents a single year, but here she has obviously run out of conventional space before the year was out. Rather than buy a second diary, she began backfilling wherever she could. In her mind, this diary *was* her year. Starting another would have been a distortion—like adding an extra month to a calendar." Evan sat down on the couch, propping a cushion under his elbow. "And if you look at it that way, then it's possible this diary was never actually finished. All evidence to the contrary, maybe it *wasn't* full, not to her way of thinking. You see, she might have gone on cross writing until…well, until the end of the calendar year. Without looking closely at the text, I couldn't tell you if she got to December 31st."

Carly sat down beside him, turning pages. "If the diary was taken from her before the year was out, it wouldn't be finished."

"Right. And that would drive her crazy."

Carly squinted, angling a page towards the light. "Most of the text is too small to make out, but I think it's mostly lists. God. It's boring stuff: shopping, housekeeping…" She turned to another page. "…car appointments?"

"Look, stop. At this point, it doesn't matter what the content is, however boring or mundane." Evan squeezed his eyes shut. "I *know* what this book represents, okay? The writer is a rigid shell of neatness and propriety, and inside…she's as cold as ice. What I want to know now…what I *need* to know…is why your father —two nights before he took his own life—went out of his way to ask my advice about this nurse? He wasn't asking me about a diary; he was asking me about a woman." His lip curled in disgust. "He was asking me about *that* woman."

Carly closed the diary. "I'm sorry. I can't tell you what was bothering him. But I can show you the room where A.L. Rouhl lived—the room where he did most of his thinking and virtually all of his writing." When Carly spoke her father's name in that formal way, she was thinking of Rouhl, the author, as another person—someone she held in awe. She wondered if she was grieving for two men, the author and the loved one, and if that was why it hurt so much. Of course, she missed her father most but wondered if there would be a time when the memories would fade and the reputation would take over.

She got up. "It's just at the end of the corridor. If there was something or someone weighing on my father's mind at the end, our best chance of figuring it out would be in there."

CHAPTER TWENTY-TWO

The entrance to her father's office was a solid panel door framed on the inside by bookshelves and Carly was surprised to find that, once again, the door was stiff at first. She stepped back, casting a glance at Evan.

"Is it locked?" He stepped to the side so he could see Carly's face.

"Locked? No. Why would I lock it?"

"I've no idea. No need to sound defensive. You know, we don't need to go in there."

Carly looked at him oddly. "Of course we do." The concern in his face made her soften her tone. "Of course *I* do."

Once again as she twisted the doorknob, she was forced to push with the flat of her hand. "Feel that. The surface of the door... Does that feel warm to you? I think that's why it's sticking. The door has expanded against its frame with the heat. It's as if all the other rooms have cooled, but the office has somehow retained its heat."

Evan touched one of the door panels. "Do the rooms have separate thermostats?"

"No. There's just the one control near the entrance to the

kitchen. When the police were finished, I turned it way down, just high enough to keep the chill out of the rooms. Didn't seem any point heating an empty house." It made her pause for a moment looking not so much at the door as through it. In her mind, she was at the moment on Saturday when she had turned the house's gas furnace down.

She had just gotten off the phone with Mrs. Crowther, politely declining her offer of help and thanking her for her services to her father. Standing there, the phone still lit in her hand, she had looked around, taking in the kitchen counter and the small indoor greenhouse window filled with periwinkle that spilled from two blue-glazed pots. The moment lived for Carly because it had brought home the reality of her father's death. After that call, turning down the thermostat had been a grim and inevitable act—a recognition of the lifelessness of these rooms, the projection of an emotional chill she could already feel.

"Car, forget this. Let's go."

She ignored that, forcing the door quickly, taking in the room on the other side. The laptop was open on the desk, the glass of port to one side. Going in, she held the door aside for Evan who edged past her, wide-eyed and alert.

"Do you feel that heat?" she said. "It's actually warm in here. How would you account for that—it being warmer than the rest of the house? The thermostat hasn't been touched since I closed up."

Evan wasn't listening. His focus was on the atmosphere. "Can you hear anything? A high-pitched buzzing? It's faint, but..."

She frowned and shook her head. She was absorbed elsewhere, leaning close to the laptop, running her fingers over it.

"I didn't think you'd hear it, Evan said. "It's a sort of ringing in the inner ear, like tinnitus; I'm probably hearing my own nerves. Still, there's a...tension? The whole room is a wound-up spring."

"What?" Carly glanced up at him. "What d'you mean?"

"I don't know. There's a sense of being below a dam that's about to burst."

Carly began to survey the room, reluctant to move away from the laptop. She could tell that the CD player was on, on a deep shelf and acting as a bookend for the two big volumes of the Shorter Oxford Dictionary—but it wasn't playing. A tiny red light glowing beside the "play" indicator begged to differ. Looking more closely, Carly could see the volume was turned up normally. A CD was visible inside. Why wasn't it playing? Or at least, why couldn't she hear it? There was nothing plugged into the headphone jack. Maybe it was jammed somehow, generating the high-frequency hiss that was bothering Evan.

Turning back to Evan, Carly took a moment to catch on; he was looking for evidence of the violence that had taken place here only five days before.

"The wall and window are clean," she said. She felt the urge to justify her father's suicide as logical and even considerate. It would have been different if her mother had been alive, but as it was, she was the only one who had been hurt by her father's final decision. Had her father assumed his daughter would understand, or had he simply not cared?

Maybe the moment of violence was what was resonating in this room and Evan was hearing A.L. Rouhl's last act. "You won't find any evidence of his death," Carly said. "The police sent people in to clean up when they were finished."

She went to the window, wanting Evan to follow. Without thinking, she righted the photograph on the window ledge. In the act of straightening it, she stopped and her head turned, her eyes focused on nothing in particular.

Evan noticed her holding the frame. "Is that a special picture?"

"Actually, I was just wondering what knocked it over, face down. It was that way when he died. You've probably figured it out: he shot himself right here at this desk."

She looked at the image, frowning. "But, yes, this picture was important to A.L. I'm not quite sure why. There was a copy of it in the file he gave me for the memoir."

Evan took it from her. "It's him, all by himself." He touched the monument behind the figure. "What's that? A gravestone?"

Carly shrugged. "It was taken inside a sort of chapel. I've never actually been inside it, but I know the location: a mausoleum down by the bay."

"Odd thing to keep by his desk. Maybe the photo was a sort of reminder of his mortality."

"Hanging around with us literary types is a bad influence on you." Carly squeezed her eyes shut in concentration. "I think... maybe...the picture had something to do with a story. That was what A.L. cared about, you know. If he cared about a *place*, it was because of the stories it had to tell. He was never that interested in a place for its own sake."

"Will you tell me about the picture? What story did that place tell?"

"I can't say I remember. Maybe he told me something about the place. I was trying to get him to come home and I tended to screen out his digressions. Anyway, it's not important." Waving her hand, she beckoned him closer to the window. "*This* is why I needed you to come in here. I want you to look outside. I want you to see what I was talking about before when we were at the pavilion. This is my magic window."

Evan held his place. "Everything in this room is important right now, Car. Tell me more about the picture. The pavilion can wait."

Carly looked at him curiously. After a second or two, she started to hand him the photograph. Instead, something caught her eye and she brought the picture close, engrossed in a detail.

She tipped the photograph aside and looked up. "That's interesting," she said, drawing Evan behind the desk.

She pointed to the laptop's screen. "Look at that. The screen saver. I think it's a detail from this photo. See this corner of the photograph—the carved ivy leaf pattern?" She framed it with her hand. "He's blown up this one detail. The colour looks richer on the computer screen because the printed picture itself has faded a little, but it's from the same photo."

Evan nodded and took the frame from her. A simple inkjet printout, it had started to turn a sepia tone in the sunlight of the window sill. It showed the elderly A. L. standing in front of a large reddish panel, finely lettered and polished. There were chiselled carvings all around so that the lettered panel was encircled. He closed his eyes for a moment.

"I don't want to upset you," he said, "but has it occurred to you that he might have laid that picture frame down so that it wouldn't be damaged?"

It took Carly a moment to understand what Evan meant. She had to look down at the window sill where the picture in its free-standing pewter frame had stood. The picture had been centered on the sill and the sill was immediately behind Rouhl's desk chair—the low backed chair in which he had died.

"You're saying he laid it flat so the *bullet* wouldn't hit it?"

"Sorry, I didn't realize how callous that would sound."

He went back to staring at the photo, squinting to make out the lettering on the stone. Carly knew what he would see; the dates were there, and words cut deeply enough to be legible: "The Great Lafayette." The rest of the inscription was partially obscured by A.L. himself. To the photographer, the name on the memorial was what had mattered. But of course, her father had no photographer. He must have framed it himself and set the timer. The Great Lafayette and the great A. L. Rouhl. She remembered her father saying something about the camera flash going off and surprising him. Maybe this was the accidental photo he had told her about, the photo supposedly taken by a ghost.

Carly sat against the sill. "I think he did tell me about the tomb, but you have to realize I was listening to him night after night. He would ramble and I'd have to choose what to put down in the memoir. There was so much. I just don't remember. The place had something to do with magic in some way. I think Lafayette was a magician. Dad told me so many stories. I wish I could remember half of them." In a much softer voice, she said, "I wish I could remember *all* of them."

Evan moved closer, letting her replace the photo on the sill. "Was your father interested in magic?"

"Yes, I guess so. I remember he showed me some tricks he'd learned. I'd be impressed, but then he'd show me how it was done and that would spoil it."

Evan was reading the sadness in her face so she turned away. They stood there, her back to him as she looked out at the still lake.

After a moment, Carly reached back, and, taking Evan's arm, guided him in front of the window frame, centering him in the cold daylight. "Look out there. I want to know what you think."

She was making Evan look out into the street and at the park beyond. He leaned from side to side, peering first at the tree branches, bare and black, overhanging the sidewalk, and then at the ice-cluttered beach. When Evan spoke, it was with an apologetic laugh. "A modest little view—peaceful. In fact, right now it looks almost like a still photograph. Your father must have enjoyed turning his chair and watching the waters of the bay, although…"

"Go on."

"Well, it's that tension again. I can't help it. I feel as though the whole world out there is on edge. You know, when animals can sense earthquakes? Nothing you can point to exactly, unless it's the unearthly quiet, the absence of life…any life…"

"Yes, I noticed that too. God...Look. No branches moving, no birds by the shore. What happened to the wind that was freezing us when we were walking over?" Carly bit her lip. She had to direct his attention. She had to make Evan see the thing that had made her stand out in the cold for twenty minutes last night—the thing that had kept her awake until morning.

"Look, Evan, let your eyes trace the path we took from the park. From the pier, along that sidewalk. See? Where the city crews have sanded? Across the street..."

Evan seemed to be having trouble getting oriented—making out the sidewalk they had taken on the far side of the road. "Look," Carly insisted. "There, where we crossed..."

His eyes widened and his shoulders flexed. "There's no cut in the snowbank where we crossed..." How had they done it? How had they got past the piles of dirty snow onto the street?

Evan leaned forward to take in the widest possible angle on the street. As his head turned to the left, she felt him start.

Evan let out a small gasp.

Carly waited.

When he spoke again, it was barely a whisper. "All right. I see it. The graffiti we saw when we stood out there... From this window, well, it isn't there now. Car, what *is* this? What's *wrong* out there? Where's the traffic? The people? Everything is so damned *still*."

Carly pulled him back against her and spoke quietly, rising on her toes to reach his ear. "I've tried thinking about it that way—that there's something wrong out *there*. But the important thing is we're seeing the world from this room, through *this* window."

Carly turned around and took in the chaotic wall of books with its untidy clutter: a barometer, a single shoe, two walking sticks, a blues harp... "This whole *room* is wrong, something seen through a distorting lens. I've been wondering..."

Evan was waiting, but Carly could feel everything moving slowly around her—the warmth, the CD player, the walls...

Her fingers brushed the desk and she looked down at its worn, distressed surface. "Evan, what did you do with the picture frame—the gravestone picture?"

"It's right there, lying flat on the window ledge." He frowned. "Isn't that where you just put it?"

Carly stood there for a moment, looking at the back of the picture with its fold out stand. "I must have. I can't remember. I thought I set it upright again."

When she looked up, she could feel the anger in her shoulders. "Evan, I think I know why the room feels so strange. Everything in here is still the way it was the moment Dad died. Even..." She was going to say that even the view from the window was the same as it had been, but the craziness of the idea seemed to reflect back at her from the glass.

"I don't know," she said, scowling at her own reflection. "In this room, it feels like it's still last *Thursday*. And when we look out this window..."

"I get it, Car. We're looking out at Thursday."

CHAPTER TWENTY-THREE

In his office on Hampton Road, Eilert Weiss was scrolling down the pages of A.L. Rouhl's final memoir. It was an easy piece to skim. Most of it wasn't about Rouhl himself, but the characters and places he'd known. There was a theme to it all: that few of us are actually what we seem at first glance. In each case, A.L. would quickly sketch in an impression of the individual—a polite Austrian carrying a mandolin case at a train station, a sexy blond teaching jazz at a university—and then Rouhl would give an accounting of how he had been surprised by him or her. He of the mandolin had turned out to have a missing schoolgirl chained to his bed; she of the blond hair worked undercover for the Chicago police.

It struck Weiss the memoir was an accounting of A.L.'s discoveries, well written, but aimed at the faithful reader who knew Rouhl's oeuvre and wanted to relive the master's greatest hits. Seen from a different perspective, it was the autobiography of a man determined to take his innermost thoughts to the grave.

Weiss came to the end and sat back with a soft, but heartfelt curse. The daughter had been right. It just petered out at the end. A.L. deserved more. Weiss hoped Carly Rouhl was a good enough editor to fill in a last paragraph that worked...something with, what did the daughter say? Poetry? What was wrong was that old Rouhl just hadn't said goodbye—hadn't given his "god be wi'ye."

He watched a flag outside the window curl in a chill and sparkling gust and tried to think himself into Rouhl's weakass, dying skin. He imagined the old guy reminiscing out loud while Carly Rouhl took dictation.

Must have been hard on the great writer. After all, he was used to his solitude, his slow contemplation. How hard was it for old Rouhl to hear the whisperings of his muse, the rhythms of his own personal style with someone else sitting there at the keyboard in his place?

Weiss remembered reading what Virginia Wolfe had said when someone asked her how she wrote so beautifully. "I hear the rhythms first," she said, "and then I put the words on the back of the rhythm." How could Rouhl *dictate* poetry? How could he say goodbye through an intermediary? Everything that made him special as a writer had died with his small motor muscles.

Ignoring the white dust from the drywall and the little crumbs of putty, Weiss propped his elbows on the window sill. His fingers pressed against his lips, the tips buried in his mustache. He watched the flag sag and sway long enough to realize that if Rouhl had attempted that paragraph—the one with poetry—he'd have done it all by himself when everyone was gone and the quiet, trustworthy impulses of his talent might have a chance to tiptoe back.

When that happened old Rouhl would have had to find the strength to type it himself. No matter how painful or slow, he'd have had to call on his inner ear, but also on the muscle memory that used to let him type for hours at a stretch.

Weiss turned back to the laptop, slouching uncharacteristically, as though, elderly and astigmatic, he was becoming a character in a play. He looked down and noticed for the first time the scratches on the plastic panel below the laptop's keyboard. He closed his eyes and thought; the scratches would have been from shirt buttons, or, for someone of Rouhl's generation, maybe even cufflinks. The idea pulled him a step closer to old Rouhl's state of mind.

Half unconsciously, he lined his wrists up with the scratches and fumbled with the laptop's list of files for a few minutes, poring over drop-down menus until he got the files sorted by "date modified," then he ran his eye up from the bottom.

Last of all, and therefore the final entry, was the suicide note, the last words of the great writer to his child. He remembered the simple tautology: "No answers, only questions."

A bit lame. A comment on life? How ironic that the great amanuensis of anecdote had no conclusion to hand on to his daughter, no wisdom or gratitude.

Unless...

Unless it was a message, a private code? Would the daughter understand the father well enough to *know* what questions dogged the old man until the end? He tried to recall the younger Rouhl's reaction on hearing the final note and decided that if it *was* some sort of key, the daughter had missed it.

Next to last came the Autobio.docx file. This was the big one he had just read, with the bulk of the last article in it, rough and inelegant, but professionally typed and largely complete. This is the one A.L. would have dictated slowly to his daughter. This was the last part of the autobiography slated for publication, first in the daughter's local magazine and then as an illustrated book for a larger public. Carly Rouhl would have to edit it carefully, trying to salvage her father's style; she'd be a biblical scholar trying to recover scripture from the tatters of a scroll.

That's when he noticed what he'd been instinctively looking for. One up from the memoir was a very small file that had been modified just this past week. It was called Questions.docx. Weiss thought about the listed date and raised an eyebrow: Wednesday. It had been added to on the day before the old man died.

He opened the document and began to read.

The interview is over and the nice young reporter from the Washington Post seems quite content. I'm now a name she can drop. Long after I'm gone, she'll be able to mention her interview with A. L. Rouhl. It'll be a good reference for her, one redolent of my long career as a writer and bright with the luster of my achievements—sadly, long past. She has spoken with a man of letters and a raconteur, his voice loud with the clatter of dropped names: John Cheever, Alice Munro, Roald Dahl...

The thing is, though, I'm getting to the end...*my* end that is, and the standard answers I gave her don't seem enough now. Nothing that I said to the reporter, nothing I've *ever* said to an interviewer, touches on the source of my talent as a writer. Mind you, I don't think I *owe* the truth to anyone. What a writer owes his reader is a performance.

But then, perhaps I *do* owe the truth to my daughter...who writes beautifully and wonders why it's not enough. Let me relieve her mind by showing how I was able to cheat my way to success. And, before she publishes and forwards my memoir to New York, let her decide whether or not to add this dying confession to the litany of evasions I have dictated to her. I thought that enduring fame was what I would want, but all along what mattered to me was a satisfying ending for myself— not because it was apt or symmetrical, but because such an ending would have the unmistakable flavor of the truth.

Weiss sat back, the weary, stooped character cast off his shoulders. He scrolled down, reading slowly, transfixed at last by the authentic voice of A.L. Rouhl.

CHAPTER TWENTY-FOUR

Eilert Weiss was reading from the screen of A.L. Rouhl's laptop. Prem Joshi came in and hefted a plastic recycling bin filled with office clutter onto a filing cabinet by the door. He looked at Weiss, who only flashed him a glance of acknowledgment.

"You look intent."

Weiss grunted.

"You might even be enjoying yourself, so it's probably not useful work."

"Probably not, but…" Weiss indicated the screen of the laptop with a tip of his chin. "You know how you know someone's finally telling you the truth? They might be full of crap, but at least it's their own authentic crap they're shovelling, so in one way or another what they're saying might actually matter. Self-delusion and ego aside, it's the way they see things."

"So what you got?"

Weiss shook his head in puzzlement. "Give me a few minutes."

"Fine, but we've got a couple of crumbs on the lift bridge drowning."

"Okay."

"Results from the autopsy on Brian Maitland? Coroner's confirming the presence of antifreeze and salt. Table salt."

Weiss looked up from the computer screen with an effort. "Just like the Brock girl, Therese Cherry."

"Not quite. They found the iodized salt in those expensive shoes Maitland was wearing, not in his lungs. His lungs were dry."

"Okay, so the Cherry girl drowned and..."

Joshi finished the thought. "Brian Maitland died of hypothermia. Fine, but they both could have died in the same location and got dumped into different parts of the bay."

Weiss was quiet for a moment. "What about the sawdust? Anything there?"

Joshi looked at his desk for the report, but, deciding he could remember, he squeezed his eyes shut and spoke slowly. "The sawdust in Maitland's clothes is mostly from oak and maple logs. The lab thinks that suggests a domestic source rather than a commercial source which would probably be pine or cedar. And the coarseness of the particles is consistent with a chainsaw and not the circular saw you'd get in a mill or carpentry environment." Joshi opened his eyes. "What would you consider a domestic source? A woodpile?"

"I guess. A cottage maybe, or someone trying to clear land."

Joshi stood waiting for Weiss to make some connection or other, but after a moment, he realized he'd lost him—his partner's eyes were drifting back to the Rouhl laptop.

"Eilert?"

"Hmm?"

"Eilert, I want to know what a caber is."

But Weiss was already reading, so Joshi sighed and left him to it.

In my mind's eye—in my imagination—I can picture one of those diners, the kind from the fifties, long and narrow with a single row of red vinyl booths fronting large windows. The windows have skinny Venetian blinds and are framed in chrome. The floor is a checkerboard and the tables jut from the wall the way broad Formica ironing boards would. I *imagine* Marcella Cole is seated at one of the tables with someone she has no business talking to—a pharmacologist from the dispensary at Joseph Brant Hospital. This is just before her trial. She'd been accused of poisoning her husband. So her talking to this young, preppy-looking guy is suggestive.

But you have to understand: I'm imagining this—a complete image, annoyingly out of focus and way too film noire, but, in my mind's eye, the picture glows as a slow, repetitive movie. I'm seeing it and hearing the chatter and clinking of dishes. And I'm noticing small details. I seem to be under a low-level anesthetic, so I can't feel my body, but all the same, I can imagine I'm actually there. You've got an imagination too, so you know what I mean. You know how it feels.

Some of us waste more time daydreaming than others, so maybe we get better at it. I don't know. Back when I was younger, I used to think I was some kind of creative visionary. I figured I was a great storyteller because I could picture things so easily.

I mean look at this—the ceiling of the diner is tin tile, hundreds of quartered circles fitted together, each circle enclosing four raised maple leaves. How's that for detail?

Here and there, a tile is replaced by a small pot light. Framing the whole ceiling, there's a single, long fluorescent tube and a deep curve of red enamel that sweeps around, and I'm right up there against its curve.

Yeah, I know—what's with that? I guess my anesthetized ass must be right up there on the fluorescent ceiling lights because I'm looking down.

I've got a theory about why I'm way the hell up there. It's cultural conditioning, see? I used to go to the movies a lot. Not

REQUIEM FOR THURSDAY

so much lately, I have to pee too often. In the movies, there's something called an establishing shot. You've seen it a million times. First, we're given this high angle view of the action, right? And the shot's wide enough that we can get a sense of the surroundings. This is before the cinematographer gently drifts us down for a two-shot. You get used to it. It's part of the language of film.

Only, in our imagination, *we* become the camera—and the sound crew.

I should have got a hint that there was something wrong with these daydreams. I came to realize that my creativity was helped along if I had something nearby, something I could touch, something that I could pack in my fist. You know, something that would get me going, get me thinking along a certain line. It could be anything: a glove, a hairpin, a razor.

By the time I came across Marcella Cole, I had gotten used to this kind of crutch and I'd become quite good at the kind of petty theft that gave me the objects I needed. I even had a devoted friend who would help me get them. At that point, Marcella was just a person of interest in the investigation, but my friend, thinking I wanted actual evidence, overreached and stole for me a sort of diary that Marcella could hardly fail to miss.

The damn thing's virtually unreadable, but as a stimulus to the imagination...

So anyway, I'm just picturing this one dreary image of Marcella sitting in a diner. I'm a writer, and it's easy for me to make up a little narrative to go along with the image.

Let's suppose, for example, that the pharmacist gets up and asks for a clean fork for Marcella. While he's leaning over the counter, Marcy peels back his sandwich and sprinkles his lettuce with a dark powder. It's nothing lethal, just enough to make him feel unwell. I'm not actually seeing this part, remember. I'm making it up, telling a story. This part of the creative process doesn't have to be visual.

Let's say that all this is happening in a tourist diner in Bracebridge. I need that detail for my story to work, you see. I figure she'll offer to drive him home to his nearby cottage, and by this point, he'll be just queasy enough to let her. Later she'll murder him.

It would be nice to imagine how she pulled that off, I mean the murder itself. It would make the story better, but I haven't come up with that part—not specifically, any more than I can name the stuff she put on his food. There's a limit to the imagination; to its first idle musings anyway. Fine details have to be filled in with research and careful writing. The easy part—the imagining—is over. You still have to give the story form and reality by choosing the words and phrases. You have to actually get it onto the page, and that's a great deal of work.

The way it works is, I know what's happening in the image I'm looking at, I have a sense of what came before and led up to that moment, and I have a pretty good sense of where the action is going. I see a picture that expands its time frame: I see the banana and know the guy's going to slip on it. It's just the creative process, right?

Anyway, that's the kind of thinking behind a lot of what I wrote as a professional—behind the kind of stuff I wrote back when I was good. I always saw myself as a fiction writer with a vivid imagination, never as a historian or a reporter. I always found it easier to at least start out with real people and places in mind.

No, it was more than that; I *needed* to start with real people or else nothing good would come to me. That limitation wasn't a problem for me. I knew no one was going to hold me accountable for the accuracy of what I wrote as long as I changed the real names and camouflaged the setting a little.

Just like every other fiction writer, I wrote drawing on what

REQUIEM FOR THURSDAY

I knew, what I remembered, what I'd experienced. And I did my half-assed research—which is what I call it when I wander around keeping my eyes open. But when my interest had been piqued by someone or someplace, all I needed was a little peace and quiet and I was off, my mind running ahead, released from the leash.

There was a period in my life when I actually *believed* all this—believed that I could write fiction. I allowed this delusion to shape my career for years, drawn on by that most blinding of irrelevancies, success. I was selling stories. When I was young, there were lots of markets for short stories.

Anyway, it turned out I was flattering myself. I would go through a lazy semblance of research and compilation, figuring I had to start somewhere with a few ideas and characters drawn from life, but I gave myself permission to daydream—you know, think creatively. I thought I was freeing myself, letting go, and that imagination would carry me forward. Quite a few novelists and story writers told me that's what *they* did. It was so much easier than journalism.

Well, damned if it didn't work. I found I could take my real-world subjects and conjecture motives and emotions for them. I would fill out what I already knew about them with good human interest stuff of my own designing and when I did, I came up with the kind of rounded narrative that good stories are made of.

My plots weren't elaborate or clever, but they had something more important, something a writer strives for—they sounded human and utterly plausible. This was the way real people thought, the way they acted, and I congratulated myself on my imaginative gift. I had it—that mysterious creative talent that allowed me to conjure up fiction. I was going to be a novelist. All I had to do was change the names of the real people who had inspired my imaginings and I'd have stories that I could call my own and sell in good conscience.

It bothered me a bit that I couldn't make up anything out of whole cloth—I had to have the underpinnings of real research, but that's what my creative friends told me they did too; John Updike, and Leonard Cohen, back when he was just a poet and novelist. It made the imaginings more authentic, less artificial.

Then, one day in the pleasant university town of Auburn, Alabama, I was at a baseball game—the Auburn Tigers against Elon. I happened to reconnect with an acquaintance I'd originally met at a local bookstore event, a kind and outgoing man named Terry who had spoken openly to me about his divorce a couple of years earlier. It had been a brief and unremarkable story about middle-aged love growing cold, but Terry's colourful drawl and squeezed putty features had caught my fancy, and I had used him in a story.

So there we were in the stands at Hitchcock Field. I sat down beside him, clutching his shoulder in greeting as, through a curtain of fine netting, he watched the home run lights swirl on the scoreboard. He looked at me quickly, and said, "Rouh!" and cursed quietly.

"What's the matter?" I asked. He'd been friendly and helpful when we last talked.

"I read the story in *Argosy* magazine," he said. "Guess I didn't realize how deep you were gonna dig." He shook his head slowly and then shrugged. "I s'pose that's what makes you a good writer. I'm not sure I could've got my wife to talk about some of that stuff myself, but, shit, *you* sure got her to open up."

"Oh," I said, wincing. "You saw my story."

Fine. I understood immediately that Terry had read the short story I'd written based on the few sad little details he'd told me, and I understood too that he'd somehow seen through the overlay of fiction and the made-up names, recognizing himself and his wife.

"She's such a close-mouthed woman," he said, "private and suspicious of people because of the way she was brought up."

REQUIEM FOR THURSDAY

Suddenly Terry's round, guileless face convulsed in pain. "Maybe she just finally had to tell someone."

He went on about his wife for a few moments, saying, "She had a *right*." He said that twice. The second time his shoulders twisted with remorse and guilt and he balled a mustard-stained napkin in his fist until I found myself looking away wide-eyed, my mouth dry.

We watched in silence as the teams changed, both of us embarrassed and at a loss for words. After only a few minutes, he got up and, without looking at me, turned to climb the steps to the exit.

Okay, I guess I should have called after him—but what would I have said? I couldn't get past the idea that there was some sort of misunderstanding, but I wasn't sure exactly what it was...what was wrong—what I had to apologize for. In the story I wrote about Terry, I had turned this pleasant, garrulous man into a selfish, abusive lover, someone who had repeatedly asphyxiated his wife to the point of unconsciousness. I'd done it because, well, you need to *embellish* a little. You need to make it dramatic.

I was ready to apologize for twisting his little confidences into something mean and sordid, for turning his real sadness into fictional melodrama. But what he had just said threw me completely. He had acted as though what hurt him was my prying. What should I have done? Should I have stood up and shouted after him that I had never even *met* his wife?

After I'd spoken to Terry in Alabama, I made a point of looking up more of the people I'd drawn on in my first few stories, published or unpublished.

I listened—in horror—as these people, one after another, deconstructed my short stories into simple facts. For the most part, they didn't know the written stories existed and I didn't tell, so they never knew why I turned pale as they answered my questions about their lives and motivations—as they described the very events I had imagined.

I went to revisit a man named Beddoes in Beaufort, South Carolina and I remember him in particular because he was a sort of exception. As we rocked together on a chained bench by the docks, he allowed me to draw out more of his experiences.

"I could have just lied," he said, "and Amelia would never have known she was entitled to the whole property," he was saying. "But fool as I am, I let it out and immediately I regretted it. If she hadn't taken that fall and busted her head on a window ledge, she could've made my life hell." He told the story almost gleefully, because for him, this incident in his life had ended well.

He couldn't know that I'd worked his hatred of Amelia Lister Lyons into a short story. I hadn't sold the manuscript yet. It was still with my publisher in New York.

"I guess there's some justice in the world," he said, and then he looked away at the bridge over the harbour mouth. His mood had changed, and he didn't want me to see it. But I knew what was on his mind. I knew that he was remembering the truth—the way it *had* happened. I knew with complete conviction that he had just been lying to me.

I knew because in the story I had written about Cal Beddoes, there *was* no window ledge. In a rage, Cal had driven Amelia's little gray head against a compressor in the pump house. Then he'd carried her dead body inside the house and, weeping with panic, he'd staged the accident, painting her torn scalp against the edge of the frame as though her head was a bloody sponge. It was a miracle he'd gotten away with it. Beddoes wasn't a clever man.

He must have wondered why I got up and walked away

without a word. I was probably dragging my ass because by that time my whole world view had turned around.

All along, I had been writing something that looked and felt like fiction. But somehow, miraculously, it *wasn't*.

What it was, was the truth. I was writing down the stuff people stopped short of telling me, or lied about to cover up some shame or guilt.

And, of course, that was the stuff that made a good story.

It won't surprise you that I went back to my motel room, opened my laptop and studied the story I'd written about Cal Beddoes, staring at each sentence as this melodrama revealed itself to be the truth. I looked for the line I had crossed, looked for the specific words, the *sentence*, that showed I was departing from what Beddoes had actually told me. I scrolled in fascination as Beddoes' self-serving lies morphed seamlessly before my eyes into what I knew were the true details of Amelia's murder.

I'd gone through it maybe three times, alternately squinting at the glow of the computer screen and frowning in thought at the cluster of palms outside my room. I think I was trying to remember what it had felt like, this dreadful insight. The palms fronds were wet, stirring in an onshore drizzle, flashing the blue of the motel sign at me. I remember that detail because it was almost as if I read the final implication of what I had written in that semaphore of blue light.

I minimized the story file and brought up my calendar. It was easy to find the week in late March when I'd written the Beddoes story because I'd done it right here in Beaufort and my travel details were all there. Then I accessed another file, one in which I kept reference material. It took a bit longer sifting through this because I'd never bothered to organize these odds and ends: notes, clippings, websites; most of which had been fleetingly useful. But at last I found it: a scan of the newspaper article detailing Amelia Lister Lyon's 'accidental' death. It was simple enough; she'd died in May.

I'd written what I was now convinced were the true details of Amelia's murder back in early March—but I'd written it weeks before Cal Beddoes had lost it and slammed her head against the rusty edges of a bolted casing.

———

It sounds mundane in the circumstances, but I still had to make a living and I had contracts to fulfill. I was writing well and my reputation was growing, but what I had begun to sell as pure fiction clearly wasn't fiction at all, and I could see myself getting into a lot of trouble pretending that it was. Still, my work was good. Too good to throw away, and if I did chuck it, what exactly *was* I going to write?

What happened next was quite simple—I took the short stories I had written, giving up the conventions of fiction and rewriting the pieces so they became literary essays. I brought the characters into the present tense and led my reader to believe I was dealing with real people and real events. He or she would understand if I changed a few names and withheld a few legally actionable details in the service of the essential truth.

It was a simple shift in style, but there were times as I worked when I shuddered with a kind of horror. As I changed a tense here or a pronoun there, I felt the distance between me and my characters shrink down to nothing. They weren't in a discrete world of my imaginings any more; they were here in this world with me. They weren't protagonists modeled on real people; these were actual human beings, and the dark and private thoughts that I had attributed to them were as real as if we'd talked over beer and cigarettes right through the night.

And readers would never know that every now and then,

the privileged details I shared with them would happen weeks, perhaps months, *after* the stories were published.

The thing is, I wasn't sure what product I was selling anymore. I could tell it was entertaining, and I had no false modesty about my skill with language. I just didn't know how to pigeon hole it for my publisher.

I shouldn't have worried. One of the manuscript readers recognized it right away. She smirked dismissively at my discomfort and with an airy gesture, she said, "You're a travel writer. Very nice. There's a market for this kind of thing."

Weiss sat back and rubbed his eyes. He was vaguely aware that Joshi had returned. He could hear the creak of the other chair behind him.

"So?" Joshi said.

Weiss looked back over his shoulder, not so much at Joshi as at the floor near his feet. "There's a bit more. I'm not finished."

"*So?*" Joshi repeated with exaggerated patience.

"Well," Weiss said, "at least it's *his* crap."

"Anything in it that actually matters a shit?"

Weiss swivelled around and folded his hands across his waistcoat. "Oh yes." He smiled. "Seems our celebrity suicide, Mr. Rouhl, took a very personal interest in Marcella Cole."

CHAPTER TWENTY-FIVE

Evan Favaro's Burlington apartment was in a condo tower in the city centre. Its glass picked up the taillight red and sodium yellow of the city, but on the lakeward side, it looked down on a little Dickensian village of boutiques and restaurants off Pearl Street. From its French balcony on the fourth floor, Carly could look down on cobblestone pathways curving through yellow pools of light from lamp post to lamp post.

Evan's home was small—a one bedroom, as far as she could tell—but the kitchen was full of expensive stainless steel and granite and the bathroom had a high-end toilet that could have flushed a basket of golf balls with a gentle whisper. The living area was a great room concept, with the kitchen exposed and facing a wall of floor-to-ceiling windows, but a corner of the living space was sectioned off with a sliding glass door as a sort of conservatory which Evan apparently used as an office. Somehow, he'd managed to crowd a computer station and full-sized table inside and both were covered with clear plastic bins full of paper, books, and magazine clippings.

Carly followed him into the cluttered floor space that remained, stepping over cables and a thick leather laptop case.

She'd never seen any of this before and wondered if it represented a different sort of man than the one she'd interviewed for her profile.

The lemon-oiled living room, she could have predicted. This workspace—not so much. Her article on Evan had worked as a celebrity puff piece as she'd intended; it had paid scant attention to the private man, which to all but the TV gossip crowd for whom the article had been written, was what mattered. Not for the first time Carly winced at the implied comparison with her father: he of the uncanny insight and perception. She had written a version of Evan that her readers expected. Maybe it was right for her magazine. Maybe it was even good commercial journalism. But it hadn't been fair to Evan.

Evan tapped the keyboard of his computer and switched on a small digital projector. A tiny fan began to hum and Carly blinked back from the furniture to what was going on.

"I've scanned a couple of useful pages of the diary," Evan said, pointing to a large screen propped in a corner against a window curtain. "Have a look at..." He focused the projector, and a detail from the nurse's diary page filled the big rectangle. Its pearly surface seemed to burn against the winter night outside.

He was presenting Carly with an image magnified to the point where the ragged edges of the nurse's pen lines were visible. Carly squinted at it. "Funny. It's actually harder to read when it's blown up big."

"But size makes the coastlines stand out better."

"Coastlines?"

She blinked again with the feeling she was constantly trying to catch up. It was the first time she'd seen Evan wear glasses. They were the skinny kind you can slip into a tube, and he had made them appear on his nose as though by sleight of hand. "Think of the words as little islands," he said. "Sometimes you can make out a word from the way certain letters—b's, d's, p's, g's and t's—rise above and fall below the main horizontal axis of the word. This nurse was writing for her own eyes only, and so she allows her cursive to dwindle down to little more than a squiggle at times. Don't look at it as sloppy—in fact, it's the exact opposite. The letters are all perfectly regular as though written by a robot, but they're simplified to the point where they constitute a kind of speedwriting, a shorthand for speed and ease of writing. She's trying to cut down on the physical strain of longhand."

"George Bernard Shaw wrote all his plays in perfect Pitman shorthand," said Carly.

"Anyway, the coastlines—the drooping g's and p's and the protruding b's and d's, the fat h's and the skinny i's—are a sort of Rosetta Stone letting us figure out what the rest of the letters must be. One lucky break: she uses a British grammar school p. That tells us she was educated in Britain or India or someplace colonial: South Africa, New Zealand. See? The p looks like an n with a long descender."

"Have you been able to make any connections between the nurse and my father?"

"We're not there yet, but at least I know what I'm looking at now. It *is* a diary of sorts, but I haven't found anything conclusive. Most people use a diary to record their thoughts and feelings. See now, this woman doesn't. She's compelled to itemize the trivial details of each day, whether they're worth remembering or not. She doesn't evaluate or entertain herself.

"About the dates: she writes much more than the diary pages allow for, so she isn't able to confine herself to the dates printed onto the diary pages themselves. She covers the original dates printed at the top of each page using small pieces of paper. See? Envelope label paper mostly—self-adhesive—and then she writes right over them. To take the place of the dates, she writes simple numbers to indicate a new day, often right in the middle of a line."

"Archy and Mehitabel."

"Excuse me?"

"They were humour pieces supposedly written by a cockroach who would jump up and down on the typewriter keys. The cockroach couldn't work the shift bar, you see." Carly realized she was babbling and shook her head. "God, how fussy. Why didn't the woman just buy a lined pad with no dates?"

"My guess would be she started out with one type of diary and, because she's a slave to regularity, she had to continue adapting the format to her needs. People like her follow patterns obsessively, sometimes ignoring the ones you and I see, but inventing their own. It's what you would expect of a sociopath who doesn't feel constrained by the rules everybody else obeys. If she fits the profile, she would go to extraordinary lengths to reduce change in her life. You've no idea; this woman might order fifty diaries at once to guarantee consistency, year after year."

Evan moved his mouse, reducing the magnification. "Look at this, see? She's not paragraphing, but actually she is. She doesn't indent or leave a line blank, but she regularly leaves just a little bit of extra space every five sentences or so. She was probably taught in elementary school that that was the proper length of a paragraph and she chooses to give slavish obedience to that rule, even when it makes no sense.

"Same with the sentences. She never uses an ellipsis or an abbreviation the way most people do in diaries, and she writes down practically *everything* she does in a day—or at least everything she can remember. My guess is that she has a specific time each evening to write in her diary. Judging from the length of the daily entries, probably a uniform ten minutes."

"Why in God's name would she keep something so trivial?"

"It's a conversation with herself, the most important one in her life, because she has no one else to confide in. This is the work of an intensely inward-looking personality. Look here:

she inventories her car before and after an auto dealership service. Two glove compartments full of junk in matching columns. Typically, little things are important to her, particularly possessions. She was probably afraid the mechanics would steal her maps or something."

"Possessions..." Carly glanced at Evan's winter pale face in the back light of the projector. Their relationship until now had been a series of missteps and awkward words instantly regretted. Why was he taking all this trouble for her? She was studying his face, watching the movements of his eyes. Then, aware she was staring, she looked down, combing her hair away from her face with her fingers. "You mean possessions like this diary?"

Evan touched the little glasses. "Yes. She'd never mislay her diary. Your father must have come by it some other way."

"Stole it, you mean."

He shrugged. "I've been reading the diary selectively here and there."

"And?"

"Well the *vertical* cross writing—it begins at the front of the diary, but of course it represents her most recent thoughts..."

"Because she was starting again from the beginning and overwriting the original words at right angles to them."

"Exactly. At that time in her life, it seems she was involved in some sort of legal mess. Lots of stuff about lawyers and motions. It must have been serious."

"Anything else?"

Evan shrugged. "The early part of the year is different. That's the original *horizontal* writing on the same pages—the *real* beginning of the diary. At that time, she seemed to have been preoccupied with her land. She was getting a new septic system put in on her property. Lots of detail about going from a big old septic tank to a new peat moss filter system."

Carly noticed the diary itself on the table under a camera

with angled lights. She picked it up. "What about people? Does she talk about her friends, co-workers?"

"There are people here—lots of them. There's one there." He tapped the screen.

Carly looked closely. "Invicta?"

"It's actually the name of a car, isn't it? She refers to people by making an association. 'Invicta' probably drove an Invicta. It's a simple code. Real names probably offend her a bit, just as people do.

Carly nodded, "So she dehumanizes them, refers to them as objects?"

"Given time we might figure out how she referred to your father, but that would require weeks of analysis."

When Evan didn't say more, Carly turned to him. Evan looked worried. He noticed her attention and said, "Look, Car, when I give advice to the police it's always in context. They have reasons to suspect someone, or they're looking for a particular type of criminal mentality.

"It was different when your father gave me this. It took me off guard. I suppose I was expecting to see your dad's own handwriting, and there I was looking at a textbook example of paranoia. I jumped to a conclusion. Several, I guess. For one thing, your dad told me the diary belonged to a nurse, so I figured it might be Mrs. Crowther or one of the day nurses."

"How do you know it's *not* Mrs. Crowther?"

Evan raised a brow and touched his tongue to his upper lip. "Because," he said, "I think I might have found the diary writer's name."

Carly tensed, unfolding her arms. "You know who this belongs to?"

"I'm pretty sure." Evan used his laptop to bring up a new page on the screen and used the mouse to zoom in on the upper right corner

"Why is this page tinted?"

"I played around with some filters to emphasize the adhesive inclusions. See that square of paper? As usual, she's put paper over the original date and written over it."

Carly could make out a rectangle the size of a raffle ticket which glowed a slightly darker shade than the surrounding page. "That scrap of paper is bigger than the stuff she usually covers the dates with."

"And look what happens when I intensify the orange tint."

Carly refolded her arms and shifted about, unable to see anything beyond the tortuous tangle of the tiny sentences.

"Remember the septic system? Well, she writes about getting into a dispute over the cost. It seems to have amounted to quite a sum of money; maybe seventeen thousand dollars. So, she pasted in part of the bill, using it to cover the date instead of the usual adhesive paper. It's a MasterCard receipt. It's very faint. The printed text from the MasterCard receipt would have been a purple colour and it's faded to almost nothing on the original page, but the orange filter lets me read some of the printing."

Evan used the shadow of his finger to point. "Look at the dotted line. That's a signature above it. Now you'd never make the name out there, but look here *below* the signature line: those two words in print..." He used his hands to shade the screen, helping her to ignore the stark, black handwriting that was overwritten onto the receipt.

Narrowing her eyes, Carly leaned forward. "Marcella..." The room was uncomfortably warm from the humming electronics, but Carly could feel a chill course though her chest as she read the second word. "Cole."

Carly looked away at nothing in particular for a moment, then stared down at the diary as though she'd just been told it was infectious. "Jesus, I think I know who this is. I remember my father talking about her—she'd been put on trial and he wrote about it. This was years ago—God, I think she was a nurse." She hefted the diary. "Marcella Cole. Yes, this has to be her. She was acquitted, but I don't know what got into Dad. He wrote all this crazy lurid stuff about her anyway. I mean, Dad wasn't above exaggerating for a good story—you could even say that it was his style—but this time... He was completely convinced she was a cold-blooded killer, and I remember he wanted to actually *name* her in his book. Of course, we told him no one could print the kind of accusations he was making, not after a jury had failed to convict her. No publisher would risk it."

"Not even his daughter?"

Carly shook her head in exasperation. "Come on, Evan, it would have been blatant, actionable libel. You know that."

"Could that be *it*, though?" Evan said. "I mean *why* he showed me the diary? He wanted me to confirm what he believed about this nurse. By this time he knew he was dying, taking his suspicions to the grave with him, leaving this woman untouched."

Carly held up the diary and nodded. "And now you've probably solved a mystery."

"We could tell the police about this Cole woman, right?"

"That's a different story, Evan. Tell them what? My father published Marcella's story as part of his last book—*without* using her real name. I could show them what he wrote, but they'd just say, 'Hmm, that's nice. Got any evidence that this stuff is true?' You see, that's the point—Dad always knew the authorities wouldn't be able to touch her, not after the acquittal. If he did see her as unfinished business..." Carly shrugged. "... well, she'll probably have to stay that way."

"Do you suppose she read his book? Would she have known about his interest in her?"

Carly gave a bitter laugh. "If she had, she'd be glad to hear about his death, whether he named her or not."

"Car, your father's condition, the one that was slowly killing him..."

"It was his immune system...the failure of his..." Carly went pale, sagging slowly against the table. "No one could ever explain how he got infected."

Evan watched her closely. "You're talking about H.I.V. aren't you? And you couldn't explain how he got it because he wasn't in any of the usual high-risk categories. But a nurse...a nurse might know how to go about infecting someone."

Suddenly Carly's back stiffened. "Jesus, Evan. Marcella Cole wasn't just a nurse; she was a head nurse with access to just about everything in the hospital: drugs, research labs, *cadavers* even. That came out in her trial; it's one of the reasons she was a suspect in her husband's death. For Christ's sake, this is..." She trailed off, shaken. "All she'd need would be a stricken man's saliva or the blood of a recent victim. It could be used to infect food, toothpaste, eye drops..."

Evan took the diary from the table where Carly had dropped it. "Car, how *did* your father get hold of this diary?" He used the book to gesture at the hellish tangle of words glowing from the orange screen. "Marcella would think of the diary as a part of her. Taking it from her would be a personal assault. If she knew, if she even *suspected* he had it, she'd never forgive...and never give up trying to recover it."

Later they went down to the dollhouse streets of The Village. They walked under the arching lights, following a laneway out to Elizabeth Street. When they reached Paradiso's dining room, Evan held a door open for Carly and the warmth and savoury aromas welcomed them inside.

While they were waiting for the menus, Carly said, "I need to *see* this woman. I mean, I want to see what she looks like."

"It shouldn't be hard to find a photo on the net."

"No, I need more than that. I want to see what she's doing, whether she's carrying on with her life."

"You mean in case she comes around here, watching you?"

"That had occurred to me." She scowled at the stemmed water glass. "Do you think I should try and get the diary back to her?"

"I don't know what to tell you, Car. It's her property, but this isn't your friendly neighbourhood caregiver. You're not going to get gratitude from her. If she could, she'd swat you like a fly. I've testified against people like her. They carry grudges for every slight they've ever experienced."

"What about *my* grudge?"

"You don't actually *know* she infected your father. Neither could he. Not really."

"You didn't know my father; he had absolutely uncanny instincts." Carly closed her eyes for a moment, then sighed. "Of course, sometimes he'd elaborate on a story so much he had trouble sorting out the facts from his suppositions. Fortunately, in his line of work it didn't usually matter all that much. He was no journalist. When you change the names…"

Carly's voice became flat and automatic as though she'd just hopped another train of thought, and Evan felt he could interrupt. "I think my advice to you is to have a look at Marcella Cole from a safe distance. But whatever you do, don't let her see *you*."

Carly seemed to come back from a million miles away. She looked down and realized Evan was holding her hand. It felt natural and electric at the same time. Her hand moved easily within his. "And the diary?"

"I can't believe I'm saying this, but I don't think you should return it. Bury the bloody thing. If Marcella even catches a whiff of it…"

"I think I'll bury it on Dad's bookshelf for now. Of course without the diary, I can't tell the police anything. It's the only physical link between my father and that awful woman."

"You said yourself there was nothing you could do." He

stroked her fingers gently with his thumb. "Car, your father shot himself. That *is* how he died."

An icy wind swayed a light somewhere outside and the shadows in the narrow walkway beyond the window pulsed in a slow rhythm. The shop across the lane was closed. A decorative pulley meant to suggest the façade of a nineteenth-century storehouse swung in ragged circles above its latticed window. She watched it for a few seconds and then closed her eyes, her brow furrowed with remembered pain. "Evan, you didn't see the change in him those last three years, the way he shrivelled and lost heart. If you had, you wouldn't be so sure who the real killer was."

At last, their hands had to drift apart, but the connection lingered in their eyes and as they rose to go, they carried a different kind of warmth out into the cobbled street. When they got near her car, not even the softness of Evan's shoulder could shut out Carly's fear of the woman she was going to approach and it drove them closer. Maybe that's all it was—Carly's need for human comfort—but in truth, she wasn't sure which one of them, Evan or herself, started the cycle of intimacies that led them past her car and into his bed. The touch of his forehead to hers, the kiss...

This time it was different. The last time they had made love, she had been annoyed at herself. She'd felt shallow for wanting his fitness club body and prime time eyes. But now her need was emotional and for the first time, she felt his strength. Her hands crossed above her head and, beneath her dark lids, her eyes rolled back. He was riding deeply into her, but he'd come to her all the way through the ugliness of her father's death and it made the joy that sprang from her belly and rippled up her ribs pure and free of guilt.

CHAPTER TWENTY-SIX

It was surprisingly easy for Carly to track down Marcella Cole. Her phone was unlisted, but she hadn't changed her name and had taken no pains to hide her home address. In preparation for taking a real look at her, Carly found some good photographs in the on-line archives of a Hamilton newspaper. Most of the stuff was about the trial and she found herself looking at a handsome, defiant woman who had obviously refused to cover her face and hide from prying press cameras.

Using her nursing credentials as a starting point, Carly was able to find out where Cole was currently working. It disturbed her that she was still calling herself a nurse, but she was in a public health role now, running a diabetes awareness program in the St. Joseph's Health Center.

She chose an overcast Wednesday morning to look in at the health centre. It had felt natural asking Evan to come along and he'd accepted without hesitation. They parked at the nearby art gallery to avoid the line up at St. Joseph's parking gate. At the last minute, Carly surprised herself by asking Evan to wait in the car.

"It'll be tricky enough being discrete without *two* strangers staring at Cole," she said.

Evan stared out the windshield for a moment, marshalling his arguments as to why he should go along. But in the end, he just nodded, speaking so quietly that she barely heard. "I'm warning you. Stay well clear of her."

She touched his arm and got out.

Carly walked along Lakeshore Road to the health centre. Once inside, she stamped her feet on their snow mat and went up to the receptionist, a twenty-something with goth-black hair, a computer screen, and a call director. She had a faint blue tear tattooed at the corner of her right eye.

"Could you tell me where I could find Marcella Cole?" Carly chose her words carefully; she didn't want the girl to hit a button and tell Cole someone was waiting in reception.

"Cole," the girl repeated, frowning and fingering her keypad. It clearly wasn't a name she heard often. "Cole. Oh yes, she's…" Her slender finger with its black nail varnish ran across the width of the screen. "Two-twelve. That'd be one up. Do you want me to buzz her?"

"No. I'll just go up." Carly thanked her, smiled, and began to turn away.

"Actually," the girl said, "there's an out of office note here. Says she's writing material at home all week to hand out to patients. There's a cell number. I can't give it to you, but I can call her if it's important."

"No. It's not important." Carly thanked her again and walked away in the direction of the entrance. Instead of going outside, though, she drifted right, walked to the end of the hallway and took the stairs.

Two-twelve was right at the end of the second-floor hall, a windowless teak door with a small acrylic nameplate. Carly read Cole's name, looked down the hallway, and then out the nearby window that looked down on the parking lot. Now that

REQUIEM FOR THURSDAY

she had her bearings, she walked the full length of the second-floor corridor and took the stairs back down. At ground level, the stairwell had an outside door with a one-way push bar. The door opened on a pathway which sloped towards the front of the building.

Carly realized she could easily walk up the slope to the top of the grade and take a path towards the back parking lot. She wasn't going to see Cole, who was supposedly working at home, but she might be able to have a glance in her office window; the upper pathway was almost on a level with the second-story windows. The stairwell door clicked behind her and she began to climb the path.

The acquittal had ended the crisis in Marcella Cole's life, but she found that people who knew her, including her employers at the hospital, had lingering doubts and that she would never again be allowed to get close to patient care, even as an administrator. They had effectively shut her out by placing her in charge of a diabetes education program. Here she was, in effect, a teacher.

Marcella had always worked, not for the money or because she cared about her patients, but because it was what one did. Work was a structure she was used to and accepting the lateral transfer allowed her to hold on to her embattled dignity. She had her responsibilities and her own office where they would leave her alone, especially if she took the precaution of entering an out of office memo into the computer now and then.

Marcella Cole looked up from her desk and turned to the window. She had picked up a minuscule movement outside. The figure on the hillside was small and partly hidden by the conifers on the slope, but motion against the untouched sweep of snow was magnified.

When Marcella made eye contact with Carly Rouhl, she was walking across to the back parking lot, neither purposefully, nor briskly because of the cold. She was ambling. For a split second, Carly looked startled and then she gave Marcella a fleeting smile to make it appear that she'd just been passing and had looked in out of curiosity. Now the Rouhl woman looked down at the path and quickened her pace.

Marcella sat perfectly still, aware that she'd given the woman a small, automatic smile in return. It lingered on her lips for a moment as she replayed the instant in her mind. She had seen the younger Rouhl smile before. Carly was her name, and she had smiled at that attractive man in the parking lot of the funeral gardens.

Marcella stood, pulled her winter coat from a wall hook, and walked calmly out into the corridor.

An elderly couple was exiting the only elevator. Quickening her pace, Marcella entered the nearby stairwell. Taking the stairs was her way of avoiding people.

Outside, she looked sharply right towards the back parking lot. A red Volvo was pulling out. She couldn't make out the occupant through the Volvo's salt-rimmed windows, but she remembered from the funeral that Rouhl drove a dark green Mazda. She stretched and looked up the snow-covered slope in the direction of Lakeshore Road.

There she was. There was Carly, walking past the parking gate. Marcella looked down at her shoes, hesitating; she hadn't had time to change into boots. She glanced up at the snowy slope and then, slipping, balancing with one arm, annoyed at having to hurry, she stamped ahead. The snow fell into her shoes and threatened to bring her to her unprotected knees, but at last, she got to the top of the slope and stepped onto the sanded sidewalk. Marcella tugged the hood of her coat up just in time as Carly glanced back. Without breaking her pace or changing direction, Carly did a complete turn. Apparently suspecting nothing, she turned back and walked on.

Marcella was beginning to think it through. To her strategic mind, what had just happened outside her office was clear—Carly had come to look at her, had tracked her down to her workplace. It was the only way the Rouhl woman could observe her without confronting her.

Marcella wondered if this was the beginning of something. Perhaps the younger Rouhl was picking up her father's vendetta against her. The old man had been so uncannily perceptive; maybe he had even guessed Marcella's involvement in his illness and told the daughter. Of course, it was impossible for either one of them to have any proof against her, so Carly could never really touch Marcella.

Carly took the crosswalk to the north side of the road and waited for the eastward light at Maple to change, then she was moving again, walking past the condos with their expensive lake views. Marcella followed at a distance, holding her hood tight across her lower face, stepping gingerly to avoid slipping in her low heeled office shoes. Her feet were painfully cold.

Carly kept going until she reached the municipal metered parking opposite the art gallery and Marcella could pick out her green Mazda there, its grill facing out towards the bay.

Marcella stopped and looked around. Beside the parking lot, there was a giant hydro tower, its girders supporting high tension lines that swung out over Lakeshore Road and south out of the city, via the beachside corridor. The high tension lines led Marcella's eye back to a bus shelter behind her. She would be able to stand there out of the frigid gusts and watch the lot unnoticed.

Around the edge of a transit poster for the Starlight Foundation, Marcella watched Carly open the passenger side of her car. A man got out. He was wearing a woollen toque and Marcella couldn't quite make out his face at this distance, but the man was poised and attractive, and Marcella guessed it was the same person Carly had spoken to at the funeral. The two of them stood talking for a moment and Marcella fancied that the man was gesturing in the direction of the hospital and health centre. Then Carly locked her car and the couple began to walk away from Marcella—past the art gallery, towards Benny's Deli and the other downtown cafes.

Marcella backed deep into the shelter, out of the wind, and leaned against the Starlight ad. A young couple joined her there while Marcella debated whether, in her inadequate shoes, she should follow Carly and her companion. A bus was coming, spraying salt slush as it closed with the curb; the young couple was pulling off gloves, fumbling for exact change.

As the bus stopped and its doors hissed aside, Marcella abruptly began walking towards Carly's car. Carly and the man were now small figures quite a ways in the distance. Marcella looked at the Mazda's windshield with its faded press sticker, a CD holder tucked up against the glass. She looked in at the parking pass left on the dash, noting the time. She pulled her coat sleeve back and looked at her watch. So Carly had only been here a half hour. Assuming she wouldn't be recognized, Carly had just come to take a look at Marcella.

Marcella glanced inside at the paper clutter of an editor-publisher's life stacked in the back and between the front seats: clipboards, flyers, local papers, notebook, file folders. There were several items—a brochure, an envelope, a press pass—clearly marked with the logo of the magazine Carly worked for: *The Escarpment*.

As Marcella ran her eyes over the front seat, she was already thinking about the walk back to the health centre. Tightening her coat around her neck and wishing she had socks on, she peered inside the car and gasped. Her eyes widened and her face contorted when she saw it, right there, tucked down against the handbrake.

It was the same narrow curve of black vinyl that she was used to seeing every evening at six o'clock. Though it was barely visible, there was no doubt in her mind; Marcella was staring at her own slender black diary.

This changed everything. Wisdom had told her all along to let Carly Rouhl be.

But this...

The diary was Marcella's intimate property. During the trial she had kept it with her to help her remember the times and dates of her alibi, and, in the confusion of arraignments, pre-trial motions, and press intrusions, it had gone missing from her briefcase. Marcella had already taken her revenge for the theft, having narrowed down the suspects to an elderly law clerk named Paulette Merrill. She had initiated the clerk's brief illness and death in a crowd of shoppers with a quick prick of her heel with a specially prepared parasol, much as she'd done with that bothersome writer A.L. Rouhl.

In an instant, the connections fell into place: it was now clear to Marcella that the law clerk must have acted on behalf of A.L. Rouhl, the grey-haired eminence who, at the trial, had stayed aloof from the noisy press rabble, drawing little attention to himself but missing nothing. *That* was why she had never been able to find the diary in the law clerk's home. A.L. Rouhl must have had it all along. And now Carly had it.

On that horrid day five years ago, it hadn't taken Marcella long to notice that the diary was missing.

In fact, she had noticed that same evening.

At six o'clock.

It would be difficult to get Carly near her woodpile, but there were other ways...

CHAPTER TWENTY-SEVEN

The blue, unmarked Ford turned north at Bell's School Road and began to climb past fields of unmarked snow that shaded off without a break into the dull sky.

Weiss was slouched against the passenger window. "So there's that coroner's report on Brian Maitland."

"Yeah. Given it some thought?"

"There was methyl alcohol in his GI tract."

"That's the antifreeze? He swallowed some contaminated water along with the iodine. It connects Brian Maitland with Therese Cherry, the Brock University teaching assistant."

"Yes, but the coroner says Maitland died of exposure, right? Hypothermia? No water in the lungs. Cherry was listed as a drowning."

Joshi checked his mirrors and began to slow. "I wouldn't worry about that. You wind up in freezing water—it's basically up to chance what kills you first—hypothermia or drowning."

Weiss breathed deeply, his laced fingers rising with his narrow chest. Joshi continued to peer out the side window, watching for the turn off. "What if Marcella's not at work? What if she's home?"

"Then we should ask her if she attended A.L. Rouhl's funeral. If she denies it, we look for the blue Lincoln. We didn't get the plate number at the funeral home, so it'll be a soft connection, but it's something."

Joshi pulled into a lane way marked with nothing more than a numbered mailbox. "I don't get where we stand with Marcella. Are we still pretending she's a fine upstanding citizen with a clean record, or do we have anything solid that justifies us knocking on her door?" He stopped and killed the engine.

"All we have is Rouhl's accusations in the 'Questions' file," Weiss said. "So if we see her, try to be polite."

"We know A.L. Rouhl had Marcella's missing diary in his possession when he died and that his daughter has it now, right? And we know that Marcella Cole was on A.L.'s mind when he spoke to Evan Favaro about the diary. If we could show that Marcella was pissed off at A.L. about the diary, it would make his sudden death much more interesting."

Weiss nodded. "But we can't be sure she knows anything about where her diary is, and anyway, we'd have a hard time explaining how Marcella could have shot the old man—we'd have to get around all the evidence that points to suicide."

"That psych prof at the university thinks Marcella is a clever killer who feels entitled to murder anyone who hurts her feelings. I figure Marcella's the one who's jerking us around here."

"Maybe. I've been doing some reading and, as I thought, there's a lurid portrait of a lady murderer in A.L.'s last book."

Joshi grinned. "And it's Marcella Cole, right?"

"I wish it was that neat. The woman described in Rouhl's book is much more accomplished than Marcella. She owns a gun, uses it twice after elaborate and lengthy plans. Both victims had been lured miles from the nearest help and conveniently close to unfindable graves before getting a bullet in the back of the head. We don't even know if Marcella owns a gun.

"Mind you, Rouhl hints at other victims who had died under

mysterious, and far less direct, circumstances—no bullets then. They were simply people who had found themselves in perilous circumstances of the killer's contrivance. And there Marcella... or the woman in the book...would be there at precisely the right moment, stepping out of the shadows to push one over a rocky path into the lake, to dislodge a carefully balanced weight onto the skull of another. Old Rouhl doesn't give a blow-by-blow of the murders, but he gives a fairly rounded picture of the killer and her motivations. That's where you can see a little of Marcella."

"Sounds pretty thin. Didn't you say Marcella's sister died in a fall? Was it anywhere near the lake?"

Weiss stroked his chin. "Yeah. The path behind one of the Boulevard mansions." He looked vaguely hopeful for a moment, then he shook his head. "And of course, that gets us precisely nowhere. Rouhl's whole damn book is a rogues' gallery anyway, each character sketch under a phony name, and Rouhl is the little boy who cried 'wolf' for a living."

"Fine. You've made your point. The book is no help." Joshi drummed his fingertips on the steering wheel.

"Interesting though. What if some of that stuff was true and Marcella had recognized herself in the book?"

Joshi shook his head. "The only way it *could* be true is if you buy into Rouhl's psychic hokum. How else would Rouhl have inside knowledge of Marcella's other murders?"

Weiss thought, tugging his coat tight against his throat. "Even Rouhl wasn't sure if he was just imagining things. Besides, the book was published three years ago, so Cole would have come after Rouhl then, not last week."

"Right. And why risk killing an old man who probably wouldn't last a year anyway?"

Weiss nodded. "When it comes to A.L. Rouhl's death, I'm still interested in the daughter. She's got something on her mind—

something about her old man's laptop. And she's taking her time handing over Marcella's diary."

"Suppose she helped her dad stage his suicide. Helped him finish his memoirs then helped the old guy write his own ending."

"Yeah, I know, Prem. I thought about that, but where does *that* get us? The law says assisted suicide is wrong, but let's be honest, the taxpayers don't give a damn unless the victim is a child in a wheelchair. Somehow, Marcella is still the nexus. She's the one who has the potential to pull this all together."

"Marcella." Joshi reached for the key and started the cruiser's engine. Warm air from the heater blasted out at their feet and the tires began to grind the frozen gravel of Marcella Cole's drive.

At the house, they got out and looked around.

"It's obvious she's not here. And we've got no warrant."

"Insufficient cause. Same problem Toni Beal had in her investigation of the Cherry girl."

"So we're trespassing."

"So far it's all a house of cards, Prem. House of cards."

Joshi held back, one eye on their car and the long, recently plowed lane way in from the road. "She doesn't seem to be interested in scenery," Weiss said. "All the windows are shuttered or curtained off."

They made a slow circuit around the house past snow-covered flower beds, Weiss noting with a fatalistic frown the confusion of footprints they had left around the perimeter of the house. "Let's have a look at the garage."

Joshi glanced at the big outbuilding to his left. "The garage is closed."

"You're a cup half empty type of person, Prem." Weiss crossed to the roll-up double door of the garage and gave the handle a tug. The door was modern and out of keeping with the old board and batten construction of the garage. "Somebody with Marcella's money would have a remote control door opener."

Joshi nodded.

"But at last…" Weiss said, stepping around the corner of the outbuilding, "…a window she didn't bother to curtain." The garage window was an old, single-glazed design with top hinges. He looked down through the bottle pane glass. "Or to lock." He pulled his penknife from his pocket, and unfolded the blade.

Joshi looked away to the empty driveway. "You can't go in there. You said we were just going to look around."

"Yes, I'm just seeing if Marcella is in here."

"Right. Sitting in her garage. You know damn well Marcella isn't here. If you were ready to confront her, you know where she works and you know she's there now."

"It's just a garage."

Joshi watched as Weiss drew his knife blade along the icicled frame. One well-placed blow with his forearm and the window swung inward. "I've seen these old frames before. I'm guessing the garage used to be a work shed. The window swings up and hooks above."

Weiss slipped a leg over the window ledge and, holding onto his hat, he shouldered his way inside. Joshi moved as close as he could without losing sight of the road and watched Weiss dusting snow off his coat.

The interior of the garage was neat and uncluttered. There was a well-organized pegboard with a few gardening implements and hooks for the clean and shining power tools—tools that looked as though they had been chosen for finish and colour rather than torque. All of the electrical cords and extensions were neatly wound and fastened, even the orange stub on the chainsaw. There was a gas-powered tiller with fierce-looking blades and a heavy-duty, self-powered snowblower. It wasn't a ride-on machine, but it appeared to have plenty of horse-power, and the rubber tires were well treaded and chained.

"This is interesting." Weiss muttered so that Joshi had to rise on his cold toes and lean in. "There's a worn eye bolt on the frame of the plow," he said kneeling behind the machine. "...and she's used it with this chain." The chain hung in uniform loops nearby. It ended in a wicked-looking grappling hook with two inward curved blades. "She's been hauling logs, using the snowblower as a tractor. I didn't know you could do that."

Joshi waited, supporting the window pane and trying to see inside. He heard Weiss grunt. Joshi felt compelled to call in an impatient, "What?"

"Just a bit of sawdust on the grappling hooks. What you'd expect hauling firewood, right?"

Joshi stepped back as Weiss's long leg appeared in the window frame. Weiss slipped down to the sunlit snow outside. "Sawdust," Joshi said with a frown. Weiss looked at him without expression and waited. Joshi's eyes widened. "Sawdust..."

They walked along the plowed pathway, Weiss pulling ahead, Joshi thoughtful in the rear. "Of course, they should have put the woman down five years ago."

"God, Prem. Not your lecture on capital punishment again."

"No. Listen. I've been thinking about it, the Dutch had the perfect refinement on execution—defenestration."

"That's where they push the poor bugger out a third-story window?"

"Exactly. Onto the pavement, two inches from the back door of the hearse. Think of the economies. That's what I call refinement."

"You're deep, Prem."

Weiss walked the neat snow cut that led from the garage to the porch of the house. It was still possible to follow Marcella's distinctive footsteps around the property; they were imprinted in yesterday's snow and dusted over lightly with today's. He looked back towards the long drive where their Ford sat alone, and then glanced once more at the front door. Weiss mounted two steps towards it and looked back down. There were some footprints heading off in the opposite direction. A secondary path had been cut leading off towards the bush. From here, he couldn't see its purpose.

Weiss stepped back down, cursing as he slipped on an icy patch. His sturdy shoes were a compromise for getting him in and out of doors in unpredictable weather, but unhelpful when he strayed off the narrow path. He crunched along the pathway that snaked away from the house. Behind him he heard Joshi, who was drawing level with the porch, muttering something in admiration of the house. Then louder for Weiss's benefit: "Nursing must pay better than I thought."

"Cole inherited wealth, married well twice and then disposed of at least one of her husbands, remember?"

"Or so the state failed to prove," Joshi muttered.

Weiss stopped and looked around to see that the thin cloud layer had broken completely, spilling a glorious day onto the fields, the air a crystal lens for the sunshine—a sunshine full of colour and contrast without a hint of warmth. The pathway itself was scarred with traffic marks, not footprints so much as long smears. These had been partially erased by the narrow tire tracks of the plow, and, he suspected, by something else. He noticed long, irregular furrows in the older snow, furrows that overlaid the tire marks in places. Simple enough: something large and heavy had been pulled along behind the plow.

He went on. Joshi was following at a distance, enjoying his own mumbled commentary about rural life. Almost right away Weiss could see the woodpile and the function of the path became clear. Strange place for a woodpile; he would have put it closer to the house. He looked over at the edge of the forested part of the property.

Maybe not so strange. The pile was closer to the trees, less distance to drag the logs. There was probably a pass-through wood box in the wall of the house where a day's supply, cut short and split, could be laid close to the fireplace. He took a moment to imagine the textures of such a life—warm fires while the wind scoured the hillside, quiet morning walks along the split rail fence—he looked down at his Reeboks—in sensible snow boots, of course.

That's when he started to notice more sawdust.

It was almost invisible under the veil of new snow, but the wind had exposed patches of reddish debris in the furrows. He bent over, paused and then glanced up ahead. The woodpile was drifted with snow as though a tattered camouflage blanket had been tugged over it. That's where you would find sawdust. He walked on, keeping to one side to protect the furrows. Already he was wondering if he had enough cause to get a forensic team out here to have a look.

The path continued, sharply cut into the snow by the corkscrew steel blades of the motorized plow. Up ahead, beside a low wall of stacked wood, the path grew darker. It wasn't reflecting back the glare of the sun as well as the section on which he was approaching. That would be the sawdust under the snow. That too made sense. This would be where the wood was cut into manageable lengths with a chainsaw and piled in cords for the winter. Sawdust was a good insulator, keeping heat in the ground. It was dark too, which meant it would warm in the sun and resist the fall of snow a bit better than its surroundings.

Weiss moved slowly up the path thinking about the man found floating in the canal with sawdust trapped in the folds of his clothing. He thought about the man's shoes: expensive Rockports suited for the nineteenth hole of a golf club.

And he thought about the properties and uses of sawdust. A shock-absorbing packing material? An absorbent cleanser for oil spills? In the old days, they used to spread it over blocks of ice in an icehouse. That way the blocks would stay frozen right into the summer when it could be hauled, block after block, to the icebox in the kitchen. Useful stuff, sawdust.

He looked around at the neatly stacked wood, each log almost exactly the same length, each cut straight and uniform. That's the kind of cut you'd get from a well-sharpened chainsaw. The idea of Marcella Cole driving the snarling chain neatly through all these logs…you had to admire her.

He knew exactly how old she was: forty-four, although she didn't look it in the pictures. The benefit of a face unlined by displays of emotion, perhaps. Botox of the heart. From what it said in the psych report he'd read, the bitch was colder than the icicles on her pine logs.

"Take your time, Eilert," Joshi was beaming. "We get paid for this." Weiss grinned back at him.

Turning back to the woodpile, Weiss noticed the curving shaft of an axe half-buried in snow. He grasped the end with his gloved hand and yanked it out. The big blade skittered to his feet driven down by its weight. "Splitting axe," he said quietly, but Joshi wasn't close enough to hear. The wedge-shaped head was fitted with two hinged claws. The force of impact would spread the claws, splitting the grain of the wood. He picked it up in both hands and hefted it. It took strength to use one of these. Hell, it took strength to lift it.

Weiss frowned in thought and took another step along the path.

He felt the spring of thick sawdust under his feet. You couldn't see much of it, but it was the cushion beneath the broadloom of powdery snow. Ahead, the path widened a little. He noticed that there was a stick protruding vertically from the bank beside him.

Weiss's leading foot went through with a convulsive poke, disappearing right into the ground. His weight shifted violently and he felt himself falling forward. He twisted around as he went. "Jesus! Prem!" His shin hit hard on the edge of an unseen pit and he plunged down into water colder than he imagined water could be.

He was in it up to his chest before the downward sweep of the splitting axe bit deep into the frozen pathway. "Help me! Prem! "His long wail broke into staccato yelps as he gasped. *"God, how could...anything feel so fucking cold! It's...like...being burned alive."* In his panic, he could hear Joshi running up the path.

Weiss hung on to the axe in sheer terror, yelling, "Get...get me out of here!" His legs thrashed at the quicksand of fiery cold. He couldn't get a grip on the side of the pit with his feet and the cold was already robbing his legs of sensation. His heart was racing as he called out again. "Prem!"

Joshi was on him, grabbing at his coat, tugging desperately, but the snow of the frozen pathway was slippery and treacherous. "Hold onto that fucking axe," Joshi screamed. "I'm losing you."

Weiss struggled to draw a breath. His body was beginning to shut down; his legs were almost useless now. Joshi was on top of the axe, wedging his shoulder against the top of the blade. In a nightmare of slippery surfaces, the axe was a single point of stillness. "Now, climb, Eilert, climb!"

At first, Weiss thought Joshi meant for him to pull himself up with the axe. He'd been trying that in frenzied panic for long seconds already. It didn't work. His soaking winter clothes were dragging him down.

Then he realized what Joshi had done. Hanging onto the axe blade, he'd skewed his body around so that one of his own arms was plunged deep in the hellish water. One of Joshi's legs was jammed against the woodpile.

Irrational fear made Weiss want to hold on to the shaft of the axe, but he knew that was a losing proposition. He couldn't remember ever being this scared. He let go one hand and reached over to Joshi's braced leg. His own legs now almost incapable of feeling, he sensed that Joshi's hand had snagged the crook of his knee under the water. Weiss put weight on it, just enough to let him get a better grip on Joshi's leg. With horror, he felt himself sag a little deeper, the icy water wicking at the band of warm skin across his shoulders.

Joshi was frantic. "Come on, Eilert. For God's sake, pull!" Joshi's body was rigid with exertion.

Weiss let go of the axe entirely and reached over Joshi's body. With one leg lurching against Joshi's freezing hand, he began to climb.

There was a loud splash and a moment of confusion. Weiss was out, but Joshi was hanging onto the axe for dear life, close to slipping in himself.

Then, in a mad avalanche of desperation and adrenaline, they were both on solid ground, gasping and writhing on the snow.

A few gasping moments passed and Joshi stirred; he knew they had to get moving or they'd both freeze to death. He managed to get Weiss to his feet, half dragging and half carrying him to the big blue Ford. He started the car with Weiss slumped in a fit of violent shivers in the passenger seat. Joshi torqued up the heater and cursed as cold air blew past his ankles. The Ford lurched towards the highway with Joshi shouting the emergency into the radio: "Police officer needs urgent help. I'm heading directly down to Jo Brant Hospital. Request immediate emergency care for full-body hypothermia."

In a few minutes, Joshi had his flashers on and the heater was finally beginning to warm the floor. "Eilert. Take off your damn clothes. Your shoes too. Come on, man. Get the wet stuff off."

Weiss grunted and began to fumble at his shoes with numb, shaking hands.

The Ford sped down the highway, the grey sweep of Lake Ontario ahead.

Weiss's face was a mask of agony as he tried to undo buttons with no sensation in his fingers. "It's a glorious day, Prem."

"That's good. You just keep talking and keep moving."

"What do you...think, Prem? Did we...just solve...two murders?" Weiss's body heaved with the exertion of peeling off his stiff coat. "Therese Cherry...Brian Maitland?"

Weiss wept in pain and frustration but his white shirt was emerging, beginning to steam as the car warmed up, and his loosened tie hung in a soggy twist from his collar. "See, Prem?" he said, baring a few inches of reddened skin that looked like it had been burned. "Piece of cake. All...we had to do...was relive the last thirty seconds...of Brian Maitland's life."

CHAPTER TWENTY-EIGHT

After the seismic shivering finally stopped it took an hour for the feeling to come back to Weiss's legs and torso, turn to a dull throb, and finally a burning sensation that was both a torment and relief. It was a long afternoon that turned into an even longer night, though in the crowded corridors and curtained alcoves of the emergency wing the difference was invisible. Joshi lingered, milking a couple of vending machines on his partner's behalf as though he thought junk food would hasten Weiss's recovery.

They sprayed his reddened skin with disinfectant which almost brought the shivers back, and covered him with a sheet as stiff as paper. The rest of the time he tried to take his mind off his discomfort by studying the wheeled white gadgets with monitors and cables that took up the corners and wall space.

Some time around two a.m., when even a detailed explanation of caber tossing couldn't keep Joshi's eyes open, Weiss managed to talk him into going home. Then he was alone in a cocoon of pain surrounded by the timeless noises of the wards.

Sometime in the endless night, he had drifted into a languor that wasn't quite sleep and opened blurry eyes to see an angel of

REQUIEM FOR THURSDAY

comfort and peace, one who coalesced into the neat suit jacket and frameless glasses of a Halton detective.

"Hey, Toni." He made a quick survey of the curtained alcove with rolling eyes and smiled weakly. "So what the hell is this all about?"

"I hear you tried to freeze yourself to death. Smart career move, Detective."

"Some say the world will end in fire, some in ice..."

"At least your brain isn't frozen."

"That only happens when I drink slushies with a straw."

They smiled at each other, Toni managing to convey concern and reproach in one lop-sided grin. Weiss tugged the paper sheet a touch higher to cover the redness and frowned. "Toni, did you send me a bottle of scotch and a card last week? Laphroaig single malt?"

"Nope. Sorry. I might get around to it this week though."

"Crazy. I've asked everyone I can think of."

"Wouldn't investigate that on the taxpayer's dollar, if I were you."

"You think?"

"So where does this leave Marcella Cole? I suppose you could sue her for having a public hazard on her property."

"Yeah, right." Weiss grimaced at some ill-defined pain. "There's a good circumstantial case tying her to my floater's death—Brian Maitland. Basically we've got a murder weapon—the cesspool on her property which was laced with salt and deliberately concealed with sawdust, the snow blower she used to drag the body. The grappling hook in the garage is positive for human blood."

"Maitland's blood?

Weiss sighed. "That's where the case becomes circumstantial. The blood on the hook is too degraded for a DNA match. Prem's started looking at Maitland to see if there's anything connecting him to Marcella's life, but so far we don't see any ties. Maybe if we could get a warrant for her house—but she's had plenty of time to clean up."

Toni was nodding slowly. "So we're looking at another judge making a tough call. Remember the prosecution won't have any of the evidence from the previous trial. Cole was acquitted then, so evidence from the previous murders wouldn't be admissible this time." Toni sat back and waited. "So what are you going to do, Eilert? It's all about you this time. You going to build a case against her?"

Weiss shut his eyes and listened to the wheels of a gurney squeak by. "It's not enough, Toni. They might even disallow what we do have because Prem and I were fishing around on Marcella's land without a warrant."

"So here we are, old friend. The bloody woman nearly had your life too, and she's still untouchable."

"Maybe if I *had* died in that water…"

"Jesus, Eilert. I'm going to try and forget you said that."

"Sorry, but I thought about killing myself five years ago. When you've reached that point even once, you don't look at life as this unalloyed gift anymore. If it wasn't for you, I'd probably be long gone."

"Will you please…" Toni Beal had her hands up, her eyes squeezed shut in exasperation. "Look, I get it. She'll never stand trial for all those lives she took, and you want it to be neater. You want someone to say 'so we were right about her all along.'"

"You and me, Toni; there we were, working on trying to convict Marcella bloody Cole five years ago when my wife… When she found a way to jump off that bridge. Maybe if I hadn't been doing my job, or at least *trying* to do my job, maybe I could have done something, been with her."

"Hey, *I* was there, sweetcheeks, and it's a damn good thing you were nowhere near the bridge when it happened. You shouldn't even have been on the recovery boat. Your wife was making war on you and she was winning. Everything she did was to hurt you and if she could have had you in her audience that night holding up score cards, she would have. Why are you the only one who can't see? It fits the pattern: she'd get herself into some real regal shit and she'd always have something personal of yours with her: your keys, your wallet, some of your goddamn clothes, so *you* wouldn't miss any of the blame and guilt. She made sure you were present—at least in proxy—for every crazy stunt she pulled. All of that stuff—just voodoo dolls so she could stick another pin in you. Sure, she was crazy, old son, but she was fucking *brilliant* at it.

"You know, Eilert, I think that's what you haven't come to terms with—not then, not now. She was just plain smarter than you, Eilert. Smarter than me too. She played us all—and what did she get in the end? *Just what she wanted.* She didn't want to cripple you. She wanted to destroy your life ever after. All you did was try and protect yourself as best you could. You and me? Hah! We were kids under an umbrella and she was the fucking monsoon season."

"Was it just me, Toni? Or did everyone know the bridge wasn't high enough? If she didn't hit the water just right, she would have survived long enough to drown in agony."

"Shut the fuck up, Eilert. She's still working you. And yeah, another thing you can't see is Marcella Cole's another one. So, maybe Marcella's time hasn't come yet. But it will. I'm sure of that. Meantime? Get her on the public endangerment charge and…"

"For Christ's sake, Toni. A bylaw infringement? Seriously?"

"It's shit, but it's all we've got and it'll get Cole on the record. Maybe someday we'll have her for murdering some other poor bastard and the prosecution will be able to make points with your frigging swim in her cesspool. You once said to me if you don't write it up, it never happened. Your work is lost."

Weiss lay still looking at the ceiling. "When we were working the original hospital case—do you remember? I was part of the team assigned to find out what happened to the main prosecution witness—the pharmacist who drowned at his cottage? A young kid with the coroner's office said something to me back then, off the record…gave me an idea. Just an idea, that's all. It was enough for a line of inquiry, but it was all too much for me by that point and none of us had any idea how to follow it up. I was being pulled in two directions back then and I wound up helping nobody—not the team, not my wife. I want Marcella Cole this time, Toni. Somehow. Anyway I can get her."

"*We'll* get her. It doesn't have to be you."

"You're right. I know. It *doesn't* have to be me—I don't give a fuck about who does it as long as she's stopped, but she almost killed *me* and she's going to keep killing until *someone* puts an end to her."

CHAPTER TWENTY-NINE

Peggy Goss was standing in the scoured snow of the plaza parking lot, looking up at Indy. The tan lab had mounted a grimy bank of plowed snow and was scratching at it with his hind paws.

"Bury it deep, Indy. I don't have any plastic bags on me." She looked small in the almost empty lot and the tall light standard made a rounded pool of light in front of her. "Atta boy. Let's you and me just forget about this until the spring, okay?" The lab looked up. "That's it," she said. "Now, act casual and come on down here."

Casual not being one of Indy's tricks, he tensed and barked at the shadowy shop windows. Only two or three of the businesses in the plaza were still open. Still barking, Indy scrambled down the bank, surfing on ice granules and his leash cord rewound into the spring coil in Peggy's hand. She pressed the brake button on the leash and held Indy close to her leg. She looked up. "It's just a nice lady walking past the shops, Indy. It's all right. Spare the poor woman. Quiet now."

All the same, Peggy watched the woman's slim figure as she stopped in front of the *Escarpment* office and peered in. The lights were still on in the office, but Peggy had locked the door while she walked Indy. Peggy slipped two fingers under Indy's collar and held him firmly. As they approached the woman, the dog, uncharacteristically, seemed to get the idea and became silent.

"I'm afraid I'm closing up," Peggy said. "Was there someone you needed to see?"

The woman was attractive, and mild somehow: a walking mannequin. "Marcella Cole. How do you do."

The formality took Peggy off guard, but she released Indy's collar, straightened, and took the woman's gloved hand. "I wanted to ask about the A.L. Rouhl memoir," Marcella Cole said, her voice as cool as the shadows. "I understand you'll be publishing another part soon."

"Well, not until April, actually. We're a quarterly, you see." Peggy unlocked the door; she was anxious to get back into the bright warmth indoors. The woman followed her into the reception area, turning back a faux lamb's wool hood. The woman stooped to give Indy a quick rub. Peggy realized that Indy was trying to back away, so she unsnapped his leash and had a good look at the visitor.

The woman was fortyish, well dressed in a long quilted coat which had an expensive-looking black on black sheen pattern. Her face was classic: straight nose, almond eyes, high, unlined brow. Her hair was perfect despite the hood, and Peggy thought that a little odd. It was in a shiny, lacquered style you could only get with curlers, both elegant and curiously old-fashioned. A gale wouldn't move those curls, but the style made the woman look thoroughly respectable.

"Not until April?" the woman said. "So long?" The speech patterns were formal and educated, with a trace of accent that Peggy couldn't place. "But you do *have* it? I mean, with Mr. Rouhl's death and all…"

"Yes. Don't worry. There's a copy on our computers ready for editing."

"Oh, okay. Good."

"I take it you're a big A.L. Rouhl fan."

"Not exactly. In fact, I've only read one of his books—the last one. A member of my family brought it to my attention."

"Oh, then…"

"Well, only part of the book actually." Suddenly, the woman turned her attention to a long-handled device on the nearby desktop. "What's that?"

Peggy frowned, unable to keep up. Her assumptions about the visitor were crumbling and she was having trouble understanding what the woman wanted. "What?"

"This thing here—what does it do?"

"Oh, that. It's an embosser, a sort of paper press. You pull the lever and it squeezes a lovely crest into the paper, a sort of coat of arms thing. It's an old fashioned idea. My father gave it to me."

"Brass, isn't it? Very heavy."

Peggy watched as the woman turned the embosser in her hand. Peggy's friendly smile was slowly vanishing. The woman was taking liberties and their conversation had ceased to make any sense. She looked around for Indy.

The dog was rooted to a spot against the far wall, his legs slightly splayed, his tail down. *Peculiar* Peggy thought. *He's standing, but he's not moving a muscle…*

While she was distracted by Indy, the embosser was already in motion—a long vertical arc that built up speed. The impact on Peggy's skull dropped her to her knees in an instant, but she didn't fall backward right away. There was enough time for Marcella Cole to see the expression of shock on Peggy's face and to hear a short gurgle in her throat. It wasn't until Marcella managed to twist the embosser from the deep, bloody gouge in

Peggy's scalp that Peggy's body was free to tumble backwards and to one side.

Marcella replaced the heavy brass piece on the desktop where it made a small red smear. She touched her fingers together as though dusting off her gloved hands and looked around. As she had ascertained earlier, the office was empty. Peggy's still form with its widening red halo would be almost invisible from the street.

Marcella stepped around the reddish-black stain and sat at a computer terminal, working quickly and expertly to erase files and track down back-ups. When she was done, she moved silently through the office, opening drawers and examining shelves. The disappointment barely registering on her face, she stood looking out at the harshly lit parking lot. Someone looking very closely might have noticed the slight movement beneath her cheekbones as her muscles strained and her teeth clenched as tightly as the brass jaws of a paper embosser.

At last, she made for the door, pausing to look back only once. That's when she saw Indy, still standing stock still against the wall. Marcella blinked once. Unusual seeing a dog completely motionless. She noted that there was an oval patch between his shoulder blades where the fur was on end. For the first time, she and the dog made eye contact. As she watched, her eyes narrowing, Marcella Cole could see the lab's lip curl.

She went out quickly into the night without taking the time to lock the office door, starting towards the shadows of the darkened storefronts. Behind her, she heard a mounting growl and from the glass door of the *Escarpment* office, she felt a single set of eyes following her along the pavement.

It was growing dark when Marcella Cole found A. L. Rouhl's house. She had to get out of her blue Lincoln and peer over the bushes to read the numbers, picking out Rouhl's doorway from the more or less identical row of porches. 124C.

Each porch had two doors separated by a red brick privacy wall. The basement windows were barely visible behind bare, snow spotted hedges, black coach lights above each one. The roof was in the Cape Cod style and the bay windows were graced with elegant arches. When it was built sometime in the sixties, it would have been an expensive address; now, with its bay view and proximity to the revitalized downtown parks and beaches, it would be worth a small fortune.

Standing there in the silent roadway, she thought briefly about destroying all that A.L. Rouhl had been and owned—and perhaps the thing that he had taken from her—all in one satisfying blaze. The notion appealed to her injured sensibilities. She looked up at the elegant windows and at the ceramic tiling of the roofline, calmly considering arson, but the tight row of attached homes made her think of circled wagons resisting her approach.

Besides, her first priority was actually getting her diary back. She imagined how it would feel, casting away the irksome spacer at last, to slip the diary smoothly into its place on her bookshelf.

She had found out where Carly Rouhl herself lived, but the green Mazda had been locked away in a basement garage, secured with a keypad code.

Then the *Escarpment* office had offered another possibility, but on reflection, Cole realized A.L.'s house would give her her best chance. Sooner or later, the younger Rouhl would show up here at her new property, parking her dark green car on the unprotected driveway or in the street.

If the diary was still inside the car... It was dark, and this time she had a small crowbar. If it wasn't there, she'd follow Carly inside.

She went back to her car and got in. She restarted the big six cylinder and rolled the car forward until, by leaning toward the passenger side, she could see the upper half of Rouhl's door and his darkened windows.

Of course, there was a chance the diary had already been returned right here, to A.L. Rouhl's house to lie among the author's papers, as if Marcella Cole's private thoughts and records were the Rouhl family's legitimate property. If the daughter failed to show, how long might the house lie fallow? Would there be cleaners, painters? People going in and out? Real estate people?

Entering the house after people had unlocked the door for her would be both easy and more dangerous. At first glance, no one looking at Marcella Cole would suspect her of wrongdoing. Experience told her that it took ages for people to catch on to who she really was—and they would *never* guess what she was capable of. She remembered the young pharmacologist, so sweet and naïve; he had actually been apologetic, embarrassed at the thought of testifying at her trial. Had it even crossed his mind that she might have done everything they'd accused her of—and so much more? A capacity for calm, self-possessed violence, she decided, was a rare gift. A pity that her victims had such a very short time to appreciate it.

Her irreproachable grooming and serene features had always been an advantage. With a moment's thought, she could invent a story that would give her access to the house and then she could wait for an opportunity to look around. She'd used the skill before. Of course, she would have to weigh the risks, the awkwardness that would come if she were confronted and her story didn't hold up.

It wasn't that she was afraid, but she did have to think about what would happen—what she would *allow* to happen. There were some things she would not countenance. The invasion of her privacy was one of those things; the unseemly attention of others to her affairs was another. In the end, A.L. Rouhl had learned that very thing, paying for his presumptuous writings with, as she had intended, years of slow decline and suffering.

And now she knew the old man had done more than peer closely at her affairs. He had also taken something of hers, something intimate and personal that had now fallen into the hands of Rouhl's daughter. The daughter's involvement too was unforgivable. Carly Rouhl, in due course, would be required to suffer and die.

She turned off the engine and sat patiently behind the wheel, allowing the warmth of the car to bleed slowly away into the black evening.

CHAPTER THIRTY

Carly arrived at her father's house with Evan just before nine, paying scant attention to the blue SUV parked a few car lengths down the road. The deep winter's evening had been dark since five. They got out of Evan's car in the driveway and mounted the steps to the late A.L. Rouhl's darkened doorway. Carly used her key and put their coats in the hall cupboard, then led Evan, clicking in his leather shoes, through the quiet rooms to her father's office.

In a few minutes, they were both standing in the little room, in front of A.L. Rouhl's laptop computer. Carly hadn't told Evan that she'd seen the same machine in Eilert Weiss's office. She imagined that one more test of his credulity would drive him out into the night, leaving her alone with her fears. At least here, surrounded by the impossible warmth of the old man's office, the bottle of port and the nagging red light of the CD player, the insanity of the room was so seamless and perfect that it almost felt right to see the computer open on the desk.

But even here the laptop would, with time—in a room that ran by the rules, that is—have lapsed into hibernation, and she would have had to use her fingerprint or a code word to open up a file. Instead, all she had to do was tap on the keys until a document popped up.

"I found this," she said to Evan, touching the keyboard. "I just looked through the file list and there it was. It's called 'Questions.docx' and I think it might be what he was hinting at in his last note to me. It's incredible that he managed to type this himself, but I guess he needed to be alone with his thoughts."

"And it explains about Marcella Cole?"

"It explains everything and settles nothing. You'll see what I mean."

Evan apparently couldn't bring himself to sit in the black leather chair in which Carly's father had died. Instead, he placed his neat, blunt manicure on the surface of the desk and bent over to read from the screen. He seemed surprised at how easy it was to read the unhurried, natural prose and at the way old Mr. Rouhl's voice seemed to ride the words along.

After a few minutes, he looked up. "This is crazy. Your dad's saying he used some kind of mind reading to write his stories."

Carly pointed to the cluttered shelves where she had found the diary. "He's saying that all this junk he collected let him intuit the secrets of people's lives. And did you catch the bit at the motel room in Beaufort?"

"It sounded like he was suggesting…"

"Don't soft pedal this, Evan. The great A.L. Rouhl was saying he wrote about real events before they had happened. That's prophecy. Nobody believed Cassandra because she was cursed, and nobody believed A.L. Rouhl because he was a storyteller by trade."

She shook her head and adjusted the screen for him. "Go on. You might as well finish it."

Evan frowned and read more.

I'm sitting here alone looking over my epitaph summed up in a
few computer files. As Keats might have put it: here lies one

whose name is writ in pixels. What I've written is not enough, of course; how could it ever be? My life was as ragged and headlong as most, cluttered with pathways refused and questions unanswered. While still a young man, I came to realize I had a peculiar talent for looking into people's hearts and lives. But like all gifts that pop out of brass lamps rubbed gleefully in our youth, it came with a curse: I was to be privy to the bright and dark secrets of others, but would never fully understand how the gift worked.

Funny thing about mysteries, though; if even one aspect of our life proves to be beyond rational explanation, if there is even one hint that all is not as it seems in our view of reality, then even a singular experience like death may hold a few surprises—a strange comfort as my years turn into minutes.

I'm dying, as fatigued by my bewilderment as I am by my failing muscles. In one of those delicious ironies I have always cherished, I was murdered by one of my own stories, by a woman on whose life and misdeeds I eavesdropped. Perhaps one day, she will be found out and people will wonder at A.L. Rouhl's ability to write about things he could not have known.

Or, mercifully perhaps, posterity will let me and my executioner, and all of those other souls I wrote about over the years in book after book, dwindle away to a foot of forgotten shelf space in the National Archives.

Finally, for all my editors and critics, who always said I overused the dash—

Evan straightened and, without taking his eyes from the screen, he stepped back against the window ledge.

"How long does the dash go on for?" he said.

"Couple of pages. Just held the key down, I guess."

"He starts off by accusing Cole of the murder of that pharmacologist."

Carly twined her fingertips tightly beneath her breasts and looked at the carpet. "Which is why this is unpublishable…"

"And it ends with that stuff about his executioner being someone he wrote about. It's obvious he thinks Marcella Cole murdered him." Evan looked at her. "I can understand that he didn't want to die with vengeance or bitterness in his heart, but what about leaving that woman unpunished to murder again? Didn't he owe *anything* to the people whose lives she could still threaten? He's buried his accusations in an obscure computer file that could easily have been overlooked completely."

"Not buried; no. He knew I'd find it. Don't you see? His suicide note was a signpost that led me to the file. I'm not just one of his readers; I'm a goddamn editor, God help me. Which means, of course, that he pretty much dumped the dilemma right in my lap. What am I supposed to do now?"

"He's not asking for revenge—or for anything."

"You're wrong about that. He's leaving it up to me whether or not to make public all this stuff about a psychic gift."

"He's left it up to his last editor. My God, Car. A.L. Rouhl! A.L. Rouhl, the literary lion… He's left his reputation in your hands. What *are* you going to do?"

Carly was staring at Evan, her eyes wide, when the door popped inward and swung aside. Holding the doorknob, her shoulder still against the panel of the door, stood Marcella Cole. For a beat, nothing moved; no one spoke. On Marcella's other arm, a black velveteen purse dropped towards her hand and she moved to arrest its fall. She still said nothing, but a small smile of satisfaction came and went in the blink of an eye.

It took Carly about as long to realize that Marcella must have recognized her at the health centre when she'd scouted her office window. Carly had left the house door unlocked and Marcella had simply followed them in.

"Why are you here?" Carly said, stepping out from behind the desk.

Marcella was wearing an impeccable black coat and black gloves—the kind of thing you'd wear to a funeral. The velveteen purse was now in both hands clutched primly to her waist. "I believe you have something of mine." She seemed calm and matter-of-fact as she leaned back against the door. It clicked shut behind her with her weight.

Carly looked quickly at Evan; his eyes were dark and slitted. He had seen pictures of Marcella Cole and now Evan was warning Carly that they were in the presence of an unpredictable psychopath. It came to her in that moment what Evan had said: "Don't give the diary back; she'd swat you like a fly." The trouble was, the diary was within a few feet of Marcella"s right elbow, back in its home on the shelf amid the clutter of A.L. Rouhl's life. It was hidden only by the jumble of junk that surrounded it—hidden in plain sight. But the camouflage of clutter was as thin as lace; sooner or later, Marcella would spot the diary's vinyl cover. Right now, though, Marcella's gaze was drifting to the desk with the laptop open on the blotter.

Marcella walked slowly forward without fear or awkwardness. Evan tugged on Carly's arm and the two of them sidestepped out of her way. There was barely room for Marcella to pass without touching them and Carly caught the scent of her fulsome perfume. She knew little about fragrances, but she remembered reading that Dorothy Parker had worn tuberose because it was used to cover the scent of corpses.

It occurred to Carly that they could easily overpower Marcella now as she brushed by—the woman was trespassing in this house. At the same moment, Carly realized that Evan had worked his elbow in front of her. She looked up at him and he was shaking his head slowly.

Marcella edged around the desk, her eyes drawn to the laptop. She blinked at its screen, still open on A.L.'s confessional farewell, and then her eye was caught by the keyboard with its scratched surface. She leaned closely, studying the marks with a deepening frown. "It's his?" she said, glancing up at Carly.

Carly frowned back, giving a slight nod. If Marcella touched the keys, Carly wouldn't be able to stop herself from leaping forward.

Marcella shifted her weight on one foot, bringing her in line with the screen. She read what she saw there, exasperation coming and going on her face.

When she looked at Carly again, she was shaking her head as though in disappointment. "I suppose the memoir will be on here too."

Evan moved in front of Carly. "You have no right being here. We're asking you to leave now." His voice was flat, unthreatening.

Allowing Evan a dismissive glance, Marcella laid her hand on the mouse.

Carly tensed, gripping Evan's arm. Evan leaned forward, his hand beginning to reach for Marcella's. "Now," Evan said, his voice suddenly heavy with threat. "Leave."

Marcella straightened, realizing from Evan's tone that the time for bluff and bafflement was over. She backed off until she was hard against the window ledge. The faux belt of her coat was just right to brush the picture frame set up there and the photo of Rouhl standing in front of Lafayette's tomb fell forward, the pewter frame making a dull click on the ledge.

Carly couldn't see what was happening behind Marcella, but she heard the tiny clatter of the frame on the window sill and she glanced down toward the small sound, her expression changing to puzzlement.

Marcella seemed unaware of what she had done, bringing her bag up close against her chest and reaching inside it with the unhurried air of a woman retrieving a compact.

By the time Carly had looked up again, the small calibre pistol Cole had taken from her purse lay in her hand carelessly.

She made no attempt to aim it or even to gesture threateningly. It simply was there, making its own statement. Had Evan lunged at that very instant, while she cupped it aimlessly in her hand, he might have had a chance of swatting it from her grasp.

Carly was stunned by the realization that all the ambiguity of the situation had just been swept away. Marcella was no longer an enigma who might or might not have been all her father claimed her to be. She was the woman who had brought about her father's death. Seeing the gun in her hand, Carly was certain of this. Marcella was the cold mechanic of suffering and death that Evan and her father had warned her against.

"You'll give me a little room." Marcella gestured now with the gun, still making no real effort to aim it purposefully, and yet Carly realized Marcella's moment of vulnerability had passed and that now she was capable of shooting them both. Evan pressed Carly back against the bookshelves, still trying to shield her with his shoulder.

"There's nothing you can do there," Carly said, nodding at the laptop. "There are copies of everything at the magazine office." In a moment of fleeting confusion, Carly realized that that wasn't true of the Question file. Only the memoir had been emailed to the *Escarpment* office. Her father's personal testament was on the laptop and there only. If Marcella somehow got hold of it and erased it, no one else would ever read her father's most personal thoughts. Certainly not the police.

Marcella gave a little smile, her attention already returning to the computer. "Yes, your magazine office." Almost immediately, the private smile was gone and she was studying the screen as though considering her options.

Cole straightened, standing squarely now behind Rouhl's desk chair. The pistol in her hand wavered, and then, as though she had made up her mind, it found them, its tiny muzzle moving minutely between the two of them before squaring up on Carly, aiming somewhere near her throat. Evan was the

REQUIEM FOR THURSDAY

greater threat...but Carly might scream loudly enough to alert the neighbours. A bullet to her throat, however...

Evan's eyes fixed on Marcella's gun, tracking its aim as he lunged forward. Marcella spun the big leather desk chair with a clatter of wheels so that it hit Evan's thigh hard. He grabbed it and tried to wrench it out of the way, stumbling with its weight.

Marcella jerked back with a scornful laugh. Her arm straightened, her hand holding the pistol steady just beyond Evan's reach. She raised her chin in patrician delight. "It looks so much easier in the movies, doesn't it? And it takes no time at all for me to pull the trigger."

Letting the chair thump back on its wheels, Evan straightened his back, bracing for a bullet he could no longer dodge.

Satisfaction suffused her features. Marcella had won and she knew it. Evan was reduced to staring at a gun so unmoving it was as if the woman's glands didn't produce adrenaline at all.

"It will have to be you first then. I can't have a, hmm...man of action getting in my way, can I?" And her aim drifted casually to Evan's heart.

The shot—when it came—was flat in the little room, the sound swallowed by the wall of books and muted by A.L. Rouhl's odd collection of gloves, baggage labels, and cell phone holsters. Carly craned to see past Evan's shoulder and the sound of the gun seemed to assault every nerve in her body: the horror of Evan's certain death, the abrupt boom of the shot filling the little room, and something else... A flash of pale light glimpsed in the reeling space between Evan's shoulder and Marcella's breast. Strange that her mind would revert to an image of her father at such a moment, but it was as if she'd caught a fleeting image of him sitting straight-backed in his desk chair. Strange too that such a hallucination should be selective, mostly obscured by Evan's body so that she couldn't see the old man's face or his upraised hand.

Marcella lurched back against the window pane with the

kind of agonized intake of breath you hear when someone cuts a finger or steps on a nail. Evan was still hunched over, holding his chest, as if he had been shot. That was, after all, the only possible outcome of the situation. Carly wanted to reach around and clutch at Evan's shirt, to touch the terrible wound, but instead, she stumbled and found her hands flat on her father's desk. From there she watched Marcella Cole die.

A bloody stain was blooming between Cole's breasts. Carly watched in astonishment as Marcella's heart pulsed and blood ran down her long bodice soaking her white rayon blouse in seconds. With stunned fascination, she watched the burgundy stain follow and sharply define the boning in the undergarment. The selective staining even brought the lace of her bra cups into sharp relief under the ghostly translucency of her blouse.

With the weeping moan of a nine-year-old child, Marcella looked down, letting the gun hang on her trigger finger and dropping her purse. In whining petulance, she remembered the gun and it began to wobble spitefully up at them again, but now her legs buckled, and her body slid down against the window ledge, crumpling into a tangle of human wreckage against the baseboards.

Carly gasped rather than screamed, as she stood beside Evan, looking at Marcella's face nuzzled against the carpet, the eyes open, but white and still. Neither one of them had looked on present death before, but Marcella's frozen features made it unmistakable. There was surprise there, and perhaps a frown of indignation?

"What…" Carly began in a barely audible whisper. "What happened? Cole shot herself? I don't understand."

Evan's eyes were wide. He had been between Carly and Marcella when Carly heard the shot, his long back blocking almost everything. "No!" he shouted, "You know that's not true. That's not possible."

Carly groped at Evan's chest, searching for the fatal wound that she had expected. "Then..."

"Carly, her gun didn't even go off. It was pointed right at *me*. You *know* that." Evan looked into her eyes as though pleading. "My eyes were on that gun and I was just waiting to die. She never let her aim wander."

Carly was struggling with the impossible. "But there *was* a shot, wasn't there? Marcella's been shot." Carly's eyes darted everywhere, searching for some implausible weapon in Evan's hands.

"Look at me! I have no gun." Evan gestured helplessly.

Slowly, a functioning part of Carly's mind was returning and she was struck with an almost superstitious wonder at this little corner of her father's room—a square yard of carpet, plaster and glass that had now witnessed two fatal shootings in a week.

She looked at the window behind her father's desk chair. There was no blood on the frame or on the wall, and none where Marcella had been standing.

She could see that the bullet hitting Marcella hadn't passed through her. There wasn't even visible staining on the carpet. She'd seen Marcella's lifeblood eerily and completely absorbed by her clothes.

The police had told Carly mercifully little about her father's death. She hadn't been required to enter the room until all evidence of the suicide had been cleaned away, and with Nurse Crowther there, she hadn't even been required to identify her father's body. For the first time, she allowed herself to visualize the horror Mrs. Crowther had walked in on. She shook her head trying to dislodge the memory of the fleeting image that had seemed to spark between Evan and Marcella like the muzzle flash of a gunshot.

When she shivered, Carly was brought back to the moment. Her shoulders gave one convulsive spasm as her eyes darted around the room.

Evan had moved to look at Marcella's body, and then he had begun staring out the window as lost in thought as Carly had been. Carly followed his eyes to the window. Through the glass she made out a single gull cruising at the edge of the mist, slowly as though against the wind. It skimmed the surface of the water, its reflection first slipping then vanishing among coastlines of slush. She realized it was the first movement she'd seen through that window since the police cleared her to enter the room.

"Evan?"

He turned.

Carly waited, but Evan's eyes had begun to move slowly about the room.

"Carly, it's getting cold in here, isn't it?"

For some reason the observation annoyed her. There were more important things to talk about. "Yes," she said. "I think so."

"We have to get out of here."

What was the matter with him? "We have to call this in to the police, Evan. Now."

Evan looked around. "My God, can't you feel it?"

At first Carly thought he was going on about the sudden chill in the room, but then he reached for her arm. "There, do you hear it?"

"What is it? What are you talking about?" she whined, on the edge of tears.

"Can't you hear…feel…the tension in the room—that dog whistle tinnitus in the air? It's back."

She shook her head petulantly, but Evan put his arm around her shoulder and Carly realized she was being urged toward the door. She didn't understand what he was talking about, but for all that, Evan sounded focussed, determined. "We have to get away from this," he said. "All of it. Hurry, Carly!"

Carly found she had difficulty pulling her eyes away from

REQUIEM FOR THURSDAY

the room with its window on a tragic Thursday, but Evan led her to the office door.

"Carly! Please!" He was dragging her now.

She barely noticed, her attention still fixed on the room, that this time the door swung open easily and without sticking.

They crashed out into the narrow corridor, thumping against the wall, Carly still looking back into the room, her eyes focused now on the desktop blotter. A curious warm light illuminated the desk pad.

Evan closed the door quickly, removed his hands slowly from the door panels, and looked at his fingers, then he turned to Carly who had flattened herself against the wall, breathing rapidly.

"Evan..." she said, her eyes wide.

"I think it's okay now. We can get to a phone now."

"No, Evan..."

At first Evan looked surprised, but then he scowled at the doorway. "Yes, I know. They're going to think I shot her. What do the police do when you present them with impossibility? This is insane. I had no gun in there—I don't even own a gun. I don't think I've ever touched one in my life. You believe me, don't you?"

"Evan!" Carly yelled, shaking him, forcing him to face her. "Did you see? In there? The laptop—my father's computer. *What happened to the laptop?*"

"Jesus, Carly, what are you talking about? Can't we get it later?"

She seemed to find some degree of control. Her breathing began to level, and she stared into his eyes with a perplexed frown. As though speaking to a child, she paced the words out: "My father's laptop...is *not* sitting on the desk anymore. It's gone."

CHAPTER THIRTY-ONE

Standing on the carpet of A.L. Rouhl's office, Detective Prem Joshi was the first to speak. "Has she changed much in five years? Do you remember her well enough?"

"Of course I do," said Weiss, looking down at the fetal body. "It's Marcella Cole. There's that perfect face. Look at it, Prem—symmetry, as though the sides of her brain were in perfect harmony. Even in death—no rictus, no grimace, no distortion, just that hint of affronted dignity."

"Yeah, okay. Nice. So, she's got a small calibre pistol in her hand. Good of her to wrap up our inquiries and all, but what business has she got, getting shot here in old Rouhl's office?"

In her open winter coat, Marcella Cole was a dark topography of folds and creases. Her blouse was a red stain laced with darker lines that had begun to blacken in the air. Weiss stood back with distaste, his hands in his coat pockets. "Carly Rouhl was one of her targets—a threat, just like A.L. Somehow, Marcella must have known the daughter had inherited the diary."

"Maybe Marcella figured Carly Rouhl would come after her

for her father's fatal illness, looking for payback," Joshi said. "Tried to eliminate her."

"You're placing a lot of faith in that 'Questions' file, Prem—which Marcella never read. That's where old Rouhl set out his suspicions about Marcella causing his illness. I'm not even sure Carly has read that."

Joshi was bent over, trying to balance without touching the edge of A.L. Rouhl's desk. "A bullet to the heart. No exit wound, so the bullet's still in there. That's a break."

Weiss held back: his mind was on the larger picture. "That would happen if the bullet hit bone," he said, "or if the bullet was partially spent before it hit her."

"Partially spent?" Joshi straightened, flexing his back muscles in relief. "What are you talking about? You sound like a man with a theory."

"I've been thinking about this too long to have just *one* theory. Have you noticed, there's no cordite smell in the room?"

Joshi looked around, inhaling noisily. "Jeez. Okay," he said.

"And no blood on the wall." Weiss didn't move, but his eyes were restless and wary.

Joshi nodded. "Well, that works, of course, because there's no pass through."

"The rug's clean," Weiss said.

"The blood was contained by her clothes. There's plenty of staining *on* her clothes—right down her torso." Joshi glanced at Weiss, frowning.

"Kind of odd," Weiss said, his weight shifting so he could angle his head. "Look, above her breasts and at her neck."

Joshi took a moment, still trying to read Weiss's features, then looked once more at the stained blouse. "Impact spatter," he said with a shrug. "Right up to her shoulders."

"The entry wound is below her breasts, Prem. How can that blood be hers? Almost all the staining is underneath in the folds of her clothes and behind some sort of heavy bodice."

"Yeah. Sort of a corset thing." Joshi backed up and waited.

Weiss turned and looked at him. Joshi was used to Weiss's invisible smiles; they would disappear under his mustache but light up his eyes.

"Okay," Joshi said. "Hard to see how the chest wound could cause spatter up high on her blouse."

Weiss shrugged and remained silent.

"Well," Joshi sighed. "Thank you for that observation. That was helpful. So what the fuck have we got? Did the daughter shoot her in self defense in her own house? It *is* her house now, right?"

"Yes, it's hers. Evan Favaro's hands and clothes will have to be tested too. Problem there is, there's no gun in evidence. We'll have to search the house and outside."

Both men stood at the side of A.L. Rouhl's desk until Joshi shook his head and began to button his coat. "Marcella Cole is dead now. Still think we're being jerked around, Eilert?"

Weiss took one last look around the room. "Just another variation, Prem—on a hidden theme."

Weiss turned to the doorway, but the twisting at his waist seemed to burn beneath his shirt. He let out the smallest of gasps.

"You all right, man? Hospitals let people go home too early these days."

"I'm fine. Healing well. And I'm fine because someone put a stop to Marcella Cole."

"It's not over yet, Eilert."

"No, it isn't. I have to pen a work of literature."

"I hope to hell you're talking about an incident report."

"Don't you see, Prem? It's shaping up; only now we have two enigmas. To get any closure on either one of them, I've got to craft a document that describes what happened in this room, a document that stays just within the envelope of plausibility. It's that simple."

Joshi watched as Weiss moved out the door with the careful stiffness of a robot. "Don't you mean it's that *difficult?*"

CHAPTER THIRTY-TWO

Detective Weiss came into the living room alone and gave Carly a quick sympathetic smile. Then he turned to Evan, who stood up and faced him. The two men looked at each other, Evan expressionless. Weiss exhaled, his face drawn and tired looking.

Finally, Evan made a small gesture towards the remaining available chair. Weiss glanced at it, but then he turned to Carly. "I wonder if you would mind if you and I went into the kitchen together, Ms. Rouhl. Ten minutes or so should be fine." When Carly nodded, Weiss turned back to Evan. "What do you think, Mr. Favaro? I won't keep her for long."

Evan shrugged. "Sure, go ahead."

Carly looked puzzled. Evan had listened as Carly had prepared a version of the truth for Weiss; they would say they had heard the shot—and discovered Cole dead. Evan had challenged the story by trying to anticipate Weiss's skeptical cross-examination. It had been an unpleasant activity, back and forth, and now here was Weiss about to test them with his own interrogation strategy.

Carly knew Weiss was trying to separate her from Evan; the other detective would come out and question Evan alone. Afterwards, the detectives would pick away at any discrepancy in their stories.

Carly knew what she planned to say, but it was up to Evan how far he would back her up—or how well. With a sinking feeling, Carly realized that the detectives stood a very good chance of catching them up in a muddle of inconsistencies. Their best defense was to say as little as possible and run the risk of sounding evasive. Carly figured Evan would realize that; she'd started to think he was smarter than she was.

Carly slipped into the breakfast nook. Weiss took the window seat against the back porch. Although she wasn't sure how his questions would come out, Carly figured there were only so many Weiss could ask, only so many angles he could follow up.

She was wrong.

The window seat had no back, so Weiss had to lean forward, his arms in his lap. "Ms. Rouhl," he said, "I have bad news for you. There's been a death at your office on Pearl. Mrs. Peggy Goss. We found her earlier tonight."

Since it was the last thing she expected to hear, it took Carly a few seconds to react. "God. Peggy? How..."

Her mind raced. She didn't understand what had happened, but she felt an instinctive guilt, as though her place should have been standing guard at the *Escarpment* office. "Oh, no. Peggy..."

Weiss watched without emotion as the tears started in Carly's eyes. "It appears she was struck on the head with a heavy object earlier this evening."

She would have been alone—alone with Indy. "Struck? My God. How did you find her?"

"Seems your dog was scratching at the office door and barking. It caused a passerby to look in."

"Indy?" Carly's knuckles were white on the edges of the table. "Oh, my God. Indy." She stared down at the moving blur of the table top. "Do you know anything about it?"

Weiss made the tiniest of gestures that might have been a negative, then looked at the corridor to Rouhl's office. "Do you know the dead woman in there?"

"I know who she is. It's Marcella Cole, a nurse."

Weiss nodded. "Your father wrote about her, didn't he?"

Carly looked up, surprised. "Yes."

"In fact, he believed she was the cause of his illness."

Carly was starting to think it through. "I'm assuming you got that from my father's computer."

"Yes, and by looking through your father's last book. It's obvious who he had in mind there, and not just to me. Anybody local would remember the trial. A few of us in the detachment helped put together the case against Marcella Cole."

That should have caught Carly's attention, but instead she was thinking about the computer screen Marcella had stared at in her father's office. "Where's my father's laptop now?"

Weiss frowned. There was that odd obsession with the laptop again. "It's still in my office." He cocked his head to one side. "Why?"

"My father's laptop is in your office," she repeated, her voice dripping with skepticism.

"As I just said. Want to explain your concern?"

"It's okay. I just need to know it's safe. It has a copy of my father's last work on it."

"Yes, I understand that. It's safe, I assure you." Weiss took a moment to continue, his instincts telling him he'd just been lied to. "Your father believed Marcella had murdered more than once. In fact, he went way beyond what the evidence supported. I know the allegations we had against Marcella and our suspicions, but your dad didn't stop there. He had her right up there in the Jeffrey Dahmer, serial killer league."

"That's right. He went after her all by himself…" There was reproach in Carly's voice. "…and then he got fatally ill."

"Do you know where he *got* the idea Marcella was a serial killer?"

"No. We talked about this before, Detective. I never understood how A.L. worked. To some of us, it looked as though he was embroidering the truth, making up stories with a dash of fact and a lot of imagination, but he never admitted to that. He would have told you he had his reasons for believing what he did and from what I can recall of the time around the trial, his hatred and fear of Marcella Cole seemed genuine enough."

"Is there any reason Marcella would have gone to your magazine's office?"

"Jesus." Carly straightened. "Cole. Marcella Cole killed Peggy. She killed Peggy and then she came here."

"And why would Marcella do that?"

"Maybe she thought she could suppress the last part of my father's autobiography. It was on the office server and she probably figured there would be a copy here." Carly swung her legs round and Weiss, thinking she was going to get up, rocked forward. Instead, Carly sat there, one hand braced on the table top, the other on her knee.

"There's something else, Detective Weiss. Marcella may have come here looking for a diary—her own diary. I'm not sure how Dad came by it, but the diary I'm talking about was here at this house, in my father's office. You'll remember you asked me for it."

"And Cole *knew* your father had this diary?"

"I'm not sure about that."

"But you think she'd break in here looking for it—and for your father's memoir?"

"We heard the shot come from the office, so she probably came in while Evan and I were in the living room."

"And Marcella was quickly followed by her killer? Is that what you're saying?"

Carly swallowed, aware of the absurdity. "Look, I know how

it sounds, but *I* didn't shoot her and Evan didn't shoot her. Neither one of us has ever had a gun, so there's your problem. Someone else must have done it."

"And you think this killer would have had time to hide or get out of the house? Before you arrived on the scene in the office?"

For a moment, they both sat still, holding eye contact. Finally, Carly dropped her gaze. "No. Frankly, I don't."

"You told the police officer you've no idea who might have shot Marcella."

"Since you know about the trial, you must know Marcella had enemies."

"Like the family of the pharmacist she was suspected of killing? Or the dozens of people who read your father's book and put two and two together? It's amazing Marcella didn't sue your father. She just might have won."

Carly, turning back to the table and waiting, said nothing. Weiss stood up with a sigh. "Well, Ms. Rouhl, we're going to do some tests. Your clothes, your hands. Mr. Favaro too, of course.

"My clothes?"

"That's not a problem is it?"

"No," Carly said, being anything but sure.

CHAPTER THIRTY-THREE

"So, now what do we do?" Eilert Weiss sat in the Headon Road office, drumming the printout from Forensics with a pair of reading glasses.

Prem Joshi was making himself comfortable dangling a tea bag in a cup of hot water, his heavy walking shoes looking as big as ATV tires propped up on a file box. "Well, we're not going to get Carly Rouhl. Not with this. If Rouhl or her boyfriend were anywhere near a gun being fired, there would be residue somewhere, and there's not a grain on either of them. Remember there was no cordite smell in the room."

Weiss looked up at him and smiled. "Yes. And the bullet in Marcella's body..."

Joshi cut him off with a theatrical yawn. "The bullet's no damn use unless we can come up with a gun to match it to. It sure as hell didn't come from Marcella's gun."

"Right; it's the wrong calibre and Marcella's gun hadn't been fired anyway." Weiss sounded wistful. "I thought maybe Favaro. He'd have the best opportunity to get hold of a gun. He works with a lot of edgy types in the media—but nothing: no sinister connections, no paper trail on either one of them."

Joshi nodded. "So all we have is the blood."

Weiss slipped the reading glasses in place and held them there as he looked down at the printout. "The trace on Cole's neck and blouse isn't her own blood." He creaked back in the desk chair. "But there's no point in trying to match it with Evan or Carly. Neither one of them has an open wound, or so much as a scratch."

Joshi was holding the dripping tea bag over his cup and looking around for someplace to put it. "But the trace blood has to be the killer's. Where else would it come from?"

Weiss shrugged, "And if that's the case, there must have been some kind of struggle to account for the trace on Marcellas's shoulders, right?"

"Fine," Joshi said. "So we've got a scenario where Marcella and the killer struggle; she manages to draw a gun to protect herself, but the killer is faster. He gets his shot in before Marcella can react."

Weiss looked at him over the reading glasses. "And the killer's blood? Where did it come from? What kind of wound would create a splash effect if Cole didn't get off a shot? Her gun wasn't fired, remember. Don't tell me you're happy with that theory."

"Shit, no. I don't even believe the struggle part. Why is nothing in the room disturbed? The place is full of loose bric-a-brac. Empty bottles, candlesticks and shit—but there's no sign of commotion. Nothing is out of place."

"Except for that picture frame."

With a tricky swinging movement, Joshi managed to dump the tea bag on the file box. "What?"

"When A.L.'s body was found last week, the picture frame behind him was lying on its face, the way it is now. It was put back in place—standing up—after the Rouhl investigation. It's possible Cole knocked it flat again when she fell."

"Helpful," Joshi sniffed.

"I'll tell you what's helpful," Weiss said. "The fact that Marcella didn't get any blood on the carpet. That's kind of unusual, right?"

"Yeah, the coroner said she was corseted up like a Victorian spinster. Her own blood was pretty much absorbed by her underwear."

"That kind of opens up some possibilities, don't you think?"

Joshi dropped his feet to the floor and raised his shaggy black and silver eyebrows in interest.

Weiss rocked forward and let his elbows rest on his knees. "Since there's no cast off blood at the scene and no evidence of commotion in the room, there's a chance Marcella was shot elsewhere and dumped in A.L.'s office."

"Maybe as some sort of tribute?" Joshi brightened. "Maybe somebody—some vigilante—was thanking old Rouhl for outing Marcella. The body was meant as a sacrificial offering at the shrine of A.L. Rouhl's genius."

"Ah, Prem, just listen to you! Bless our multicultural hiring practices. You put that so nicely. If I use it, you'll get full credit. If not a Pulitzer Prize."

Joshi primped a little, smoothing his hair back. "It's hardly a tidy conclusion, but it works better than anything else we got."

Weiss sighed, swung around to the desktop, and pulled a heavy package towards him. Rouhl's computer had been rewrapped in plastic and bound in neat loops of clear adhesive tape. There was a large label tucked under the web of tape. "I'm taking A.L.'s laptop downstairs," Weiss said, standing up listlessly, still lost in thought. He picked up the package, settled it under his arm, and stood there studying the clean, new floor tiles.

Joshi watched him. "Having second thoughts? Think maybe we should keep the computer longer?"

"Hmm?" Weiss looked at Joshi, and then down at the laptop nestled against his hip. "Oh. No, it's nothing." He started for the door, opened it and stepped out into the corridor. He meant to pull the door closed behind him but stopped with the door half open. He stood there for a moment until Joshi's head appeared around the door jamb. "You're worrying me," Joshi said.

Weiss grinned. "You're right to be worried. It just hit me what A.L. Rouhl had in mind for his death scene—what he was writing for us all along. You ever heard of a 'locked room mystery,' Prem? There *is* another gun in all this, isn't there? Just one."

"Damn. You being quixotic again?"

"I just thought of another test for the lab to do and Mercer is going to love this one. Back up, Prem. I've got to use the phone."

CHAPTER THIRTY-FOUR

Peggy Goss's funeral was a surprising affair—the small gathering of family was outnumbered by friends and colleagues who spoke of a long and busy life, spent almost entirely in Halton County. Carly looked at them all, some writers and photographers she hadn't seen for months. With a twinge of envy, she realized that it had been Peggy and not she who had been the glue holding the office together. Peggy, who was always there. And then she thought about her father's travels and wondered if Scott Fitzgerald had been right; life was, after all, better viewed from a single window.

The arrangements had been paid for by Peggy's most recent employer. In that role, Carly had suggested the Talbot Memorial Gardens as a last resting place.

Afterwards, Carly asked Evan if he wanted to see where A.L. Rouhl's ashes would be interred. They walked the icy pathway towards the bay until they were beneath a canopy of pine and Carly took Evan's elbow to stop him.

"Here," she said.

Evan looked at the shadows of pines on the untrammelled snow. "It's a lovely location. There's nothing here yet."

"There will be. I've hired an architect."

"An architect? Are you serious?"

Carly nodded. "Something modern and dignified, of course, with a stone bench out front where people can sit and look at the lake through the trees and maybe even read a few of Dad's words. Something about the 'cartographers of reason,' perhaps."

"The tomb won't be anything like the neighbour's, then?" Evan looked up and across the path. The backlit dome of Lafayette's mausoleum was a ragged shape sheared out of the sky.

"Well, only in one way. Lafayette made provisions for his dog. Well, there's going to be a spot here for Indy right beside the bench. The rest of the design is up to the architect."

There was nothing more to see except the marks of amber crumbs and dry pine needles on the snow, so they crossed over to the shadowed steps of Lafayette's tomb. The doorway offered protection from a wind that was light enough to be invisible, but brisk enough to be felt. Carly unsnapped her hood, placed it on the top step, and then sat on it. Her long legs were covered and her boots looked warm.

"Evan, tell me what happened that night when A.L. asked you to hold the diary."

"But I did tell you. There was tea, a few biscuits and the sound of Nurse Crowther moving about in the kitchen. He gave me the diary and he waited."

"And you told me what he asked of you—and what you said to him."

"The rest was just pleasantries, Car. My getting settled on the couch… Nothing helpful."

"Evan," Carly was looking at a point somewhere beyond his left shoulder. "While you were sitting there holding the diary…"

"Yes?"

"What was *he* holding?"

Evan frowned and seemed about to protest the question. Instead, he looked away in thought for a moment. "He…"

His eyes came back to her. "Your dad was holding my teal coat. It's so funny you're asking that question. I never would have remembered it, but that was just one of the strange things about the situation. When I first came in he was out of his chair, standing there looking frail and stooped, but he insisted on taking my coat. I thought it was touching. Very gentlemanly and old-school. He even made an effort to help me off with it. And then…"

"He held on to it, didn't he."

Evan laughed. "Yes, actually he did. He took it with him when we sat ourselves down, and put it to one side while we talked."

"You said he was holding it."

"He didn't have it in his lap or anything. It was on that side table thing, but he kept his grip on it the whole time. An absent-minded thing to do. You know how old people…"

"There was nothing wrong with my father's mind, Evan. What you saw was a deliberate choice."

"Car, what is it?"

Carly seemed fixed on the grain of the polished granite step. Her hands were deep in her coat pockets. "You know, Dad would hide away in that cluttered office of his and stare at his wall of books and his odd collection of stuff. And that's where all the magic happened. You know: the *genius* of A. L. Rouhl. You saw it. The shelves in his office were full of random objects: bits of fabric, wrist watches, an old walking stick, Marcella Cole's ridiculous diary…"

"Sure. His souvenirs," Evan said.

"When I think about it, there was always something close at hand—some *thing*…sometimes in his hand—the way your coat was." Carly shifted, her eyes slowly climbing the steps. "I think that while you were looking at the diary, he was reading *you*."

"A.L. was touching my coat—to get an impression of me?"

"You've read enough of Marcella's diary to know the diary itself didn't give away anything important. Maybe for him, the boring lists in the diary were irrelevant. Hell, he could have got as much from her shoe. What's important is that it was Marcella Cole's diary. It was something she touched every day for close to a year. I think my father saw more about Marcella Cole in that diary than he could ever prove. The things he wrote about her—he saw all that, just as he saw that she was responsible for his own death."

"Careful, Car. Great writing is not clairvoyance."

"Maybe that's just what Dad did do—confuse them, I mean. Just think about it; how would he be able to sort out all the sensations—knowledge, imagination, surmise, speculation, vision. Maybe to him, all those sensations *felt* the same. Real genius is always a mystery and his own gift was the thing Dad could never understand. Imagine how it must have been for him; from moment to moment. he couldn't tell what it was he was doing: dreaming, remembering, guessing... I honestly think my father had lost the ability to discern truth from invention. He'd made a few lucky guesses and he was beginning to believe in prophecy."

Evan searched her eyes until a stray thought made him look away. Carly turned and realized he was looking back at the site of the Rouhl tomb. "I've been wondering if the whole diary thing—your dad calling me up, asking me to come to his house—if it wasn't all part of his message to you. You know; like that 'Questions' file. Maybe he didn't need me to validate his opinion of Marcella, but he knew that I was connected to you, and it was *you* he was thinking of at the end of his life. What if the diary was just another part of his message, another way of letting you know something?"

"Know what? That his talent was just a trick? Magic performed in front of a kid?"

"Or that he believed it to be. But even if he'd lost faith in his imagination, even if he felt the need to rationalize his talent as vision and prophecy, do you think less of him for that?"

Carly looked at Evan in silence, feeling the appalling emptiness of Lafayette's tomb behind her. At last she said, "No. Not at all. It's still magic, isn't it?"

She needed to turn away from him until she could be sure of her voice. She stayed that way for a few minutes and found herself listening to the chop of footsteps approaching from the path. And then a solitary runner came around the corner. He was wearing an insulated track suit and he looked up as he passed. He made a quick gesture of acknowledgement and Carly waved back. Then the man turned out of sight and the footfalls began to die away into the pure sound that only distance makes.

Evan broke into her air of distraction. "Weiss has to come after us for Marcella's death, doesn't he?"

Carly was three steps up, looking down at him. "Try and see it from Weiss's point of view. He has no murder weapon. Cole died from a bullet wound and neither of us had a gun. The tests will show neither of us fired one. How far can he go with that?"

"What about our point of view?" Evan answered. "We saw her die, Car."

"I'm not a detective..." She smiled, and the sparkle of a secret pleasure moved in her eyes. "...but I know a little bit about storytelling."

"Okay. Fine. So tell me a story. But how do you make the story work?"

"A story by *Carly* Rouhl? Would you like that? For me to write my own piece of...of... creative nonfiction?" She kicked back a crescent snowdrift and frowned up at the overcast. "Then let's start by taking us out of the picture.

"Suppose you and I were just bystanders at Marcella Cole's death; bystanders who didn't need to be there. But Marcella Cole? Now, *she* did need to be there. She was standing behind my father's chair—the chair Dad died in. She was where she needed to be. Maybe, in one of his little reveries, Dad would say that he 'saw' her there."

Evan smiled. "Ah, prophecy."

"She had to be there, you see, to die by my father's bullet—by the bullet *he fired*."

Evan reached up to snug Carly's collar. "Well, you're right about one thing, kiddo. You're no detective."

She took his hand and pressed his fingers against her cheek. "But, oh, my father would have loved to write that ending to his life. He had the guts to do it too. He wouldn't shoot Marcella out of vengeance, mind you. Not even to stop her from hurting others—he didn't write stories with morals. He wasn't that kind of writer, not the kind you give a Nobel Prize to.

"He claimed that all he ever did was tell people's real stories. But—man!—he could polish them up beautifully, make the stories seem dramatic and complete. He could tease out the ironic twist or sense of rightness. Reality can come across as mundane, you know. It's all about how you write it. *An ending that works*. You see, *that's* something I understand. That's something *he* understood."

Evan laughed. "But wait a second; the ending *doesn't* work. Your dad died last Thursday. Marcella died days later."

Carly's eyes drifted from his. She turned and glanced up at the painted iron panels and brass lock of Lafayaette's mausoleum. "Dad found ghost stories unsatisfying because ghosts can't *do* anything. They come out of their timeless limbo, shake a few insubstantial chains, swear revenge, and go back, unable to thrust a sword or push someone over a cliff. Ghosts can't touch us—all they've got is their timelessness... which is, of course, the best damn vantage point imaginable. Imagine being able to see events from outside the flow of time. You'd be looking down on traffic from a helicopter. You'd see causes and results all in one glance."

"Whoa. Wait a minute. Ghost stories? Why are we talking about ghost stories?"

"Because you're right. Prophecy isn't enough to make it all work. Hey, can't you see my old man as a ghost? If anybody could make a ghost story satisfying. it would be A.L. Rouhl. You see, as a ghost, he couldn't physically stop Marcella, but he could *watch* her—watch her move through time. He could watch her past, her present—and even her future. And what do you know! Marcella's path through life would eventually bring her to his *own office*. Better than that—she'd stand behind his desk chair. Imagine! For a few seconds, Marcella's life line would intersect the path of the only bullet Dad had ever fired in his whole life—the one that killed him."

Evan was looking at Carly, but she knew he was imagining the old man as he had seen him that Tuesday night with his sea captain's scowl.

"The amazing thing is that Marcella did come. She brought herself there—for her own reasons, of course. Okay, now—so there's my father's spirit—looking down, or up, or whatever it is that ghosts do, and he sees that this is a moment when his bullet just happens to be aligned with Marcella's heart."

"Hey, Car. The bullet that killed your father…it was fired last Thursday."

"I'm getting there. So, here's the trick, sweetie—a ghost can't *do* anything. Ghosts are bad plot devices because they can't pull on a steering wheel or switch trains onto sidings. They can't touch us directly, you got that? They can't shoot guns all by themselves."

"Yeah, yeah. So what would a smart ghost like your father do about that?"

"You mean a ghost who knew how to write a satisfying ending? I think Dad would see Marcella Cole standing where she needed to be, right there in his favourite place, in the room he'd made his own—and then, in that one room, for just a little while...he'd make sure it was Thursday. And he'd make sure it *stayed* Thursday, just long enough—you know: with his glass of port sitting there and his laptop open on his desk. Because, you see, that's *when* Cole needed to be there.

"Do you get it now, Evan? A *ghost* can't do anything, but a *bullet* can. A ghost can't *fire* a bullet, but a dying man can. All the ghost needs to do is stage manage *time*—and time is a ghost's strong suit."

They sat there in silence for a minute or two, Carly's thoughts shifting focus. She was acutely aware that at last, she was thinking the way her father would have thought. She was letting herself go, trusting her heart. She was writing a story. "My God, Evan, think of it. A man kills himself *and* his murderer with one shot. The power of the story...

"My father was a gruff and even embittered man, looking back at his life and his gift. But he was also a man taking something with him to the grave: the secret nature of that gift. Maybe it was his idea that he was special, that he had spent a career bending the limits of the possible, and it made him think that, like Lafayette, he could cheat death...or at least *use* it, the way he had used the lives of so many people."

Remembering at last that Evan was watching her, Carly grinned. She was surprised to see that he didn't look judgmental or skeptical. Fine, he was humouring her; humouring was all she needed right now. Evan had the kindness not to smile derision at her—but all the same, she felt the helpless, euphoric way she did when he *did* smile at her.

It felt right to lean forward and kiss him, but then she remembered they were in a cemetery and paused. Of course, Evan wasn't as finely tuned to symbolism as she was, because now he was brushing her lips with his. Then his hand was on her head drawing her into a hard thrusting kiss that drove back the cold and all her fears.

She was glad her father had had a chance to meet him, to get to know him.

And hold his coat.

CHAPTER THIRTY-FIVE

It was late on Saturday morning when Weiss called. Carly's cell phone tootled a tune from the top of a pile of cardboard boxes on her father's dining room table and Indy barked at it. Carly had expected it to be Evan. He'd asked her out and they needed to connect.

"Where are you now Ms. Rouhl?" It was Weiss's voice.

"I'm at Dad's house, putting some things away."

Weiss was quiet for a moment, long enough for Carly to hear low voices in the background. "I'm at the *Escarpment* office with some of our people. Could I drop over there?"

"I'll be here at the house for a while. I have an appointment at one."

Weiss was at the door a few minutes later and Indy came barreling out of the kitchen to defend the front hall. Carly gave Indy a reassuring pat and opened the door. Weiss stepped in, took off his hat, but lingered at the doorway turning the brim in his hands and grinning down at Indy. Carly had the hall cupboard open for Weiss's coat. Weiss looked at the rack of hangers for a moment then put his hat back on. "Would you take a short walk with me?"

"A walk? Where?"

"Just across the road."

Carly looked past him at the sanded street and the frozen park beyond. After a moment's puzzled hesitation, she snatched her coat off a hanger. Weiss bent to fuss over the dog. "Can you leave Indy?"

"He's good." Carly shuffled Indy off in the direction of the kitchen. "Indy? I'm leaving you in charge. Don't answer the phone." Indy strutted back a few feet and flopped against the wall to watch, his left ear vigilant.

Taking her time putting on warm boots and gloves, Carly noticed that Weiss had never bothered to take his own gloves off. The detective closed his collar and led the way down the driveway. At the sidewalk, he began to walk up the street, turning only to encourage Carly to follow. He walked with his elbows slightly bent as though his armpits hurt. Carly saw Weiss's unmarked patrol car tight against the drifts.

As they passed, Detective Joshi opened the driver's side door and stood, looking across the roof of the cruiser. Weiss touched his cap, but Joshi was looking at Carly, nodding his head politely. He wasn't smiling.

In a few seconds, she and Weiss were beyond the last car and Carly was surprised to see that Joshi was content to remain behind, staring after them. Whatever this little walk was, Joshi was in on it and had been forewarned.

Weiss and Carly continued along the plowed sidewalk until, at the end of the block of townhouses, Weiss started to cross the road towards the lake. The traffic was light and the sidewalks on the wind blown bay side were deserted.

After another minute of aimless walking, Weiss stopped and looked across at a children's play area in the lakeside park; then he glanced down at Carly's boots and, as if deciding that they were up to plodding through snow, he stepped off the sidewalk.

Carly followed, looking around at a structure of wood and

plastic in primary colours that was supposed to be a playground pirate ship. There were swings nearby that had been chained up out of reach for the winter.

Carly stood watching as Weiss carefully perched himself on an icy wooden beam. "Why are we standing in a playground? It's damn cold out here."

Weiss glanced quickly around. "Let's call it neutral territory. I need to see who's listening. And so do you."

Carly had a look for herself. There was no one in sight. Cars continued to pass by, but the beach was a ragged no-man's land of piled-up ice, and, with no leaves to rustle or move in the breeze, the parkland was unnaturally still.

"Let's suppose," Weiss began at last, "that I could place Marcella Cole at the *Escarpment* office when Mrs. Goss was killed. That would simplify things, wouldn't it? We'd know Marcella was a murderer and we'd have Peggy Goss's killer." Then he added, "Or perhaps it wouldn't simplify things at all."

Carly blinked and her head jerked back. "You can *prove* Cole was there with Peggy? How?"

"Well, *if*, for example, there was dog fur on her right glove. It would be easy enough to check that against a reference sample of Indy's coat we have from your father's suicide investigation. Such a test would have to be requisitioned, of course. By me."

Carly cupped her ears against the cold. "Indy?"

"Right now, let's just call it dog fur."

"Detective Weiss, you know I didn't shoot Marcella, right? I mean, you must have an instinct."

"You know, Ms. Rouhl, yours is a funny situation. It's one that doesn't happen all that often in my line of work. If Marcella is what we think she is, then we're left with no real victim crying out for justice—just a dead serial killer who can do no more harm and is finally punished for what she's done to others —and of course, we have your father's sad but understandable suicide.

REQUIEM FOR THURSDAY

"We both know that Marcella Cole is tainted. The psych evaluation from her trial five years ago said that she had a form of obsessive personality disorder and she only escaped conviction for murder because a key witness died. With some recent evidence that we've just obtained against her, a defense lawyer would have a good chance of defending whoever shot her."

Carly felt a wave of relief. "If you know what she was, then you also know that there are several people out there who might want to shoot her, whether she was actually convicted of murder or not—people who lost loved ones to her. Maybe even people who read my father's book and were convinced he was right."

"The portrait in your father's last book isn't unambiguously Marcella Cole."

"Look, Detective Weiss, there are people who would have known it was her. You said so yourself; a lot of people knew who my father was writing about."

"Well, yes, Ms. Rouhl, but somehow, I can't work up any enthusiasm about some third party assassin...some aggrieved relative or other who just happened to track her down to your father's office."

Carly gritted her teeth and turned her back on Weiss. She rested a gloved hand on the bulging prow of the yellow plastic play ship. "So what then, Detective?" she asked quietly. "You're not seriously going to set *me* up as her killer? You know I've never owned a gun. I called in the alarm. I waited for you to arrive."

"Yes, all very good. And if I was inclined to 'set you up,' I don't expect I'd be able to take it very far. But since we're alone out here, I'll tell you something, Ms. Rouhl." Weiss got up off the beam. "With apologies in advance—I might just choose to make your life difficult and expensive for a while."

Carly's head spun around. "What? Why? Why would you do that? It's..."

"Malicious prosecution? You're an obvious suspect, Ms. Rouhl. Under those circumstances, you could hardly make a case that I was harassing you." He shrugged. "But in a way, you'd be right. Not that I bear any real malice towards you, you understand, but I do need to know what you know, and I think you're going to make me put pressure on you. You know—make me lean on you, and on your Mr. Favaro, of course.

"What has either of us done to make you believe we're lying?"

Weiss looked up and squinted at the overcast. "You've both co-operated, and you've both given reasonable accounts to the police of your movements up to and after the discovery of the body." Weiss tried hooking his thumbs in his coat pocket, but the effort seemed to pain him.

"But as soon as I saw your face back in the living room, I knew you and I were going to wind up doing a little dance around the truth. So, let's get our cards on the table quickly, shall we? There's a file on your father's computer that implicates Marcella Cole as his killer, and I think you've read it. Blaming Marcella somehow for your father's final illness, you might conceivably have a motive for shooting the woman."

Weiss gave a half smile. "Bringing her to your father's office before shooting her? Now *that* would have been profoundly stupid, so…Well, I admit it. In accusing you of the shooting, I'm just being difficult."

Carly looked around desperately as though appealing to some invisible jury. "But then…"

Weiss cut her off. "Then let's be direct, Ms. Rouhl. I know something's going on, and it's making me more than a little bit crazy. So I thought I might make you crazy until you help me out."

"Jesus Christ, Weiss. I can't write your report."

"No? Well, why don't we start with the bullet?"

"Oh come on, I'm a bloody civilian. I know squat about bullets."

Weiss nodded in sympathy. "No, of course. How *could* you know? How could you have any idea..." Weiss stepped carefully across the snow and put his face inches from Carly's. "...*why would the bullet from a gun in a police lock up end up in Marcella Cole's body?*"

Carly just stared.

A minute passed with the gusts snatching fitfully at their clothes. Weiss backed off and looked down at his gloves. "Yes. Imagine my surprise when I got the lab report back. And it doesn't end there. There were traces of blood on Cole besides her own. The blood is a match for your father. Perhaps you have an idea where that might lead us. Now, if you have anything to tell me that might bring this into focus for me, I'd be a happy man."

Carly felt lost, but the change in Weiss's voice made her feel she was being given room to move. She needed the time. And she needed to understand what Weiss was bringing to the table. "What gun are you talking about? Why would I know anything about a gun you have in lock up?"

Weiss raised his brows in wonder. "You see? I'm going back and forth on this. *Now* I'm wondering if you are as ingenuous as you appear. I'm talking about the gun your father used to kill himself—that preposterous little derringer."

Carly actually staggered a little, making the snow creak. "Dad's gun?" She could have guessed what Weiss was going to say, but listening to her own imaginings begin to congeal into reality made her skin prickle. Had her father felt like this when he caught himself crossing the line between daydreaming and *knowing*?

Weiss shook his head. "My God, you're good...if you're lying, I mean." He narrowed his eyes and looked at Carly. "But then I don't believe you are. Not *actually* lying, that is. Liars are often afraid of overacting, so they tone it down a bit. You've been shading off into burlesque, waving your arms about, getting red in the face. Nothing personal. The fact is, genuine indignation frequently comes across as burlesque."

He touched his gloved hands together. "Come on now, Ms. Rouhl. Let's work something out. I need to know I'm not being made a fool of."

"So that's all this is? You brought me out here so you could *threaten* me and deny it afterwards?"

"Yes, I did that. But we're also here so that you can tell me the truth—and deny it afterwards, if you choose to. Seems fair, don't you think?

"Look..." Weiss went on, beginning to pick away at his coat buttons. He still had his gloves on and something about the attempt was causing him pain. Eventually, he had to remove his gloves, placing them on the beam, and Carly realized with surprise that his hands looked reddish, as though they'd been scalded. Now his coat hung open.

With the air crystalline and bitter in the fitful onshore breeze, Weiss began undoing his vest and shirt buttons, the pain in his hands distorting his brow. With the last button undone, he hoisted his shirt and vest exposing a pale chest to the frigid air.

Carly stood rooted, stunned. Weiss had red patches on his torso as well, as though he'd spilled hot coffee on himself.

Weiss stood there for a few brief seconds, ignoring the cold, and then quickly started to cover up again. "I'm showing you that I don't have a hidden recording device, Ms. Rouhl. Also, if you look around you, you'll see that there's nowhere someone with a parabolic mic could hide."

He patted himself down as though looking for a lost key. "I suppose you should check my pockets. Recording devices can be ridiculously small these days. If you did, you'd find this." He reached under his coat to his jacket pocket and pulled out a small digital recorder. Carly recognized it as the one she'd seen in Weiss's pocket when she was being questioned. "A small light indicates it's recording," Weiss said, demonstrating. "Note that it is now *off*."

He re-pocketed the recorder, shivered, and continued to do up buttons. "Excuse me. I'm going to have to put myself together again. When I'm done, I hope you'll make me a peace offering. Then I'll make one to you. You see how it works?"

Carly looked around. It was true. If she was going to be a fool, Weiss had given her a secluded place to do it. She was reminded of some labour negotiations she'd been involved in. They'd called it "no commitment bargaining." Say whatever you want; no one will hold you to it.

Carly reached up to grasp one of the chains from a swing and looked down at the snow. "If I told you Evan and I...that we actually witnessed the shooting," she said, "you'd love that, wouldn't you?"

"Of course. Why wouldn't I?"

"Because then I'd have to tell you that there was no shooter, and you'd want me to explain further."

Weiss shrugged. "Let me play along with you here. In this line of thought, where might the bullet come from if not from a visible attacker?"

"Shit." Carly shook her head in frustration. "Look, Marcella was struck right in front of me. I could see her lurch back with the impact. I saw the blood start to flow, the expression of surprise on her face. Do you hear what I'm saying? If I knew one iota about ballistics, I'd have to say..."

"What? What would you say?" Weiss gave a little laugh. "Please, go on. I expect I'll be disappointed with you later, but right now you've got my attention."

"I'm so glad." Carly watched a car go by in the distance. "The bullet must have come from where Evan was standing, but he didn't have a bloody gun. Nothing! Despite everything that I just said, I swear neither one of us shot her."

The weary smile on Weiss's face was relaxing slowly. "My, my. And poor Evan, where was *he* when this happened?"

"Right in front of me. This might sound ridiculously noble under the circumstances, but any 'offering' I might make to you isn't going to feature him, all right?"

"At this point in our exchange, such things are possible."

"What you need to know is, Evan didn't have a gun." Carly put a glove to her brow. She was thinking about the fine line between imagination and prescience—the line her father couldn't define. Right there in the frozen playground, Weiss was putting together the same story she had told Evan. "Are you sure about the derringer? About the gun that killed my father?"

"Ballistics in Toronto is sure. The bullet we took from Marcella's heart matches your father's gun. Of course, when faced with the impossible…"

Carly nodded. "I've wondered about that. What happens then? What *do* people do when they're faced with an impossible situation?"

Weiss stared for a few seconds, then said, "Ms. Rouhl, I have absolutely no idea. They look for someone to blame, I suppose."

"Someone like you? You're worried they're going to call this whole thing a botched investigation, aren't you?"

"I've considered that. And then, Ms. Rouhl, we'd have nothing that even resembled justice being done, would we? Fortunately, I never actually handled the bullet in my report on Cole's death, so the first suspicion about the derringer would have to be aimed at the poor crime scene investigators, and the lab technicians. God knows what you would accuse *them* of. Loaning out a piece of evidence just long enough for it to be used for another murder?"

Carly watched Weiss's eyes. "Now might be a nice time for *you* to throw out an offering or two."

REQUIEM FOR THURSDAY

Weiss nodded and thought for a moment. "Well, you've told me a story that amounts to an impossibility, so let's put that aside and maybe I'll try out something slightly more plausible. But first, I have to remind you that we found traces of your father's blood on Marcella. Not much, but enough."

Carly stood her ground, but her eyes were wide with astonishment.

Weiss shrugged. "Yes, you're right. Any case against you would be at best an ethical nightmare and at worst, a farce. I just needed to know what you would say under pressure, and frankly, it wasn't helpful. So, let's say Marcella was shot *before* the derringer came into our possession."

"But that would have been last Thursday, before my father died. You've had the derringer since he died."

"I'm glad to see you getting into the spirit of this, Ms. Rouhl. It contradicts what you just told me about watching Marcella die, but let's say it anyway...for now. At least it's your turn again."

Carly had the growing realization that she was being asked to collaborate—to co-write a story. "So if I continue to say officially that we just *found* her body there..."

Weiss nodded slowly. "It would be a start. Even if we say that Marcella was shot with A.L. Rouhl's derringer, we still have a long way to go with this yet. There's the question of the bullet that actually killed your father. Where is it?"

Weiss continued. "Now, if Marcella *had* been standing behind your father when he fired the fatal bullet—on Thursday, you understand—well, my equation would balance. You see, the bullet in Marcella could have served to kill your father too. Oh, and amazingly enough, this peculiar little story would explain why there was so little blood on the wall behind your father when we found him."

"Wait a minute. You're talking about my *father* killing Marcella Cole with his own suicide?"

"Yes, and you're reacting with what, interest? Not shock or disbelief? I've looked at your father's death every which way, trying to account for a series of inescapable facts. And here, Ms. Rouhl—here is where you must concede that it would be *possible*: that one bullet killed your father *and* Marcella Cole. Your move, as they say."

Carly stared.

Weiss waited for a moment and then added, "You know, Ms. Rouhl, someday the biographers will come sorting through your father's life, hoping it makes a good story. But it seems to me that writers aren't policemen or even publishers. A writer's fame is only enhanced by a bit of drama, by a whiff of scandal. Hemingway used a shotgun. Blew his head off, so the story goes. If such a story ever leaked out to the press, it would only spark renewed interest in your father's work."

Weiss's tone was mild and accommodating. Perhaps if it hadn't been, Carly would have been shocked. Pure hypocrisy on her part, of course—the smart, sensible person she had always been was at war with the fabulist she had always admired in her father. A mocking denial was almost out of Carly's mouth, but then she realized that this *was* all about storytelling…and about Weiss's paperwork. She hesitated, realizing how her father would have loved the irony of the situation.

At last, she said, "Marcella Cole was unfinished business to my father. He as much as said so in that 'Questions' file you referred to. Given the future he was facing, it's…not inconceivable…that he'd be willing to take his life *and* hers. It has the poetic bullshit A.L. was good at."

Weiss shrugged. "Okay, so let's try that out. Marcella Cole was in your father's office, perhaps trying to recover her property—her diary. Your father had some idea that Marcella was responsible for his illness. She moved around behind your father's chair, perhaps threatening him with her pistol. His own derringer is very small—your father manages to palm it, covertly raise it to his mouth, tilt his head just so, knowing the bullet will pass under his skull...and he takes his revenge? The bullet finds the region of his murderer's heart. An extraordinary notion." Weiss was actually smiling. "But then, your father was an extraordinary man as I've sensed from the beginning."

Carly said nothing. It was as though she and Weiss were on the same side. Or was he a good cop, with a lurking bad cop? Was he actually trying to trap her?

Weiss picked it up. "Well, now... a third party—there would have to be someone else involved, you see—not an assassin now, but an accomplice after the fact. Someone would have to remove Marcella's body. Perhaps someone trying to protect the reputation of a great man. This person then hid the corpse. It would have to be out in the cold, of course, to stabilize the body. You wouldn't be able to freeze her though, because the lab people can tell. Cellular break down and all that. A car might work... in an underground garage maybe?"

And who, Carly thought to herself, *would this accomplice be, but a loving daughter with easy access to the house and driveway—assisted by her boyfriend, perhaps? A daughter who didn't want her father's name associated with a murder-suicide. No, wait; it would be a suicide-murder, wouldn't it? A.L. would be picky about the wording.*

"And then yesterday," Carly said, "this third party put Marcella Cole's body *back* in the office? Jesus, Weiss. Who's going to believe..." Even as she said it, Carly realized she sounded disappointed.

Weiss cut her off. "Before you say anything more, look at the position we're in. I say *we*, Ms. Rouhl. The position you and I are in. We've got gun powder on your father's hand, an indisputable exit wound in the back of his head, and we've got the one and only bullet that's a match for his derringer in Cole's fucking heart. So it's going to be the weirdest goddam murder-suicide I ever heard of—but, don't you see? The evidence! The evidence is satisfied."

And then Weiss gave the merest tilt of the head. It wasn't much, but Carly knew Weiss was telegraphing a concession: "Perhaps with all of *that* cleared up, my department won't squander precious man hours trying to pin accessory to murder on... Well, our third party, whoever that might be."

"So that's your offer? You'd be prepared to leave it at that—a murder-suicide—and leave Evan and me alone?"

"I might be prepared to write it down that way. I couldn't actually call it self-defense, of course, but if Cole was threatening your father at the time, we might call it justifiable homicide. You'd be surprised how important paperwork is in policing. I'm actually rather good at writing reports. A rare and useful gift, writing, eh? Your father hated Marcella, and the story we just told has the one fragile virtue of fitting the evidence. Except, of course, for one thing..." Weiss's voice trailed off into silence and he waited.

Carly's eyes darted back and forth, looking for the flaw. At last, she cursed under her breath. "Dog hairs on Marcella's gloves. She was at the *Escarpment* office yesterday. That means Marcella must have been alive after my father's death."

"Of course, I might be wrong speculating about a couple of dog hairs matching your Indy; that particular test hasn't gone to the lab. I've been getting a lot of flack for too many speculative forensic tests lately. The significant thing is, it *seems* Marcella hasn't been at work for a week. There's an out of office memo on the health centre computer where she works. And no one has actually *seen* her during that time. Have they, Ms. Rouhl?" Weiss tugged on a single glove and waited.

Carly remained silent. She had seen Cole at the health centre. The painful silence seemed to go on forever and it cost her dignity. It was easy to rationalize a lie, of course. Somewhere along the line, their conversation had ceased to be about truth. Strangely, though, to Carly it still felt that they were talking about justice.

In her mind, she could see Marcella Cole in her office, looking up and catching Carly's eye. She could even remember the token smile of acknowledgement on Marcella's face. When the silence of the frozen shoreline and the stillness of the playground had become too much to bear, Carly gave Weiss a single authoritative nod. Okay, no one saw her. Somehow nodding a lie was easier than speaking it.

Weiss seemed…not pleased so much as relieved. "Well then, I'll try writing something along those lines. Given that there doesn't appear to be any other viable theory, it might be enough to bring the Marcella Cole investigation to a conclusion. There will be several of my colleagues happy with that—and anxious that the press doesn't catch wind of it."

He turned away and began to trudge across the snow towards the roadway. Before he got to the plowed sidewalk, he stopped and paused to put his second glove back on. "Of course, there may be more to this—matters that have no business being in a police report. It would be satisfying if, some day, over a glass of scotch—someone sent me a very nice bottle of single malt—you could tell me a story with a little more…poetry? Off duty and off the record, you understand. Maybe it would make me feel better about not being able to solve Peggy Goss's murder—officially, I mean. Her family deserves some justice too." He tugged at his hat. "You *are* a writer aren't you?"

"And if I told you a different type of story—a ghost story, say—you'd believe what I told you then? Over our glass of whiskey?"

"What I'd want to hear is what you'd say when nothing is at stake. The threat of time in prison can make people less than candid."

"I notice you didn't answer my question, Detective, about *believing* what I told you."

"Believing you? You're a writer, for God's sake, just like your old man. All that matters is that the story sounds complete. You know, satisfying."

"Ah," Carly said, "I get it. You'd want a beginning, a middle, and an end."

Weiss smiled. He did it with his eyes, but the mustache bristled. "I don't know about that. Complete is hard enough."

"Maybe the whiskey would help. I told you my father used to drink the hard stuff when he wrote—back when he could write like an angel and make up stories that had the ring of truth itself."

"Yes, I remember."

Carly gave a small laugh. "It wasn't port back then. *His* drink of choice was scotch too." She closed one eye and thought. "Laphroaig, I think it was called."

Weiss's eyes suddenly ranged out over the bay and his smile vanished. A second or two passed before he seemed to come back into the moment, and then, with the briefest nod in her direction, he continued his walk in the snow.

The End

Watch for *Book 2: Requiem For Noah* coming soon. You won't want to miss it!

ABOUT THE AUTHOR

Doug Cockell was born in Edinburgh, Scotland and did graduate work in Literature with acclaimed novelist and playwright Robertson Davies at the University of Toronto. Doug has taught Literature, Art, and Media Studies in Oakville and Burlington and was awarded the McLuhan Distinguished Teacher Medal for showing the common visual language shared by illustration, the movies and computers. He has offered courses through The University of Toronto, Brock University, and The Art Gallery of Burlington. In addition to being an author, Doug is an accomplished artist who came to art through his love of the great Twentieth Century illustrators, delighted by their charm and whimsy as well as their skill.

Requiem For Thursday is Doug's debut novel. However, it is not the only novel he has written. So, add this author to your watch list because you won't want to miss the collection of well crafted murder mysteries Doug has in store for you.

Doug enjoys hearing from his readers and he'd love to know what you thought of Book 1 in the Requiem Series. You can reach him via email at douglascockell@gmail.com

CPSIA information can be obtained
at www.ICGtesting.com
Printed in the USA
LVHW111926080920
665365LV00013B/171/J